A COMFORTING KISS

Marcus slipped out through the double French doors onto the terrace and was arrested by the sound of sobs.

She wept! He stared at Arabella, her slender figure doubled over and her head down on her arms on the wrought-iron railing of the terrace. Pierced to the core by her unhappiness, he was frozen, unable to move. He never imagined that beneath that glittering façade, behind those laughing eyes, such wrenching sadness could exist. He moved forward.

"Arabella," he whispered, as he turned her around. She straightened and tried to pull away, but he enfolded her fiercely in his arms and felt her melt against him.

He let her cry, rocking her gently and talking in hushed tones. He told her everything would be all right, that he would fix everything.

At that, she tried to pull away again, but he would not let her go. He looked down into her drowned green eyes in the pale light from the music room. The crashing chords of the piano coincided with heavier rain that poured down outside the overhang, looking like a silvery curtain. The pain and fear in her eyes were too much, and he lowered his face and gently kissed her mouth, tentatively at first. Any hesitation and he would have released her instantly.

But there was no hesitation. Her bare hands stole up around his neck and she pressed herself to him. . . .

Books by Donna Simpson

LORD ST. CLAIRE'S ANGEL

LADY DELAFONT'S DILEMMA

LADY MAY'S FOLLY

MISS TRUELOVE BECKONS

BELLE OF THE BALL

Published by Zebra Books

BELLE OF
THE BALL

Donna Simpson

ZEBRA BOOKS
Kensington Publishing Corp.
http://www.zebrabooks.com

ZEBRA BOOKS are published by

Kensington Publishing Corp.
850 Third Avenue
New York, NY 10022

All Kensington titles, imprints, and distributed lines are
available at special quantity discounts for bulk purchases
for sales promotion, premiums, fund-raising, educational or
institutional use.

Special book excerpts or customized printings can also be
created to fit specific needs. For details, write or phone the
office of the Kensington Special Sales Manager:
Kensington Publishing Corp., 850 Third Avenue, New York,
NY 10022. Attn: Special Sales Department. Phone: 1-800-
221-2647.

Zebra and the Z logo Reg. U.S. Pat. & TM Off.

First Printing: November 2001
10 9 8 7 6 5 4 3 2 1

Printed in the United States of America

This is dedicated to John Scognamiglio, with eternal gratitude and respect for his unfailing kindness to and generosity towards a fledgling writer.

One

Biting her lip to keep the tears from coming, the Honorable Miss Arabella Swinley, daughter of Baron Swinley, deceased four long years before, stood in the shop with her head held high. This was the worst thing that had ever happened to her, even including hearing that her father was dead, for after all, she had barely known the old man, though he had professed a careless affection for her on the few occasions when she did spend a day or two at Swinley Manor as a girl. This was worse . . . much worse!

"Annie, we must leave," she whispered through clenched teeth.

Her maid, looking confused, placed the gloves her mistress had intended to buy down on the polished countertop.

Arabella, quivering from mortification, steeled herself to go. With one swift, heartbroken glance at the stiff couple who had pushed in front of her at the counter, she turned.

And faced a wall.

She stepped back and looked up. And kept looking. He was the tallest man she had ever seen, and she was of no mean height herself, for a lady. But he was much taller, over the six foot mark, surely, by at least a few inches. And with shoulders that would make Weston weep.

"I believe this lady was first," he said in a loud, booming voice, as if he had had to make himself heard often over long distances.

The couple at the glass display counter turned and glared. The clerk had the grace to look abashed, but it really was not the poor man's fault that Lord and Lady Snowdale had cut Arabella, elbowing past her and taking her place at the counter. She wanted to sink through the floor at that moment, but it was to get worse still.

"I beg your pardon," Lord Snowdale said with a haughty expression on his pudgy face. He glared up at the man who had spoken so loudly. "Were you speaking to us, sir?"

"I was. If I am right, you deliberately snubbed this young lady," the man said, frowning down at the elegantly dressed couple. "Now, what can have induced such finely dressed and appearing folk to give what, if I remember correctly, is called the 'cut direct' to this girl?"

His voice was cultured, but my, was it loud! Other people in the dim shop were turning to see what the commotion was, even as they inspected cloth and made their selections. One older gentleman put an eyeglass up to his eye and harrumphed loudly. Arabella gave an embarrassed smile to the clerk and started to back away, hoping to make it to the door and bolt. She was not generally hen-hearted, but she was sure she knew why she had been given the cut by the Snowdales, and she did not want her humiliation canvassed in public. She wished those who did not know to stay in the dark, if that was still possible, after her mother's outrageous behavior at the country manor of the Farmingtons.

"Do not leave, miss. You shall have your gloves." The loud gentleman smiled down at her and winked, his eyes glittering in the dim interior of the shop. He threw a gold coin on top of the gloves on the counter and said, "For the young lady's purchase. *If* she is served first, as she should be."

"Well! I have never been so insulted . . ." Lady Snowdale started, spluttering frostily.

"No insult intended, ma'am, but I do wonder what you meant by your behavior?"

Could he not just let it go, Arabella thought, sending a pleading look up at the stranger. His response was a friendly smile.

Lord Snowdale, despite the considerable size difference between him and his adversary, said, "See here, young man, I do not know from what backwater you have arisen, but this is London, b'God, and we have courtesy and a way of doing things that perhaps you colonial chaps don't understand."

Arabella, rooted to the spot now as much by her obligation to the stranger as by a queer sort of fascination with the proceedings, gazed at the unnamed gentleman. Not only was he tall, but she had to admit that despite the aspersions cast on his manner by Lord Snowdale, he was not merely good-looking, but charismatic. He had dark straight hair unfashionably long, and though his suit looked to be of recent vintage, its cut was more generous than any London tailor would countenance, meaning he likely did not need to be shoe-horned into the sleeves, though the looser cut did not conceal a kind of massive strength and intimidating breadth to the man.

He had been accepting his change from the clerk and counting it, but now he glanced at the viscount before him. "So you have twigged to my recent arrival from 'the colonies,' as you put it. Interesting. But at any rate, *sir*, where I come from courtesy does not include making a lady wait." He scooped up the gloves from the counter and presented them to Arabella with a flourish.

If it were not so desperate a situation, Arabella would have found it funny, the way Lord Snowdale goggled up at the tall man in front of him, and the sight of Lady Snowdale cackling in the background like a . . . well, like a chicken about to lay an egg. That homely metaphor suited the plump woman and the clucking sounds she emitted.

But her reputation was at stake. Arabella assumed her frostiest, most aristocratic manner, and said, "Sir, I cannot accept the gloves from you, as you must know. I thank you for your concern, but I assure you it is misplaced. You . . . you misunderstood the situation. His lordship and Lady Snowdale did not cut in front of me. They had . . . had been there first, and . . . were merely browsing before coming back to make their purchases." She clutched her hands together to stop them from shaking as she fabricated her story, hoping to rescue a hopeless situation from becoming even worse.

Allied against the common foe, Lady Snowdale nodded to Arabella with approval and then whispered to her husband, in tones loud enough to be heard, "We must have been misinformed, Rupert, for surely a young lady with such perfect manners could not have done such a thing as we heard she did to Lord Conroy. It is all a hum, I swan! She is everything a modest young lady should be, that is quite clear."

Lord Snowdale nodded to his wife. "You must be right, m'dear." He bowed to Arabella. "I do apologize, Miss Swinley. If we cut in front of you at all, it was not intentional."

"Not at all, my lord, it does not matter in the least. As I said, I believe it was merely a misunderstanding." Arabella, her heart pounding, congratulated herself on her good sense in turning such a desperate situation around. Perhaps, oh, perhaps this had saved the day! She curtsied to the Snowdales, who moved off at a majestic pace, eschewing their shopping for the day after saying that they hoped they saw her the next night at the Parkhurst ball. When she glanced up, it was directly into a pair of amused gray eyes.

"What did you do to offend them, I wonder? And what does this Lord Conroy have to do with it?" the stranger said. He stuck out his large callused hand. "By the way, I am Marcus Westhaven, and I—"

"Sir, it is the worst manners to introduce yourself to a lady, as any simpleton knows," she said, furious that he had made her the object of such a scene. Some people were still staring, and he stood there like a great idiot with his hand still stuck out. "And I could only make it worse by acknowledging such an inappropriate introduction! Come, Annie," Arabella said, whirling on her heel and leaving the shop and her lovely gloves behind.

Marcus Westhaven stood staring after her. How very beautiful she was, and yet a little termagant, by all indications. Flashing green eyes, blond ringlets, a turned-up nose, and the sweetest little pursed-up mouth he had ever seen. The complete London belle. He chuckled and shook his head. What a little firebrand! He glanced over at the clerk and shrugged. "Keep the money," he said, tossing the gloves back on the counter. "Someone may as well profit from this absurdity."

He strode from the stuffy, dim shop out into the street, for his business had already been completed when he had seen the two snobs push the young lady out of the way and take her place at the counter. It had made him burn as injustice always did, and so he had stepped in. He had certainly been too long out of England. It had apparently been the wrong thing to do and the girl, a "Miss Swinley," it seemed, had been more concerned about kowtowing to those old frauds than in being properly thankful for his intervention.

He marched down the street, still a little uneasy in the presence of so much traffic; gigs and phaetons and barouches careened along the road as sweepers darted between them. He had not remembered it as so damned crowded, but then it had been many years since he had trod the streets and roads of his native land. Hawkers shouted of their wares as they rolled barrows and carts heaped with produce and flowers and all manner of goods. And besides the noise there was a smell that assailed his nostrils every minute of every day, a smell of excrement and rotting fish and smoke, and over it all the stale odor of unwashed bodies and greasy hair was impossible to avoid, as impossible as stepping around the rotting cabbage and horse manure in the gutters.

London. How far removed he was from the stillness of the Canadian wilderness, soaring pines, the howl of the wolf, a breeze stirring the leaves as he paddled down a gurgling stream with George Two Feathers, his best friend these past years. The funny thing was, those smells—horse excrement, rotting fish, smoke—they were all a part of the wilderness, too, but he supposed it was not in such overwhelming power. And in the wild they were cut with the scent of pines and fresh air and water, always water, pure and clear, scrubbing man and beast alike to a vigorous cleanliness. He longed for just one good, big breath of that air, so he could hold it deep in his lungs.

And yet there was a vitality in the London scene that entranced him. It was an overwhelming assault on his senses every moment of every day, and he was feasting on it in a way, fascinated by every small detail down to the rags on the little street urchins and the wilting violets a flower girl sold on the corner. He stopped and gave her a gold coin; she gazed up at him in awe, but then a look of world-weary suspicion darkened her young face and she bit it. He laughed heartily and moved on as she realized it was the real thing and called out an almost unintelligible thanks.

He could not say if he would want to stay—he was interested for the moment but had the feeling the longing for fresh air and wide spaces would at some time overpower him—but for the time being he was ensconced at the Fontaine, one of the city's more modest hotels. His future depended in a large part on the health of a very old man, and he was not really certain what outcome he desired.

Arabella removed her bonnet and handed it over to Annie before sinking wearily into a chair in the front drawing room of the Mayfair House, loaned to her and her mother by the in-laws of their cousin, Truelove, now Lady Drake. What a morning it had been! March in London had always been her favorite time. The Season was just starting; there was the hustle and bustle of buying new clothes and accoutrements for all manner of entertainments, and there was the excitement of seeing friends again, and looking forward to balls and routs and musicales, Vauxhall, the opera, picnics at Richmond. Two and even three engagements in a day would not be unusual, with morning visits in addition. The frenetic pace suited her, for she could not abide idleness and had more trouble assuming the correct degree of languor considered appropriate for a young lady than in attaining any other social accomplishment.

But this Season was different.

First, there was the question of whether she would even be able to stay in London for the Season or not.

If the Snowdales' behavior was any indication, it was quite possible that she would be forced to leave in disgrace. She had saved that particular awkward scene, but how long could she continue if word got around? It was all her mother's fault.

Lady Swinley chose that inopportune moment in her daughter's reflections to enter the drawing room.

She was much shorter than her daughter and thin, with a pinched, ungenerous face and hard eyes. Her marriage to the Baron Swinley—she had been Isabella Trent of the Dorset Trents, a very good family indeed—had been thought by her family to be a step below what she could have expected, but somewhere deep inside she had known herself to be lucky. She had married a man of wealth and property and limited intestinal fortitude. The vulgar would no doubt say she had promptly assumed the breeches in the family, but she had looked upon it as merely her due, to take a measure of control to herself and learn quickly how to ensure her husband's acquiescence.

Her only child had turned out to be a daughter, and after that the baron had not bothered her much for a second child, which suited her just fine. She considered that she had done her duty in bearing one child; it was too bad Arabella was not a boy, but there was no help for it. Secretly, some wondered how such a plain woman had borne such a beauty as Arabella, but she considered that there was a family resemblance. Most thought that it was limited to that pinched look about the mouth when Arabella was displeased about something.

Lady Swinley entered the drawing room with a book of plates in hand. "I don't know how we are to do it with our finances at such low tide, but you simply must have a new spencer on the military line. Ever since Waterloo every gel is wearing these military duds with shakos and gold frogging. Perhaps you could sell your pearls . . ."

"No!" Arabella snapped. "That is the only thing Papa gave me personally and they were his mother's. I will not sell them."

Lady Swinley pursed her lips, and the drawstring lines around her mouth were even more pronounced than usual. "Do not take that tone with me, young lady, I . . ."

Arabella stood and said, her voice shaking, "Mother, I was cut by the Snowdales."

The book dropped from Lady Swinley's hands. She sank into the chair just vacated by Arabella, quick to see all the ramifications of such an occurrence. "Cut? Oh Lord."

"Yes, cut! And it is all your fault. If you had not pulled that absurd trick on Lord Conroy . . ."

"I had no choice," Lady Swinley retorted. She sprang up from her seat again and faced her daughter. "You were no closer to eliciting a proposal from the idiot than you were when we left Lea Park after *that* debacle. And how you let Drake slip through your fingers only to have him wed your simpering, silly little cousin Truelove Becket I will never know!"

Rage toward her mother warred with her pique that the previous autumn on a visit that was supposed to see her wed to the eligible, handsome Lord Drake, viscount and heir to the Earl of Leathorne's considerable estate, he had been snatched from her grasp by her cousin Truelove Becket, who had accompanied them on the visit as companion to Arabella. And yet she could not still the tiny, sensible voice that reminded her that she had decided that Drake would not do for her. A retired soldier wounded at Waterloo, the viscount was undoubtedly handsome, but the legacy of that famous battle had been a physical limp and frightening nightmares that had plagued him every night. She did not want to go into marriage as some man's nursemaid!

She had discouraged his attentions, but it appeared that marriage had cured him, or *something* had. When delicately questioned about it, True, now heavy with their first child, claimed he had not had the nightmares since before the wedding. He was cured, and she, Truelove, was wealthy beyond the wildest imaginings of a vicar's daughter from a tiny Cornwall village.

"Let us not quarrel about that, Mother," Arabella said. She supposed her mother did have some grounds for a sense of ill usage. Arabella should have been Lady Drake by now instead of her cousin, True, having that title. It was something Lady Swinley had long talked of and hoped for as the best possible match for her daughter. But by the time Arabella had decided she must make a push to attach him, True had the upper hand, and Arabella had found it beyond her ability to bring the rather imposing Major-General to heel. If that was not quite how things had come about, it was how her mother viewed it, laying the blame equally on her daughter and their cousin. Ultimately it came down to the same thing: they had lost a fortune.

And simply put, the Swinleys were destitute. Lady Swinley swore that when her husband died four years before, she had no idea that they would be so poor. The title had lapsed due to there being no male heir in sight, but what should have been a stroke of good fortune for his wife and daughter did not aid their finances a bit; the manor house was mortgaged up to the very top of the crenelated roof. A brilliant marriage on Arabella's part was supposed to rescue them from penury, but somehow one Season followed another—Arabella had not yet known that her marriage was supposed to pull them out of the soup—and the right man, wealthy, titled, and handsome, had never come along. Why should they worry though, both mother and daughter thought? There was always Lord Drake. Isabella Swinley and Jessica Prescott, Countess Leathorne, were bosom bows from their school days and had planned, loosely, the match very early. Once Drake was back from the war and had resigned his commission, the visit was planned with the match in mind.

But somehow, Arabella and Drake had not hit it off as they should have. And then with the nightmares and Drake's apparent preference for petite, mousy Truelove, Arabella had decided that Lord Nathan Conroy—Drake's best friend, staying at the Leathornes' home on an extended visit—was a more likely conquest. Not as rich, but much more susceptible to Arabella's flirtatious ways. And so while Drake suffered through a bout of fever and delirium brought on by his despondency at Truelove's supposed impending nuptials to another man, Arabella and her mother had taken Lord Conroy's invitation to depart with him to his family home as a sign that he, not as rich as Drake, but still wealthy, could be had.

"I will not tax you with losing Lord Drake if you will not raise the issue of Lord Conroy," Lady Swinley bargained, picking up the book that had fallen from her fingers at Arabella's announcement of the Snowdale snubbing.

"Agreed, Mother," Arabella said. For she could not look back on that visit to Lord Conroy's family home with any degree of comfort, even though she still held herself blameless in the disaster that had made them flee from the mansion in late January.

Lord Conroy's mother, the indomitable Lady Farmington, made Lady Swinley appear as gentle as a ewe lamb. And she was fiercely protective of her son, so Arabella, only staying at the family estate on sufferance and made to feel it every day, could not openly pursue the alliance with Conroy. And he, being a mama's boy and rather afraid of his dragonish mother, and alarmed that he had displeased her by inviting the Swinleys in the first place, had backed away from the preference he had clearly demonstrated for Arabella when they all were at Lea Park.

That was when Lady Swinley had made her disastrous and desperate plan, unbeknownst to Arabella. But it did not bear thinking about; it was all water under the bridge. She was still furious with her mother, but it would do no good to berate each other. Their situation was desperate and she needed to find a wealthy husband this Season, or they would be in deep trouble.

And so she told her mother the tale of the morning, and the snub by Lord and Lady Snowdale, and the gentleman stepping in.

"But you put him in his place, I hope?" Lady Swinley said.

"Yes, of course! I said it had just been a misunderstanding, and that the Snowdales were there before me. They spoke to me very kindly after that, and hoped to see me at the Parkhust ball tomorrow night."

"That is all right then. I told you all would be well!"

Arabella just wasn't sure. If the Snowdales had heard of the Conroy debacle, then others had, too. And the Snowdales might realize later that she was covering for them in the store that day to make up to them, not just out of class loyalty, which everyone of the *ton* understood.

It was the one part she felt a little uneasy about. She did not regret doing what she could to repair her reputation in front of the two aristocrats, for she had clearly handled it the only way she could, even though they *had* cut her. But she could not look back on her treatment of the large gentleman with any degree of composure, though she did not tell her mother that. Lady

Swinley wouldn't understand why she felt badly about snubbing the good-looking stranger to gain points with the noble couple.

But she did feel a little uneasy. It was kindly meant, defending her, and then purchasing her gloves. But could he not see that it just was not done? Where had he been that he could think that acceptable in anyone's eyes? She had enough trouble without adding *fast* to her list of faults in *tonnish* eyes. She had been hoping that no one had heard of the terrible outcome of their visit to the Farmingtons', but Lady Farmington had no doubt spread it among all her friends, luckily a small group. Arabella's only hope was that she had made up enough ground with the Snowdales that they would deny the charge against her in public if it should ever come up again. And that would only work as long as the Farmingtons were not in London.

If only her cousin True, now Lady Drake, had been able to sponsor her in London this Season, as she had offered. But Drake—overprotective, Arabella thought—would not hear of his pregnant wife suffering the fetid air of London in her "delicate" condition, and so she was staying in the country at Thorne House, their home near the Leathornes, his parents. The most he would do was convince his parents to let Lady Swinley and Arabella borrow their elegant Mayfair home for the Season, rent free. It was a valuable boon indeed, but it still would not pay for a new wardrobe and all the other things they needed to present a good front and make Arabella seem a worthy wife for a wealthy man.

She stiffened her back and looked down at her mother, who was lost again in her perusal of the book of dress patterns she had brought in. It was up to her this Season to rescue herself and her mother from penury. Maybe she did not owe her mother any allegiance.

After all, the woman had abandoned her throughout most of her childhood, leaving her at the vicarage, Truelove's family home until her marriage to Drake.

But Lady Swinley needed her daughter now, and Arabella would be there for her. Maybe then her mother would be proud of her. She turned and left the room without a word.

TWO

Arabella smoothed ice blue gloves up over her elbows, checking for tears and wear spots as she did so—after all, they were last year's—as she distractedly listened to her mother, who paced behind her while Annie fussed with her hair.

"Now, I have been visiting everyone I know these last two days, and I must say I don't think anyone has heard about . . . about the Conroy affair." Seldom did she refer to that embarrassing time, but when she did, it was as "the Conroy affair." She still did not regret her actions, although the outcome had mortified her. "With a little luck we should be able to manage as long as Lady Farmington or Lord Conroy do not come to London for the Season. I have heard that Lady Farmington has come down with some indisposition; we can only hope it is a lasting one."

"Or fatal," Arabella said, grimly.

Ignoring her daughter as she usually did, Lady Swinley said, "I have made a list of the eligible men who are rumored to be looking for a wife this Season."

A list of men; a list of potential *husbands*, rather. And not one of them would have laughing gray eyes and broad shoulders, Arabella thought, then caught herself. She would not brood over that impossibly rude stranger! It simply would not do, since she was likely never to see him again. He was clearly not of sufficient social status to attend the same balls and events as Baron Swinley's only child would. That was evident in his lack of manners and ignorance of correct behavior.

"As well, I have made a second list of those men I think might be persuaded to marry, though you haven't had much luck lately in that, have you?" Lady Swinley gave her daughter a cold look in the mirror, then resumed her pacing, gazing down at a paper she held in her hands.

Sighing, Arabella batted Annie's hands away, took up her bottle of scent, and dabbed just a little behind each ear and in her modest décolletage. She gazed at herself critically in the glass and pulled down a curl, letting it drape artfully near the neckline of her dress. Now she looked perfect. "Mother," she said, glancing up at Lady Swinley with a frown. "It is not like it was in your day, when marriages were always arranged and all the girl had to do was sit back and look demure."

"In my day ladies knew how to capture a man's interest, my girl, regardless of any arrangements made on their behalf!" Lady Swinley snapped. "Men have always needed to be manipulated; nothing has changed in that respect. You would do well to assume a fragile air, but no! You insist on being healthy and vigorous. How is a man supposed to feel protective toward you if you don't look like you need protecting?"

It was an old argument, and Arabella stayed silent.

"Now, first is the Duke of Haliburton's seedling. He is the matrimonial prize this Season, and if you would apply yourself, I think you could get his attention; it is rumored he has shown a weakness for blondes. He's a little younger than you, just two-and-twenty, but old Haliburton is convinced he is going to stick his spoon in the wall and wants to see the succession assured. So they'll be looking for a healthy gel like you, mayhap."

Arabella frowned at her reflection in the mirror.

"That is Bessemere, right? I have met him. He seems—I don't know. So very unsure of himself." Weak-willed was what she meant. Rumor had it that he was completely under the thumb of his dominating mother, and that did not bode well for his wife. Just look at what had happened with Lord Conroy.

"And what does that matter? With a firm hand he could be molded into the ideal husband." Lady Swinley consulted her paper. "He is a bookish sort; likely would not bother you too much once you had begotten the heir. Problem there is his mother will likely be screening any gels that capture his interest, and she is a tough one."

"And she is a good friend of Lady Farmington," Arabella said, feeling a chill go down her back.

"Hmm. Thought there was a falling-out there. I shall have to check into that." She made a notation.

Standing finally and brushing her dress into the correct folds, Arabella gazed at herself in the cheval mirror at the end of her dressing room. The gown was from last year, but she and Annie had worked feverishly on it, supplying the ice blue silk with a frothy overskirt of white lace—very expensive but purchased at a warehouse, so much cheaper than the mantuamakers would sell it—and it really looked new. She gazed at her slender figure with approval. Blondes were in fashion this year, and her looks had always stood her well. Without being vain, she knew it was her chief attraction, that and her vivacious manner. It had never been difficult to gain male attention, and never had it been a more vital skill than this Season.

"Next—do you remember from last Season Count Arndt Verbrachan?"

"I remember him," Arabella admitted. He had flirted with her on numerous occasions, but had never seemed interested in marriage. He was good-looking in a dark, cold way and older, probably in his forties.

"It is gossiped that he is on the lookout this Season for a wife." Lady Swinley stopped pacing and gazed at her daughter critically. She gave a nod of approval finally, after pulling the bodice of Arabella's dress down just a little and prodding her small breasts into more showiness. "He is very, very wealthy, but as foreign nobility he will not be looking among the upper titles for his bride, even though it has been rumored that Princess Elizabeth conceived an infatuation for him some years ago and would have been glad to marry him. But he is not a prince, after all, nor even a duke. If it is true that he wishes to marry, he is a good possibility."

Picking up a fan from the dressing table while Annie brought her Kashmir shawl, Arabella chose her next words carefully. "I have heard—" She looked down and bit her lip. "Mother, it has been whispered among some of the girls that there was some suspicion that he was responsible for the disappearance of an opera dancer that he had under his protection."

"Pish-tush! Foolish gabble. And even if he was, those kind of girls take that risk. A man does all sorts of things with harlots that he would never try with a girl of good family."

Arabella shivered and stared at her mother in disbelief. "Mother! She disappeared, maybe died!"

"Slut. Likely all she deserved."

Stunned, Arabella realized that protest was hopeless. Her mother's opinions were ever a mystery to her. Apparently in Lady Swinley's mind, the life of one opera dancer was of no account, nor did the poor girl's fate portend ill for any wife Count Verbrachan might choose. She would just have to keep her own counsel on the subject of Count Verbrachan.

Lady Swinley stared down at the paper in her hand

and then said, "The most likely, I must say, is Lord Pelimore."

"Lord Pelimore?" Arabella slipped the silken cord of her fan around her wrist and allowed Annie to drape the soft, multicolored shawl around her shoulders. "He is sixty, at least!"

"And what is wrong with a mature man?" Her mother threw down the paper and stamped one foot on the carpet. "First you complain Bessemere is too young and now Pelimore is too old! There is no pleasing you, and I do not know why I take all of this trouble—"

Arabella sighed, picked up the paper and handed it back to her mother. "Tell me about him, then."

Lady Swinley's voice took on the enthusiasm reserved for one topic, money. "He is very, very wealthy—he owns a brewery, you know—and just out of mourning for his son, who died last year without issue. His current heir is his nephew and he despises the fellow; he can't even stand to be in the same room with him. So it is a certain thing that he is looking for a second wife—Nellie died more than twenty years ago—and he will need one of breeding age." The baroness took her daughter by the shoulders and looked her over critically one more time. "Perfect. You are perfectly lovely, as usual." A rare smile lit her face. She squeezed Arabella's shoulders and released her. "His age is in his favor, my dear, because he will not want to waste any time and will likely choose a bride early in the Season."

The ugliness of the discussion hit her that moment and Arabella felt a dull dread sweep over her. By this time next Season she would be married and likely with child by a man she would not love. Not everyone was as lucky as her cousin, Truelove, who had fallen in love with Lord Drake and had had her feelings reciprocated. It was almost nauseating how happy True was, and yet she could not sneer at her cousin's joy. Arabella felt an envy she had never experienced before. What must that be like, to be so in love?

Anyway, she thought, squaring her slim shoulders and heading out the door, she was not likely to experience that, as she had joked with True, until she had married, presented her husband with a couple of sons, and then taken a lover. Or perhaps she was just not capable of the emotion so cloyingly described by the more putrid poets. She was her mother's daughter, after all.

On the way to the Parkhurst ball Lady Swinley kept up a steady stream of chatter. There were other eligibles, of course, and it would be worthwhile looking at them, but they must focus early on one, for they had little time. This Season was it; Arabella must be engaged by the end of it, or the vultures—meaning the moneylenders Lady Swinley owed—would close in around them. They could not be choosy, they must settle on one husband, and soon.

Arabella steeled herself to enter the Parkhursts' London mansion, lit up in glittering candlelight and with flambeaux at the door, with liveried footmen lining the walk. This was it, the first ball of the Season. Here she would find out if the horrible scene at the Farmingtons' country mansion had made the gossip rounds and if she was to be cut *en masse.* They had visited friends already, and had received their invitation to this ball a week ago, but that could have been delivered before news of the debacle was related to the Parkhursts. The next few minutes would tell the tale of their London Season.

She felt as though everyone in the world must know about it, and could not help reliving over and over again the awful moment of being ejected from the Farmington mansion on a frigid January evening. Lord Conroy had been peeping out from behind his formidable mother, and if Arabella hadn't been crying, her tears crystallizing into ice on her chilled cheek, she might have felt like laughing. It was like a scene from one of the more ludicrous of romances—the innocent maiden wronged and then thrown out into the night by a wicked aristocrat. And yet the thought made her indignant, too. One moment Nathan was ready to propose and the next, he was standing back and letting his mother toss the object of his supposed affections out of the house! What kind of man would do that?

She mounted the marble steps and entered the house behind another group of people, a couple she did not know. At last in, she listened, her ears burning while the butler announced their names.

"Baroness Swinley and the Honorable Miss Arabella Swinley," he intoned.

The entire company gasped and drew back in horror as one, and a wave of whispered condemnations—

"Arabella, what are you gaping at? Come," Lady Swinley hissed, grabbing her daughter's wrist and starting down the steps.

Obediently, Arabella followed her mother down the steps into the crowd, who had, in truth, ignored their momentous arrival. She was relieved that her little daydream was not reality, but it was still to be seen how they would be greeted by the Farmingtons' intimates. And what if Lord Conroy should have come to London for the Season? It was quite likely, despite his mother's purported indisposition, and yet she had not even thought of it until now. Oh, Lord, how she hoped he didn't!

Lady Swinley led the way to their hostess, who stood with her husband and a group of their friends. "Lady Parkhurst! How wonderful you look tonight, and Letitia, too!"

The young lady just named, the Parkhursts' spinster daughter, thirty or older and still unwed, nodded coolly.

Lady Parkhurst smiled and took Lady Swinley's offered hand. "How nice of you both to attend," she murmured. She turned to Arabella. "Lady Snowdale mentioned meeting with you at the Nash Emporium." Her smile was malicious. "You had a brave defender for some imagined slight."

Managing a smile, Arabella said, "Yes, was that not absurd? It just shows how a situation can be misunderstood so very easily!"

"I suppose," Lady Parkhurst murmured.

So, the Snowdales had spoken of the scene, but had clearly not retailed the gossip that was behind their snub, nor had they revealed the snub itself. Could she breathe easier? Would she and her mother escape without condemnation? Why had the Snowdales been so circumspect?

Arabella drifted away as her mother headed for a line of chairs along the wall where a couple of her bosom bows, other women acting as chaperones, were seated. Strictly speaking she should stay by her mother until claimed for a dance, but she was no green girl in her first Season. No one would look askance at a girl of three-and-twenty without her chaperone clinging to her skirts.

The first ball of the Season. It had been many years since her first ball of her *first* Season, but she could readily identify the wide-eyed looks and pale complexions, and the snowy dresses of this year's new crop. There were blondes and brunettes and a few unfortunate redheads, and it seemed to Arabella that there were an excessive number of truly beautiful girls to add to the few diamonds from the previous year who had not made a match.

"Have you ever seen so many frightened children?"

Arabella jumped at the voice almost in her ear, and whirled to find her friend, Miss Eveleen O'Clannahan, at her elbow. Eveleen was redheaded with sprinkling of reddish freckles across her narrow nose, though the rest of her complexion was the color of thick Devonshire cream. She was as tall as Arabella, but rather more voluptuous. Arabella gave her friend a quick hug and then put her at arm's length.

"Eveleen, it is so good to see you! My, but you look marvelous!" She scanned her friend's gown, a rich and lustrous azure, trimmed in expensive Mechlin. She wore sapphires around her neck and wrist, with diamond earbobs. Oh, to be that rich, Arabella thought, envious of her friend's fortune. "I believed, from your last letter, that you had determined not to do this—what did you call it? The 'annual farce of searching for a man one can bear to be near for more than a few seconds'?"

Eveleen chuckled. "That was until my father threatened to forcibly take me back to Ireland and confine me to my great-granny's farm. As long as I pretend to search for a husband he will let me stay in London with just Sheltie to protect me."

"Sheltie! Where is the dear old thing?"

Eveleen glanced around and pointed to an extraordinary-looking woman who seemed, at first glance, to be a bundle of rags, until one looked closer and realized it was only a multiplicity of shawls that made her appear so. She was a great-aunt of Eveleen's, dark Irish with a thick brogue that put off the more superficial of the London crowd. Anyone who got to know her fell in love with her multiple eccentricities and marvelously original conversation. She was broody and fey and claimed to see visions, like some Gypsy from a caravan. Arabella waved—the merest genteel fluttering of her hand—and the woman peered at her, then waved gaily back before returning to a conversation with another lady. In fact . . . no, Arabella would not believe it. But yes! It appeared that Sheltie was reading the woman's palm, right in the middle of a London ballroom!

"You are lucky," Arabella said, enviously. "Your own establishment, with just darling Sheltie to deal with."

Eveleen gazed at her friend with an expression of understanding in her brilliant blue eyes. "Ah, but I am a spinster of many more years than you, my girl, and independently wealthy."

"Eve, my dear, you are twenty-nine, not thirty-nine!"

Lady Swinley bustled over at that moment. "Why, hello, Eveleen." She looked her daughter's friend over critically. "Put on a few pounds, have you not?"

"Mother!" Arabella gasped.

"Never mind; listen to me. Lord Pelimore has just entered. Look lively, my girl. He has created quite a stir." She hustled away again, with just a motion of her head toward the stairs.

"My heavens," Eveleen exclaimed. "Have you ever seen so much flashing teeth and eyes and batting eyelashes? You would think the man was the catch of the year instead of an ugly, snuff-addicted old man! I had heard he was on the lookout for a wife, but I never envisioned this . . . this hubbub! I pity the poor girls who must go after him. What did your mother want, bringing him to your atten—" Eveleen's words trailed off as she gazed at her friend.

Arabella stayed silent; she could not meet her friend's gaze.

"Never say—do not tell me you are entering the matrimonial stakes for old Lord Pelimore?"

"I am afraid so, Eve. I very much fear it is true."

Three

"What on earth could induce you to do such a mad thing, my dear girl?" Eveleen's voice, faintly inflected with an Irish lilt, was filled with incredulous wonder. "You are not thinking that at three-and-twenty you are past anything better? If so, I assure you that you are not quite at such desperate ends yet."

"Some of us are not independently wealthy and *must* marry," Arabella said, stung into a precipitate reply by her friend's mocking tone. She glanced around hastily at the crowd, hoping no one had heard their indelicate conversation. One did not speak of money, even if one was desperately in need of it. It just was not done.

"Oho! It is money, is it?" Eveleen regarded her silently for a moment. She had always been blunt, and no subject was off limits. "Are you and your mother under the hatches, then?"

It went against the grain to confess all, but if not to Eve, her dearest and closest friend, then to whom? "We are." Arabella lifted her chin, desperately trying not to feel the shame attendant on poverty. "And it is up to me to repair our fortunes, and we only have this Season to do it." It did not even need to be said, she knew, that all must be kept in confidence. Eveleen might like to listen to gossip, but she was not without sensitivity, and she was fiercely loyal to her friends.

"How comes it that even with no other heirs to snatch

Swinley Manor from under the widow and child's bottom, that you and your mother should be so undone?"

Eveleen referred to the fact that the barony had lapsed after Lord Swinley's death. There was no male heir known, and so the manor house and land, including farm, timber, orchards, and other enterprises, had stayed with Lady Swinley. It was a gray area in law, and there was some dissenting view that the Swinley title and lands should revert to the throne, but there had not been much interest from any quarter, and there was really nothing to take that was not encumbered with mortgages. Arabella did not honestly know what had happened and said so to her friend, her words smothered among the hubbub of lords and ladies arriving and chattering to friends they had not seen through the long winter.

"Mama claims that Papa left the estate in a bad way," Arabella continued, moving out of the way for Lord Stibblethorpe, a clumsy and usually drunken marquess, well known for his corpulence and smell. Luckily he was already married, or her mother would have included him on the list. She drifted back toward Eveleen and they both turned to watch the marquess make his way through the crowd like a fishing scow among elegant sailboats. "But it just seems so unlikely," she continued. "I mean, I did not spend overmuch time at Swinley Manor as a child, you know. Mama didn't have much use for a little girl under her feet, and so I spent most of my holidays at my cousins' home in Cornwall. Their father is a vicar, and I stayed at the vicarage for some months every year. But I just wonder how it can be that Papa left things so involved when it is the only thing he did—managing the estates, I mean. I do not remember any sign of gambling; he spent little time in London, and then only at Mother's behest. So what can have happened to all the money?"

Eveleen shrugged. "I cannot imagine, my dear, but I am sorry to hear about your troubles."

Lady Swinley was at that very moment giving her significant looks that urged her to go greet Lord Pelimore, still enveloped by a crowd of frothy pale gowns and bare white arms, all belonging to girls being introduced by their hopeful chaperones. But Arabella did not think that was the way to gain the old man's attention. All of those girls would blend into one another after a few seconds; he would not be making any choice this very evening anyway. There were better ways to gain a gentleman's attention, as a veteran of the London Season knew.

"Who is that good-looking, very rough gentleman over there who is staring at you?"

Eveleen's voice broke Arabella out of her reverie, and she glanced over to where her friend looked.

It was him! It was the fellow from the shop; and she had thought never to see him again! He was dressed in evening clothes this time, very correct in black, Beau Brummelish, and even more devastatingly handsome. And yet there was still that about him that made Eveleen call him "rough." His straight dark hair was still too long, his hands, no doubt, still calloused, and he seemed to be fresh from some wild place where evening clothes and evening manners were irrelevant and faintly silly.

And yet he did not look silly in evening clothes. He looked rather magnificent, rugged and powerful like a handsome wolf among a flock of bleating sheep. And he was staring at her with arched brows and a significant look.

"That is no gentleman," Arabella said, acidly, turning her gaze away and clutching her shaking hands together to stop their quivering. She told her friend the story of how she had met him, and how he boldly had introduced himself after that and tried to buy her gloves for her. Eveleen was the only one to whom she had confessed the whole story of her disgrace at the Farmington estate—she and Eveleen corresponded throughout the winter—and her subsequent worries about being ostracized from London company, so her friend understood the background of her snubbing by the Snowdales already. While Arabella spoke, she wondered if he was still looking her way, and then called herself a widgeon for even caring.

"So you do not know him, properly?"

"No, not at all. We have not been formally introduced. I cannot imagine what he is doing here, but I would not put it past him to march in here unannounced and uninvited like some—"

"Well, he is coming this way, regardless," Eveleen said, her voice holding a hint of laughter.

Flustered and panicked, Arabella glanced around. He was indeed coming their way across the marble floor, and with that devilish grin on his face, as if he dared her to run. Well, she would not run from him. She was not afraid of him; what was there to be afraid of but this strange fluttery feeling in her breast, a feeling she had never had before and could not identify? She would meet him with equanimity and put her nose up at him, give him the cut! That would put him in his place.

He was coming; he was going to accost her in the middle of the Parkhurst ballroom . . . he was going to . . . going to walk right past her! With a taunting grin on his face and a wink of his eye, he walked right past her and joined Lady Parkhurst.

Arabella snapped her fan open and applied it vigorously to work on cooling her flaming face. She caught Eveleen's laughing look. "The man is impossible! He knew I thought he would accost me, and deliberately walked this way to taunt me!"

"Impossible," Eveleen agreed, eyeing him as he appeared to charm Lady Parkhurst. He bowed low over the hostess's hand and kissed it. "Impossibly tall, impossibly handsome, impossibly irresistible."

Tartly, Arabella said, "If you think him so, then you should take him in hand and tame him."

Smiling, Eveleen drifted away, saying over her shoulder, "Perhaps I will. I have a feeling it would be worth the effort."

She joined Lady Parkhurst and the unknown gentleman, throwing one last, saucy look back to her friend. Arabella put her nose in the air and retreated to the chaperones' area.

Finally the dancing had begun, and Arabella had been engaged for almost every dance so far. She had always had her own court of admirers, and they flocked to her again this Season, complimenting her, flattering her on her looks and new dress. If the compliments were more in the line of how little she changed over the "passing years" she would ignore that for now.

At first it had felt like any other Season, but then her mother dragged her away to the ladies' withdrawing room and angrily asked her when she was going to get down to the business at hand, which was catching a husband, most likely Lord Pelimore, before some other widgeon had him locked up tighter than a dowager's jewel chest.

Pleasure in the evening was over, and Arabella set herself to charming the gentlemen, but it seemed that the harder she tried, the more difficult it became. Apart from her looks, it had always been her gay flirtatiousness that had attracted the men, she supposed, but she could not seem to find the right lightness. She felt herself trying too hard; her laughter sounded forced, her banter strained, her voice feverish. More than one gentleman had fled her company the moment the dance was over with just the barest of civility.

All the gentlemen clustered around the newest diamond, a Lady Cynthia Walkerton, another lovely blonde; she flirted and teased and had her choice of men begging her for the next dance. The Honorable Miss Swinley, diamond of years gone by, was left on the sidelines watching more than once as the evening wore on, for after all, she could dance with no gentleman more than once or twice and her court was soon depleted, especially as more and more gentlemen drifted off to the card room or to Lady Cynthia's side.

And so she tried harder. Working through the figures of the dance with Sir William Drayton, she gaily said, "So, Sir William, how pleasant to see you again this year. Shall some lucky lady find you ready to settle down in parson's mousetrap this year?"

"P—p—parson's mousetrap?" The man goggled visibly. "I d—d—don't intend to m—m—marry this year, M—M—Miss Swinley."

He had never stammered before. How odd. They parted and came together again to the beat of the lilting country tune as the flickering lights of the chandelier winked and twinkled above them. "Ah, but no gentleman *intends* to marry, isn't that true?" She smiled up at him, putting all her effort forth to be charming and witty. He paled.

And just at that second she caught the mystery gentleman's eyes on her—what was the name he had introduced himself by?—from his position on the sidelines, as if he could read what was happening. She swiftly looked away and gazed up at her dance partner with a lingering smile that made his eyes goggle again.

"T—t—true? I d—d—don't know."

The moment the dance was over, Sir William escorted her back to Lady Swinley's side and bolted off to the card room, not to be seen again that evening. So far, she was having a lot of luck with the gentlemen, all of it bad. And always the tall gentleman's eyes were on her. He seemed invariably to be in her line of sight, and she freely admitted that he stood out, quite literally, head and shoulders above the other men.

His hair, still that same unfashionable length from the day before, was dark and straight, falling below his collar onto his shoulders, and his features were strong, his nose slightly beaky, his cheekbones high. Arabella had to admit to herself that he epitomized masculine good looks, to her thinking. But there was more to him than just his looks. There was an intelligent sharpness in his eyes—they were a clear gray, she remembered—and his air was confident without being swaggering, as if he was comfortable with himself on all levels and did not need to make a show about it.

But it was his smile that stayed in her memory even when she looked away from him. It transformed his face as sunlight does a landscape, changing it from brooding to beaming in one breathtaking instant.

And she would have to stop mooning about an ineligible man who infuriated her for some inexplicable reason. She was there to meet the man she would marry, whoever he might be, and she must get down to the serious business of finding him. She could not count on good luck forever. Myriad things could go wrong: Lord Conroy could come to London and speak openly of the whole mess, or some intimate of the Farmingtons' could speak of it, or word could get around about the Swinleys' financial dilemma. Any one of those events would be death to her plans.

Eveleen joined her that minute, fresh from the dance, her cheeks glowing from the exercise and her blue eyes bright. "That will do, Captain Harris," she said to her scarlet-coated escort. "You may go and flirt with the younger ladies, now that you have done your duty by the confirmed spinster."

The man bent close to her ear and murmured something, a gallantry, no doubt, and she giggled and tapped him lightly on the arm with her fan. He turned and retreated in the direction of blond and beautiful Lady Cynthia. Eveleen took a deep breath. "Well, and so you are unclaimed yet again?"

"You make me sound like a parcel that no one wants," Arabella said, waspishly.

Chuckling, Eveleen said, "Why do you think they call us 'on the shelf' when too many years have passed and we have not married? We are goods, chattel to be bartered while we have worth and forgotten when we are no longer fresh."

Arabella glanced at her friend in shock. "That is revolutionary talk."

"I am Irish; it comes naturally." Eveleen, her eyes blazing with mischief, scanned the ballroom as she spoke. "Look," she said, nodding toward the chaperones' area. "There is Leticia Parkhurst. Thirty-one, rich, titled, and yet she is not married. Her fault? She waited too long, and now no one wants her. And yet I happen to know that despite her sour looks, she is intelligent, witty, and once she has had a glass or two of wine, outrageously funny!"

"But this is just the way things are," Arabella said, ever practical. "A woman only has so long to have children, and must marry young. And a woman *must* marry! What would we do if we did not marry?"

"Paint, write, teach, doctor, soldier, travel, work, play—all the things that men are free to do without the constraints of womanhood. If only we were allowed! The pity is, that women like Leticia have been so inculcated with society's pressures, that she feels herself a failure for not marrying, as does her mother and all of our set."

"And the other things men do without constraint?" Arabella could not help herself from asking, though she blushed at the turn her thoughts were taking.

"You mean love? Or at least, *making* love?" Eveleen said, bluntly. "Would it not be lovely to do that without constraint, choosing whom one wanted, dallying here and there like the fat bumblebee drifting over the lovely flowers." She had a dreamy look on her face.

Shocked to the core, Arabella gazed up at her friend. "I . . . I do not know what to make of you when you speak like that, Eve."

"Of course you do not. You have been indoctrinated into the belief that women have only one purpose, and that is to bear some man's children. We have no passions, no desires." Eveleen's handsome face was set and grim, her eyes no longer dreamy or mischievous, though a smile was still pasted on her lips. "If we paint, we are patted on the head and told how nice it is that we can dabble; if we are politically astute, our only recourse is to marry and bully our husbands into being our cat's-paw. Any hint of passion and we are condemned as loose. It is outrageous and unfair."

"I did not know you to be so bitter, nor did I realize that you like men so little." Arabella felt a little of her world shift. People were so hard to read. She would have ventured to say that Eve, a woman she had known since her first Season four years before, was exactly what she seemed, a care-for-nothing flirt who enjoyed making her way through the London Season dancing and having a wonderful time. She had known from early in their acquaintance that Eveleen intended not to marry, but had viewed it as just some private quirk, and not a broad philosophy. But it seemed that there was some guiding principle to her life that Arabella did not understand. "With that feeling, I am surprised you wish to stay in London so badly."

"Do you think I stay here for this?" Eveleen said, sweeping one graceful, gloved hand out to indicate the expanse of the ballroom. "No, this is why my father *lets* me stay, else he would drag me back to Ireland and forcibly marry me off to some toothless farmer who does nothing but scratch and spit. He is hoping that my dowry will catch me an English title, though I would rather see Bedlam than marry some thin-blooded, knock-kneed English coronet. Do not mistake me; I like men well enough—they have their charms and purposes—but not to wed."

"Then why do you stay?"

"I stay because of a band of like-minded women who work for the freedom of other women." There was a glint of hard determination in Eveleen's glistening eyes.

"What do you mean 'like-minded women'? And freedom from what?"

"Like-minded women—women who believe that others of our sex have more reason to exist than merely as men's chattel. And the freedom we seek is freedom from—" She stopped and chuckled. "Well, now, I think your uncouth admirer is watching you again."

For the first time since he had come to her attention, Arabella had actually forgotten the stranger's whereabouts, and she looked up in shock to find his laughing eyes upon her. He was standing with Lady Parkhurst once more, and they were talking about her. He pointed, actually *pointed!* The height of ill manners.

Lady Parkhurst appeared to ask him a question and he nodded. They started toward Eveleen and Arabella. She looked away, feeling the color flood her face, as her friend watched in amusement. Infuriating man! He was likely taunting her again and would pass her by on some pretext or another. She would ignore him. She would—

"Miss Swinley, may I present Mr. Marcus Westhaven?"

Four

He bowed over her hand. "I have seen this enchanting young lady before, Lady Parkhurst, which is why I inveigled you to introduce me."

Arabella swallowed, tipped her head up, and said, "We have met? I must admit, I have no memory of such a meeting."

Lady Parkhurst was watching avidly, and Eveleen was barely stifling her laughter.

"Oh, but you must, for Lord and Lady Snowdale have retailed my blunder throughout the company. I am now known for rescuing maidens definitely not in distress."

His gray eyes danced with merriment and Arabella felt her lips curving up, responding to his liveliness. He was impossible to resist.

"Since you clearly have no partner for this set," he said, with a mocking grin, "may I ask you to sit this one out with me? I am not yet familiar with the latest dances, having been out of the country for some time."

He was laughing at her for having no partner! Arabella felt a swift burst of anger. She could not give him the setdown he deserved in front of Lady Parkhurst, but she longed to; oh, how she longed to!

"I would be delighted," she said, through gritted teeth. To refuse would be uncouth, and above all she could not risk her reputation this Season. She must be seen as the epitome of culture and manners, a lady through and through, if she was to catch a husband, even so elderly and decrepit a one as Lord Pelimore.

"If you ladies would excuse us? Lady Parkhurst, Miss O'Clannahan, your servant." He bowed gracefully and took Arabella's arm, leading her out to the refreshment room. He obtained a glass of champagne for her and a stronger drink for himself. "Shall we stroll in the conservatory? I believe it is open for that purpose."

Silently, Arabella nodded. Why had he approached her, she wondered.

They walked in silence through the large glass doors and into the moist warmth of the conservatory. Lord Parkhurst had traveled extensively, spending some time in India, and was known for his collection of exotic plants. All were labeled and named, with a card relating the plant's history and culture. They strolled the walkways, toward a tall palm that dominated the end of the room.

"What a fascinating plant," Arabella said, desperate at last for innocuous conversation. She was finding that her pulse would not return to its normal sedate pace, with him so close and her arm claimed and firmly held close to his body. She felt a shivering awareness of muscle under his coat, muscle and sinew that he kept firmly restrained in the stultifying atmosphere of London. He hinted that he had not been in England for a very long time, which perhaps explained the aura of wildness that clung to him.

"So, Mr. Westhaven, have you been to India?" Perhaps he was some rich nabob, and if not titled, had deep pockets nevertheless. That would explain his uncouth manner, yet apparent acceptability in the ballrooms of London.

"No, I have never been there. Not much of a one for tropical climes."

"But you said that you have not been in England for

a long time. The West Indies, perhaps? But no, you do not like tropical climes." Arabella nodded to another couple who strolled by, sipping champagne.

Westhaven directed her to a bench and they sat. But he did not let go of her arm. She was starting to feel suffocated, but whether it was from the cloying humidity of the conservatory, or the overpowering nearness of Mr. Westhaven, she could not have said.

Finally he released her arm, but laid his own along the back of the bench. His naked fingers—no evening gloves, shocking breach of manners!—caressed her bare shoulder, and the touch of his callused hand felt as intimate as a kiss. She shivered.

"No, I do not like tropical climates, or I do not think I would, anyway. I have been in the Canadas these last years."

"Canada!" Arabella felt a true stirring of interest beyond the polite social chitchat one engaged in. She gazed up at him avidly. "Have you ever met an Indian?"

"If you mean a native of that Continent, yes. You know, it is merely a silly mistake that has us calling them Indians. There is no reason in fact or fancy for that appellation. Yes, I have met them. I lived among them for a time."

Arabella stared at him in disbelief. "And they did not kill you?"

Westhaven put back his head and his uninhibited roar of laughter vibrated through the glass conservatory; Arabella felt that the very windows were rattling, and she was confused. Had she said something so dreadfully funny?

"Did you know that they fought on our side in the recent war—not the continental war, but the war with America? One of their great chiefs, Tecumseh, was a hero of that effort. *Died* a hero, as a matter of fact. He was called, among our army, the 'Indian Wellington,' though I think the compliment was really to Wellington. Brilliant strategist was Tecumseh, and a truly great man."

He gazed at her kindly, the smile still on his lips, and caressed her shoulder briefly. "They are not butchers, my dear girl. They are just people; they might have different habits and culture than we do, but they have families that they care about, and they work hard to provide for them, and they have disagreements that cause them to go to war, and they sometimes settle their differences without war, with treaties and agreements. They are just *people.*"

Arabella bit her lip. She felt foolish, and she *hated* feeling foolish. She stiffened and moved away from the heat that radiated from the large man at her side.

Westhaven looked down at her, and his expression became more serious. As if he were reading her mind, he said, "Do not feel stupid. Nine out of ten people I meet think that the natives of North America are 'savages,' inhuman, somehow. It is just ignorance, but you cannot know what you have not been taught and so there is no shame, my dear." He shifted to move closer to her again. "In fact some explorers added to that belief with their reports of native culture. What they did not understand, they labeled 'savage.' I have studied history; it does not seem to me that the worst crimes ever laid at the feet of native North Americans rival some of our own barbarisms, even up to the present day and the hangman's noose. In fact, one of the most civilized men I have ever met is a native gentleman by the name of George Two Feathers."

She assimilated what he was saying, relaxing a little now that she knew he did not censure her for her ignorance. The information he was giving her was new, and required some thought. "Why were you in the Canadas? What did you do?"

"First," Westhaven said, setting her champagne glass aside with his own glass, and taking her hands in his, "I want to apologize for putting you in a sticky spot in the Emporium the other day. My excuse must be that I have been away so long, I have become rusty with my manners."

Arabella gazed into his gray eyes and felt all her anger melt away. "I—there is much there that you do not understand, and that I do not wish to discuss, but thank you. I accept your apology."

He smiled. "And—?"

"And what?"

"Do you not have something to say back?"

She thought. She had accepted his apology and thanked him very prettily, she believed. What more was there? Oh, she could not think while he caressed her hands in that intimate manner! "No. What more would I have to say?"

"I thought you might want to apologize to me for biting my head off when I was only trying to do you a service."

"Apologize?" she cried. "Apologize? I do not think I have anything to apologize for! If you had not stuck your big nose in where it was not wanted—" At that moment Arabella saw his grin. Infuriating man! "Oh! You are roasting me. Very well, I will do this handsomely." She sat up straight, looked him in the eye, and said, "I apologize for biting your head off when you only thought—great, hulking simpleton that you are—that you were doing me a service." She felt a lighthearted desire to laugh, something she had not felt yet this Season.

"Well, how can I argue with that! What a *handsome* apology, indeed!" He rolled his eyes.

"Now tell me what you were doing in Canada." She was very conscious that he retained her hands in his firm grip. His hands were large and strong and very, *very* warm. A strange, foreign trill of something like happiness trickled down her spine and fluttered in her stomach.

"Your wish is my command. Let's see, where to start. The beginning I guess. That is always safe." He relaxed back and crossed one leg over the other, keeping her hand in one of his and laying his free arm over the back of the bench again. "I am a civilian, but I have always been fascinated by maps and mapping and have some experience as a cartographer, so about eleven years ago I went over independently to see some more of the world and ended up attached to an army regiment as a hydrographer—that is a mapper of waterways. I don't know how familiar you are with the geography of North America, but there is a collection of lakes in about the center of the continent that is enormous! Breathtakingly large, like inland oceans, and beautiful, silvery in the morning, and like glass when calm. We started mapping them, their shorelines and tributaries, and then a few years ago the war started, and they found a use for my knowledge of the area and my unique, uh, skills."

"Did you like it?"

"Like it? I loved it." His eyes became misty, like an early morning fog rolling in off a lake. "Canada is like no other place you have ever seen. Everything is so big there! The trees, the forests, the lakes, the rivers—everything is on a grand scale, and fresh and clean, as God must have meant the earth to be. You know, we believe that God gave us the earth to look after, to superintend, as if we are masters of all we survey, but the native inhabitants of North America believe that the Great Spirit created the earth and all on it to coexist. They feel that the relationship is more like kinship than mastery. That difference of opinion has led to some of the major disagreements between European and native." He paused and looked down at their joined hands. His rough fingers caught the delicate silk of her glove.

"Kinship—that is fascinating. Tell me more," Arabella said, breathless and eager. His voice was deep, and he conveyed all the grandeur of the New World in his words. It intrigued her more than she would have believed possible. She felt she could listen to him all night.

He smiled down at her, searching her eyes. "If . . . if you really wish."

"I do," she said. "I want to learn more about Canada. I have heard so little, but what I have heard made me wish to know more, to see it through someone's eyes."

"Very well. I have explored for years, but there is still so much to see, so much to do! West of the lakes, many miles west, there is a series of great mountains to rival the Alps. I have heard that they are huge and soar to great snowy peaks and plunge to deep valley gorges where wild, white water tumbles. My dream is to see them, to find a way to the Pacific through them."

"Why have you come back to England?" Arabella asked. She was feeling winded, as if she had been scaling one of those enormous mountains, breathing that wild, free, fresh air. How marvelous it must be, how absolutely invigorating. If she were only a man, she would—But he had not answered her question. "Why have you come back, Mr. Westhaven, if you love it so?"

He reached out with one large hand and caressed a ringlet that scraped her bare shoulder. His hand was so warm she could feel the heat radiating from it, and yet the very heat made her shiver.

His eyes met hers and held them. "I have come into an inheritance, or am about to, anyway."

Arabella felt her pulse quicken. He was inheriting money? If he should be rich, and perhaps coming into a title—the possibilities frightened her a little. She had never felt this immediate interest in a man, a man at the same time fascinating and infuriating. If he were rich and titled and looking to wed? A vision of marriage to a man of such frightening charisma and overwhelming power entranced and yet alarmed her. "How . . . fortunate for you. Are you . . . will you . . . is it a large inheritance?"

He chuckled. "I am not sure how much it is yet. I am a very poor man, you know, so any money will seem like a lot." He gazed at her steadily. "Does it matter?" he said, softly.

Treacherous shoals, she thought. No man, and especially not this one, wanted to be valued for his purse alone. "Of course not! It was just a casual question."

His gray eyes hooded in the dimness of the conservatory, he said, "I think it will be a couple hundred. Not more than that."

A couple of hundred pounds. It may seem like a lot to him, but it was nothing, the merest pittance. And she was sitting in the conservatory with him speaking of nonsense when she should be out circulating and finding her future mate. Disappointment fueled anger, anger at *herself* for being caught up in his marvelous dream of traveling to far-off places, and anger at *him* for not being eligible. She did not have time to lose her sense of purpose this Season!

Marcus saw her nose go up, and almost felt her chill. For a few minutes he had seen her warmth, a vivacity he found entrancing. She was genuinely interested in Canada, he thought; on some level the wildness of it appealed to her.

And by God, she was beautiful, especially when her green eyes sparkled and she shook back her blond curls impatiently as she listened, enraptured. Smooth skin, slim, supple figure, exquisite of face and form; he felt the pulse of attraction even as he watched her pert nose turn up and felt her withdraw from him. Apparently he was not rich enough for her, mercenary little baggage. What a disappointment.

He was not surprised when she stood. "We—I think this number is over, and we should be getting back to the ballroom."

He stood and stretched, flexing his muscles, feeling them begin to atrophy from the unaccustomed lack of exercise. Her eyes widened as she almost unwillingly gazed at his body, eyeing his shoulders. She licked her lips and swallowed, and he felt an inevitable stirring in his loins at her interest. Damn, but he wished she were another type of woman, one available for seduction. The blush on her pretty cheeks told him much about her own awareness of the physical attraction that existed between them. She might be innocent—in fact he was sure she must be—but there were passionate depths to her that were unexplored. But he would not be the one to plumb them; that honor would be reserved for the rich husband she was no doubt laying her snares for. Too bad.

He escorted her back into the ballroom just as the set was changing. Her next partner claimed her and she was led into the line, just as her friend, Eveleen O'Clannahan, drifted toward him. Little Miss Swinley had an almost comical look of dismay on her face, and he wondered what she was worried about.

"Mr. Westhaven, you and my friend disappeared for quite some time."

He grinned at her. "Do men and women not lose track of time in England, when they are finding each other's company fascinating?"

"Is that what happened?"

"Certainly. She was asking questions about my experiences in the Canadas. Tell me, Miss O'Clannahan, is Miss Swinley wealthy?"

The young woman's reddish eyebrows raised in surprise. "That is a question I cannot and will not answer, sir. And it is not the done thing to ask, you know."

"Now, if there was one woman in this room who I thought would enjoy flouting convention, it would be you," he said. Miss O'Clannahan was the type of woman who would do well in the wilds of Canada, he thought. From their brief conversation earlier, he thought she had a mental toughness that she hid from the world.

"It is not convention I would be flouting by giving you that information, but friendship. *That* I will never abandon."

He bowed slightly. "I honor your circumspection, and your loyalty."

"I can tell you a little about Arabella if you are interested." She glanced at him sideways, and took his silence as consent. "Arabella Swinley is the daughter of Baron Swinley, who died a few years ago. Before his death she spent little time with her parents. From what I can gather—for you must know, delicacy forbade me asking direct questions—her mother, Lady Swinley, had no use for her before it was time for her come-out, so she spent all of her school holidays with her cousin Miss Truelove Becket, now married to a wealthy viscount down in Hampshire, somewhere. I think Miss Becket was a good influence on little Arabella, but since she has been with her mother, she has learned to think differently about some things. I worry about that."

Marcus glanced sideways. This was a new side to Miss O'Clannahan, whom he had taken for a rather cynical, hard-edged young woman. "Her mother is not a healthy influence?"

"Her mother," the lady said, acidly, "is a mercenary,

money-grubbing—I have no words for what I think of Lady Swinley and her effect on Arabella."

At that moment, Arabella sailed by in the arms of a young man. She was smiling up at him and gaily laughing, but even from a distance Marcus could see a hint of desperate eagerness in her flirtation. "Who is that fellow?"

Eveleen peered rather shortsightedly at Arabella's partner. "Oh, that is Bessemere, next Duke of Haliburton. Poor fellow, he is this year's prize. Rather like a stud bull, don't you know? Everybody's preferred stock."

Marcus gazed at him with disdain. "That child? He looks frightened, as if the world is out to bite him. He would not last two minutes in Canada. What makes him such a prize?"

"He is the next Duke of Haliburton," Eveleen said, patiently. "He is the Marquess of Bessemere, in his own right wealthy, and when he becomes Haliburton, he will have access to millions—literally, *millions* of pounds. And it is rumored they are looking for a match for him this year. But his mother will never choose someone like Arabella. She is wasting her time on him. She is too lowborn and too poor."

"Do you mean she is flirting with him to try to gain his attention?"

Miss O'Clannahan turned and placed her hands on her hips. "See here, Westhaven, just how long have you been out of the country, and what *have* you remembered about all of this?"

Marcus was silent. He remembered Arabella's eyes when he said he was about to inherit, the way the green had deepened to jade. So she truly was nothing more than a money-grubbing little schemer, he thought with disappointment, and his burgeoning feelings for her must be nothing more than physical attraction, and the tendency to imbue the desired object with graces and attributes.

Eveleen O'Clannahan was watching him, he could feel it, and he met her steady gaze.

"You blame her for her ambition?" the young woman asked.

"How can I help but blame her for fortune hunting? You yourself called the *mother* mercenary. I despise people who only care about wealth. It was one of the reasons I was not sad to leave this country."

"And no one anywhere else in the world does this, or something very like it? Do parents in other lands not wish their children to marry well, to be wealthy and happy, whatever that means in another culture? Somehow, I cannot believe it."

"But *we* have made a sport of it," Marcus protested. "Like hunting. In England we hunt for the inedible merely for the sport. You will not find anyone in Canada doing that. There, we hunt to eat. There is so much about this country I do not like." He watched Arabella sail by again, her whole focus on the young man holding her in his arms. He felt his stomach convulse in a queer twist of jealously and revulsion. "How can she," he burst out, crossing his arms across his chest. "She is so intelligent and witty and beautiful and lively and—and she is worth *more* than that, damn it, so much more!"

"Do not condemn, sir, what you do not understand. I urge you to get to know her before you decide what she is. You could be surprised." Eveleen, with one last look at Marcus, turned away from him and drifted off to join other friends.

Five

Arabella buried her nose in the massive bouquet of white roses that sat on a table in the hall, and sniffed deeply. What a glorious scent! She eagerly read the card and felt a jolt of disappointment. They were from Lord Bessemere. She should be in alt, for such an offering meant she had made an impression on him, though a personal visit would have been better. And she had liked the young marquess. He was not bad-looking, she supposed, and his character was one of studious gentleness. For the longest time he had seemed almost frightened by her gay chatter until she had hit on the subject of books, not something she knew a lot about, but that was never a reason to shy away from a subject, she had learned, since gentlemen invariably wanted to lead the talk anyway. Then his eyes had lit up and the rest of their dance, a waltz, had gone well.

No, her disappointment was not because she had not liked him; she had. But she had hoped a floral offering would come from another gentleman she had spent some time with. She searched among the bouquets and cards. Sanders, MacDonough, Lewisham, Andrews—not there.

Nestled among the larger bouquets, though, she saw a tiny basket and fished it out. It was small, just the size of her two cupped hands, and it was made of some strange white bark and with a twig handle, all lashed together with what looked like leather thongs. It had a kind of rough, sturdy beauty all its own. Nestled in the basket, in moss, was a small bouquet of golden buttercups. A moment of fierce longing swept over her, a longing for her childhood. These were the very same flowers she and True and Faith, True's younger sister, had been used to gather down by the river when they were all children at the vicarage where True's father made his home.

Tears pricked the back of her eyes as she turned the basket around, noting the fascinating texture of the bark and how it contrasted with the soft waxy petals of the buttercups. Who sent this? She saw a note slipped down in the basket and pulled it out. It was damp from the moss, but she could still read it.

"To the Belle of the Ball, from a secret admirer."

Her heart thudded. It had to be from Westhaven; the rough bark was as unique as he was, rugged yet attractive. Somehow she knew it was his offering, and her heart was touched. As she stared at it she relived the thrill of his hands touching her, his gray eyes looking deep into hers, as though he were seeking her very soul. She had never been stirred like that, had never felt as though—

"What is that you have there?"

Her mother had come upon her, her slippers silent on the marble floor of the hall of their borrowed Mayfair town home. Flustered, Arabella said, "Oh, 'tis nothing, just a . . . a small basket with a nosegay of buttercups from . . . from a secret admirer, it says."

Lady Swinley grabbed the basket, glared at it, and said, "Paltry offering! Who would send such a piece of trash?"

"I . . . I don't know."

"Buttercups? Must be a poor man."

"I think it's rather pretty, don't you, Mother?"

"Pretty?" Lady Swinley's hard eyes narrowed. "My girl, any man who was really interested in you would send something more than mere country flowers. He must know you will be besieged with offerings, and any man who wanted to fix your interest would try to dazzle you. Buttercups? Ha!"

Frowning, Arabella considered her mother's words and reluctantly decided they held a great deal of sense. Should a man not be trying to impress her? Was that not the game men and women played, until each could single the other out from the crowd?

Lady Swinley threw the basket down on the table and sailed away, calling over her shoulder, "Come, Arabella. We have much to do today, so no dawdling."

But Arabella could not resist rescuing the small basket. "Brock," she said to a footman passing, "could you have this taken up to my room, please? Have Annie set it on my bedside table."

"Yes, miss," he said, taking the basket.

For the rest of the day Arabella was on tenterhooks, wondering if *he* would visit. Gentlemen came and gentlemen went, but Westhaven did not make an appearance. Oh, well, she thought. She had mentioned that she was to attend the Tredwell musicale that evening; maybe he was invited, too, and she would see him there. She did not want to think why she was so intent on seeing him again. He was an infuriating man, alternately teasing and maddening and charming. And there could be no future. He had said himself he was poor enough that a couple of hundred pounds seemed like a lot of money to him.

But he was not at the Tredwell musicale that evening, nor at the Silkertons' Venetian breakfast the next day, nor at the Smythe-Jones ball the next evening. But Bessemere was, and so was Lord Pelimore.

Lady Swinley, impressed by the massive bouquet of

white roses Bessemere had sent to Arabella, advised her
to try for the younger, wealthier man, but if there was
no definite sign within days that he was attempting to
fix his interest with her, she was to transfer her attentions to Lord Pelimore, who was, after all, a baron and
quite wealthy. She sat with Lord Pelimore, danced with
Bessemere, and spent some time talking to both.

With Lord Pelimore she merely listened while he retailed story after story of his youth and the high adven-
tures he had had. By his own admission he had been a
rascal, a bon vivant of the old king's time, when every
gentleman still wore a wig, and men's clothing was silk
and lace to rival a lady's. She could not help but let her
mind wander to the memory of a tall, broad-shouldered
man dressed in sober black, so masculine as to make
all other men in the room appear effeminate. Could
she picture *him* rigged out in lace and satin, carrying
the *de rigeur* gentleman's accessory of the last century,
a fan? No, she could not, but if he did he would somehow contrive to make it look manly, like the brilliant
feathers of a peacock beside the dull plumage of a pea-
hen.

The next night at the Connolly ball, Eveleen sought
her out in the withdrawing room while Arabella removed her shawl and left it with Annie, her maid. Lady
Swinley had already hurried off to accost a crony she
had not yet seen that Season. After a brief hug of greeting, Eveleen said, "And has your rough-hewn swain
come to visit you since the Parkhurst ball?"

"My—" Arabella colored. "I do not know who you
mean, Eve."

The older woman chuckled as she took Arabella's
arm and strolled with her into the ballroom. It was already full, and the noise of a hundred or more chattering people echoed from the high vaulted ceiling as the
heat from their bodies created a swirl of air. "Oh, Bella,

how can you say that with a straight face? You are looking around the room for him this very minute, are you not? I thought perhaps he told you he was to be here."

Arabella's color deepened and she stopped her quick scan of the ballroom. "I will not pretend to misunderstand you; you mean Mr. Marcus Westhaven. I have no more interest in Mr. Westhaven than he has in me, so you can stop fishing for information."

"So little interest as that, hmm? I happen to know that he was invited tonight."

"Really? Is he here? Have you—" Arabella stopped abruptly, cursing her unruly tongue.

Eveleen fought back a smile. "No, he sent regrets, apparently. 'Unavoidable business' was the excuse, I think. He has a letter of introduction, you know—I have that from Lady Connolly herself, who is some sort of aunt or cousin to me—which is why he is invited. Some regimental captain from the Canadas, very well connected, etcetera, begs Lady Connolly to 'be kind to him.' "

So that explained his forays into the upper echelons of society, Arabella thought, with disappointment. He must have asked all of his contacts in the regiment for letters to people they knew in London. She realized that she had been cherishing secret hopes that he would prove to be the long-lost scion of some noble house, but that was clearly ridiculous, given his poverty.

"Let us not talk of men tonight," Arabella said. She looked her friend over, from the jeweled headpiece of emeralds in her hair to the tips of her slippered feet. "I have missed you these last couple of days. You look marvelous in that green, Eveleen. It becomes you."

With a humorous smile, she replied, "And that lavender becomes *you*. Now we have canvassed clothing, what else shall we speak of?"

Arabella knew what she wanted to ask her friend, but

she could not bring the subject up. She must turn her mind away from such unprofitable lines and concentrate on the business of the Season, which was to find a gentleman and marry him. Preferably not old Lord Pelimore. They took a place at the edge of the ballroom, near a magenta draped window that was open just a little to let in the still-cool spring air. The room was already hot, and before long it would be stifling from the body heat of hundreds of energetically galloping couples. The Connolly ball was well attended and would likely be called a "squeeze" the next day in the papers. That would be considered a compliment.

Sighing, Eveleen said, languidly, "I suppose you really must marry this Season?"

"Yes. It is imperative that I find someone and attach him before too long. We . . . my mother is depending on me, Eve." Arabella smiled and nodded at a couple of young ladies who passed her, arm in arm. She scanned the crowd and saw Bessemere with his mother, the formidable Lady Haliburton, formerly an intimate of Lady Farmington. Would she have heard? Could the Farmington debacle ruin her chances with young Lord Bessemere?

And there was still Lord Conroy to be worried about. He always attended the Season; it was life and meat to him. Why was he not yet in London? Was it because of his mother's indisposition? Could she count on his continued absence? Surely not. After all, the woman would recover sometime. But even when he did come, could Arabella perhaps hope that he would be as little willing to have his private affairs bandied about society as she was, and so he would stay silent and not ruin her? It was her best hope for salvation.

"And what has your mother ever done for you that you are now responsible for her?"

There was a fierceness in her friend's voice. Startled,

she gazed into Eve's blue eyes and said, "What . . . what do you mean?"

"I mean, why is it up to you to repair the family fortune when it was not you who lost it but your parents? Does it not seem unfair to you? How can you go like a lamb to the slaughter?" Eveleen waved a fan in front of her face, hiding her scowl.

Shocked, Arabella said, "Well of course it is up to me! Is that not what has always happened? Many a young man has married an heiress he was not fond of just to 'repair the family fortune,' as you said it."

"And what about love? What about finding that one man who makes your heart pound and your palms damp? You should not seek a fat purse at the expense of your young life!"

Arabella's mind immediately flew to Westhaven and how his mere presence sent her senses reeling. She shook her head. She must teach herself not to think like that. It would hardly be fair to her future husband if she did, and it was certainly not seemly in a maiden to think of his square shoulders and muscular body and—She turned her mind away from such thoughts. "I am surprised at you, Eveleen. I had thought you did not even like men, and here you are speaking of love like some green girl, dewy-eyed and in her first Season." Her voice sounded acid, even to her own ears. Love was for other women, not for her. She had never felt it for any man, and doubted she would at three-and-twenty if she had not as a susceptible girl.

"I do not dislike men, quite the contrary. I just do not think there are that many good ones out there. But have you never seen an example of love, my dear?" Eveleen's voice had gone from fierce to gentle, so soft it was almost drowned out by the increasing noise of the crowd and the sound of the orchestra tuning up in the gallery above them.

But she heard her. Yes, Arabella thought. She had
seen true love, quite literally. Her cousin, Truelove
Becket, had found the real thing with Lord Drake, the
man she, Arabella, was supposed to marry. She could
not understand it herself. Drake was good-looking, certainly, with the kind of "golden god" looks that women
swooned over, but when Truelove fell in love with him
he was also crippled from the war and suffering through
a period of mental turmoil, nightmares so horrific he
screamed the house down most nights. Arabella had
been appalled and frightened, but True had fallen in
love with him despite his problems.

Such self-sacrifice was not for her, though. She was
far too practical to fall for mere manly good looks,
though to be fair True had fallen in love with her
husband's character, she claimed, not his title or his
looks. That was Truelove, though, not her. She
needed a more pragmatic reason to give up the single state. She needed cold, hard cash, a title, and
land. Love would not pay off her mother's debts, nor
keep her in the style in which she preferred to live.

She frowned at her friend. "Of course I know that
true love does exist. I suppose I am only surprised that
you would believe in it, Eve. You seemed so cynical the
other night, about affairs between men and women."

"Not cynical, my dear, but I do think that society has
warped relations between men and women. I acknowl-
edge the need for a degree of financial comfort, but
society has made that into the way we separate the worthy from the unworthy."

"How can that be, that this is wrong? Have we not
created society? It is a reflection of the strengths and
weaknesses of both sexes, is it not? We need men's protection. We need their income to support us, and they
need . . . they need our, well, our children."

"Why do we need their protection?"

"Well, other men—"

"Exactly! Society has dictated that an unwed woman is in need of protection from *other men!* Is that not deplorable?" Eveleen's eyes were dark with anger. "Why is it that a woman alone is seen as suitable prey for men's depredations? That we are somehow lacking in morality if we choose to be alone?"

"Well, setting aside that, women need a husband to take care of them financially."

"And why is *that*? I will tell you; it is because society has dictated that a woman of quality cannot look after her own money, nor make her own way in the world except among the lowest paid and most looked-down-upon professions, like governessing or teaching, or as companion to other women. They think we are not capable of handling money, or government, or of succeeding in any of the paying arts beyond a little genteel piano playing or sketching. It is abominable, I tell you! We should be free to pursue our interests and make our living just as any man is." Her azure eyes blazed with fire.

If Eveleen's vision of the perfect world—a world where women were on an equal footing with men—were only the reality, Arabella thought, allowing herself a glorious dream for just a moment. Then she could travel, like Westhaven, to the far-flung reaches of the empire. She would go west, to the Canadas, and explore those lofty peaks and cavernous gorges, she would traverse mountain passes, making her own way free and unfettered by societal disapproval.

It sounded thrilling, but—ah, there was the rub. It was not and never would be the way of the world. She shook her head. "I do not understand half of what you say, Eve," she said, dismissing it all from her mind. She was too practical to regret what could never be. "To return to our original topic, though, I know that love is possible, but for someone like me, not probable. I do not have the luxury of time, you see, and I have never found anyone I could love. So why should I not benefit myself in marriage like everyone else does? It is the way of our world."

"Perhaps you are right," Eveleen said, musing. "But," she finished, with an arch smile, "have you really *never* found anyone you could love? Honestly?" A gentleman in scarlet regimentals, a Captain Harris, came to claim Eveleen for a dance, and she drifted away with one long, lingering look at her friend.

The evening progressed, and Arabella forgot—or at least, attempted to forget—her conversation with Eveleen. She danced most dances, trying to master the art of not looking too desperate when she felt like time was dwindling and she must make every second count. Her social education should have stood her in good stead, but she felt awkward and did not know why. She felt suddenly like she did not belong, as if her desperation were a leprous disease that made her unfit for good company. Bessemere, now that his mother was present, was tongue-tied and inarticulate in her company, and nothing Arabella could do would set him at ease. Had he heard of the Lord Conroy embarrassment? Just thinking of it made her feverish all over.

Lord Pelimore was courted by many, now that it was known he definitely would be choosing a new bride this Season. All of the mothers were throwing their plain daughters at the baron in the hopes that his standards would not be too nice, so Arabella did not push too hard, relying on her looks—which in all modesty she knew to be good—to attract his attention. He might be old, but he was still a man.

And it was working. The modest looks she threw his way, the way she was always just on the periphery of the crowd around him, it was drawing his eye more and more to her, and she knew with a certainty borne of experience that he would soon single her out. Did she want that? She supposed she must. What other option did she have?

Always in the past she had done such things, the flirtatious glances, the demure coquetry, to test her skills, to ensure that the allure was still there and working for her. Men had been drawn and then released; it was like fishing when she was a child. She didn't even like fish—at least, not to eat—but catching them had been fun. Faith, her cousin, the same age as her almost, had never understood why she wanted to let the fish go after catching them.

And she had released many a gentleman fish, only to see them swim almost directly into the nets of another fisherwoman. Lord Sweetan, her would-be fiancé from the previous year, was already engaged. He was said to be in London, but they had not yet chanced to be at the same event. She could only be glad; their last interview had not been pleasant. She drifted over to the chaperone's area and joined her mother. Lady Swinley was magnificent in dark plum satin—last year's dress, just as Arabella's was—and wore an ostrich plume in her turban.

Just as she was about to speak to her mother, someone touched her elbow and she whirled, her heart thudding. It was Lord Pelimore, and she felt foolish for the hope that had leaped into her heart. She knew *he* was not coming that night; had not Eveleen already told her that?

"Miss Swinley," the aging peer said, with a bow, "I do not often dance, as you know, but if there is a space on your card free, I would be most pleased if you would sit one out with me."

Lady Swinley's eyes shone with triumph, and she said, "My daughter would be delighted, sir. Your gracious condescension has undone her, thus her silence. In fact, her next dance is free." She nudged Arabella with her elbow.

"Uh, yes, my lord. As a matter of fact, I do have this dance free, the only free one on my card, I fear." It would not do to look too available. No man desired what no other man wanted. They were competitive beasts, like dogs eyeing a bone. Each wanted the choice bits, and the choice bits must be what everyone else wanted. My, but she was utilizing animal metaphors of late! She smiled and curtsied, and Lord Pelimore took her arm and escorted her to a seating area in an alcove behind a marble pillar, out of sight of most of the crowd. Arabella felt faintly uneasy, but the gentleman released her arm and sat wearily down. It appeared all he wanted was some peace and quiet.

"Hot in here," he said, mopping his brow with a handkerchief. He blew his nose in it, then retrieved his snuff case, offered her some, and when she refused, took a great snort himself. He sneezed repeatedly and blew his nose once more before putting away the hand-kerchief. His nose was a little bulbous, and threaded with red veins.

Snapping open her fan and waving it languidly to hide her repulsion, Arabella murmured, "Yes, it is a trifle warm."

"How those young gels do giggle," he said, critically, gazing at a gaggle of seventeen-year-old girls, all in white as befitted them so early in their first Season.

And I suppose I am ancient, Arabella thought crossly, suddenly *feeling* old. She was three-and-twenty, and be-ing courted by a man old enough to be her grandfather.

There was silence for a moment, and when Arabella stole a glance sideways it was to find Pelimore staring at her. She smiled.

"Won't beat about the bush, m'girl. Not getting any

younger. Not that I'm as old as that Lord Oakmont. Friend of m'father's, b'lieve it or not. Have you heard the news?"

Bewildered, Arabella shook her head.

Pelimore pulled at his breeches and shifted uneasily on the marble bench. "Oakmont," he continued, "he's ninety-four, I b'lieve. Going to stick his spoon in the wall any day, it's said. Frantic search for the heir. Some great-nephew has come forth. Don't want that to happen to me. Been thinking about that ever since m'son Jamie up and died last year. Thirty-eight, and he dies b'fore his pa. Ain't right. Not at all. So, I'm in the market." He gazed at her with squinted eyes, as he would size up a prize bit of horseflesh. He nodded once. "I'm in the market for a wife, y'see."

Arabella fidgeted in her chair. It almost sounded like he was going to make her an offer right then and there! She should be grateful for this blunt approach, since she wanted no sweet words from the elderly man, but she was not ready for the proposal yet. Desperately wanting to put off the moment, she picked up the subject, settling her skirts around her and fiddling with her fan. "That is the Earl of Oakmont, I believe, of whom you speak. I had not heard that he was on his deathbed. Poor man."

"Oldest peer livin' it's said. Too damned old, if you ask me. Outlived everyone else. My da, now he died at a sensible age. Sixty-eight, he was. That were thirty years ago."

"Really," Arabella said, faintly. Thirty years ago. And Lord Pelimore would not have been a young man even then.

"Oakmont's great-nevvie's come forward, like I said. Been in India all this time, I hear. Nabob, now; rich in his own right and brown as a nut, so they say."

"Someone has seen the Oakmont heir?" Arabella said.

"Lady Jacobs had it from some fella who knew some other fella what was in the solicitor's office what handles old Lord Oakmont's estate. Guess they're doin' all the checks ta make sure the fella is who he says he is. Disappeared for some years, doncha know. Can't be lax about that kind of thing. Primogeniture, an' all that. Rights of inheritance—mighty important. Which brings me back around to my own dilemma, you see—"

"Is the nephew an older man, have you heard?" Arabella asked, gripping her fan tightly, not wanting to hear, yet, about his dilemma. Perhaps this nut brown Croesus, Oakmont's heir, would be not past middle age and on the lookout for a wife. Perhaps there was still time to find a more acceptable husband—more acceptable to her stomach if not to her purse. She felt quite queasy at having to entertain a proposal from the gentleman beside her. Her cousin, True, had explained a little about the intimacy of the marriage bed, and the thought of lying with this old man and allowing such familiarities was repulsive to her. She would have to submit to it, she supposed, and yet . . . and yet—

"Can't be *too* old," Lord Pelimore said. "Not like me."

Arabella, caught off guard by his unusual self-deprecation, relied on her social instincts at that moment, and burst out, "Oh, but, Lord Pelimore, you are not old! Why, you cannot be a day over . . . over forty, surely!"

She heard a snort of disbelief, and from behind the pillar strolled Mr. Marcus Westhaven, looking very much at his ease and as handsome as ever in unrelieved black.

Six

"What do you want, young man? Private conversation, doncha know?" Pelimore's voice was querulous as he glared at Westhaven, who lounged against the pillar as if he had nothing better to do.

He had heard that ridiculous piece of flattery; Arabella could see it in the merriment in his gray eyes. The reluctant joy she felt at his presence was tempered by the knowledge that he must think her a mercenary flirt. After all, it must be obvious to anyone who happened to observe what was going on between her and the baron; everyone knew he was on the lookout for a wife. But what did she care what Mr. Westhaven thought? He was nothing to her. She tossed her head haughtily.

"Lord Pelimore, may I present Mr. Marcus Westhaven?"

"Westhaven, Westhaven . . . I know I have heard that name lately, but where?" Pelimore, his thick eyebrows beetling over his dark eyes, stared up at Westhaven.

"I am sure I do not know, sir," he replied, politely. He turned his smoky gaze toward Arabella and bowed low. "This dance is just ending, Miss Swinley."

His voice was rich and low, and she felt a thrill shiver through her down to the toes of her elegant silver slippers.

"May I see your dance card?" he asked, holding her gaze with his.

BELLE OF THE BALL   69

Arabella flushed and hid it in the folds of her dress. She had implied to Lord Pelimore that it was quite full, when in fact it was almost empty. She felt the humiliation of that sharply, especially now, with Marcus Westhaven. "I . . . I must have lost it somewhere."

"Why no, I think it is still on your wrist, along with your fan. I see it peeping out of the skirt of your elegant gown." Westhaven leaned over and plucked it out of the folds of her lavender dress, pulling her wrist as an unwilling hostage, encircled as it was by the ribbon attaching the card. "Ah, what luck." He took her little pencil and wrote in his name, with a flourish. "There. Walk with me, Miss Swinley."

With a look of apology to Lord Pelimore, Arabella stood and put her arm through Westhaven's. In truth, she could think of nothing she would like more than to walk with him and talk with him—infuriating man though he was—but at what cost? She had been close to a proposal, she thought, even though she had been trying to avoid it. She must have been mad; she should have encouraged Pelimore, should have allowed him his say. Then she would now be engaged and could relax for the rest of the Season with the security of betrothal. What had she been about, discouraging the man she felt that inevitably she must marry? Lud, but she was so confused! It was almost as if her mind and her heart worked independently, battling over what she *should* do and what she *wanted* to do.

Her mother would be furious if she heard that Lord Pelimore had been interrupted in the middle of an "interesting conversation," and by a nobody like Mr. Marcus Westhaven. Well, Arabella rationalized, if Pelimore was close to a proposal, he would not give up merely because of this. It never hurt the gentlemen to have to chase a lady; it was all part of the sport, as much as her own flirtatious ways were. And her mother need never know, after all. All would be well. And in the meantime, she might as well enjoy this half-hour with Mr. West-haven.

She walked away, gazing up at his stern profile, the hard line of his jaw jutting aggressively forward. From her angle she could see the silky sheen of his long hair and wondered if it *felt* like silk to the touch. Absurd thought, but still, her fingers twitched with longing. She tightened her hold on his arm.

If only he were rich, she thought, with a deep sigh of regret. If only.

Marcus stayed silent at first as he strolled the ball-room with Arabella Swinley on his arm, conquering the unreasoning anger he felt. For some reason it infuriated him to hear a bright, vivacious, intelligent girl like Ara-bella Swinley making up to that old relic, Lord Peli-more. He knew the truth, had heard the gossip. Pelimore was looking for a wife to bear him an heir because he couldn't stand his nephew, who stood to inherit the title and estate after the death of the baron's only son.

But did he have to choose the best and the brightest of London belles for such a mundane chore as filling his nursery? Let him choose some other girl, not this flower, this blooming, lovely English rose! And speaking of flowers—He guided her to a private nook and re-leased her arm. He gazed down at her. "Did you receive my flowers?"

Stiffly, she said, "That little basket? Yes."

Snob, he thought fiercely. He was wasting his time on her, and she did not deserve his consideration. "That 'little basket,' as you so slightingly call it, was handmade of birch bark by a native girl of seven, and given to me before I left as a precious gift! She is the daughter of

my friend, George Two Feathers, and I cherish it." He
heard the grating anger in his own voice, but didn't
give a damn about how he sounded. What had possessed him to give Mary's sweet gift to someone who
could not appreciate its value?

She had the grace to look abashed and her cheeks
flamed red. She glanced around their private alcove,
avoiding his eyes. Her lips trembled, and she stuttered,
"I d—do like it, Mr. Westhaven, I . . . I p—p—put it on
my b—bedside table."

He swallowed hard. What was it about her that made
him want to shake her and then kiss her? Why did he
bother with her at all? And yet he could not seem to
stay away; something about her drew him. He softened
his voice, and said, "I picked the buttercups myself, you
know. Their color reminded me of your hair, how it
would look in the sunlight." He reached up and
touched one ringlet, winding the glossy curl around his
finger. Touching it to his lips, he inhaled the fragrance
that drifted from her.

Nervously she shied away from his touch, avoiding
his gaze, and with a shake of her head, pulled her curl
from his grasp. If only they were not in so very public
a place, he thought, if only! He would show her she
need not shy away from him, need not fear his lips and
his hands. A little shocked at the direction his mind
would take when he saw her innocent blush, he folded
his hands together and glanced around. The temptation was strong to find out if the rose blush on her
cheeks was warm to the touch, but though in a nook,
they were still in the ballroom, with people parading
past every few seconds. He reined in his wandering
thoughts.

"They are the very flowers I used to gather with my
cousins," Miss Swinley said, her voice faint and breathless. She calmed down, took a deep breath, and spoke

again. "I lived at the vicarage, their home, for much of my childhood, and we would go fishing, and swimming and gather flowers. My cousin is a great herbalist and knows the names of everything. In fact she saved her husband's life—he was not her husband then, but they married soon after—with an herbal infusion of white willow when he fell ill with the—" She stopped, her green eyes wide, and looked up in confusion. "Oh, I am babbling. I do apologize, Mr. Westhaven."

"No, don't apologize," he said, smiling and touching her shoulder with a brief caress. He felt her shiver. He was entranced, charmed against his will, and knew why he had not been able to get her out of his mind for the two days he had spent away from London on unavoidable business. When she talked of her childhood he caught glimpses of a sweet girl, unaffected and good-natured, the girl she may have been before London society changed her into an automaton, a performing doll. What a jumble of contradictions she was, part schemer, part dreamer—or was that just his desire for her coloring her character with charming traits? "What else did you do at your cousin's?" he said, wanting to draw her out.

It seemed he had breached some wall in her, coming upon her so suddenly as he had. He had broken through, briefly, her stiff, social facade. For a quarter hour she spoke of the vicarage down in Cornwall, a memorable trip to Polperro when she was eleven, riding the vicarage pony, visiting the poor with her cousin, a vicar's daughter. She lost her self-consciousness after a while and chattered as happily as a child, with just occasional prompting from him. She was lively and animated, green eyes flashing, her hands in use when she talked of her first riding experience, which ended with her on her bottom in a thistle patch. He roared with laughter. He was completely at his ease with her.

And he thought he was as happy as he had ever been in his life.

He had come back to England with every expectation of enjoyment, but so far the trip had not proved as enjoyable as he had expected. He had looked up old friends only to find them stuffy and stultifying and full of annoying and wrongheaded assumptions about Canada that they would not allow him to correct. Somehow they presumed to know more about the country he had just come from than he who had spent the last eleven years there. Galling in the extreme.

And the business he was there in England to resolve could not be called a happy one, by any means. He was not even sure how he felt about the inevitable outcome. So altogether, the visit to his homeland had so far not been an unqualified success. This moment, in a London ballroom with the Honorable Miss Swinley, was the happiest part of his trip "home" so far. He watched her lovely, joyful face, alight with mischief as she recalled pranks she had pulled and trouble she had caused as a child, with very little evidence of remorse. He thought he would have liked her as a child much better than her cousin, True, who sounded altogether *too* good.

He took her arm and guided her out of the alcove, taking her on a stroll around the ballroom. The noise and heat were overpowering, but if it was the price he must pay for a half-hour with this girl, then he would gladly pay it.

"How big is Canada, truly?" she asked, her eyebrows knotted together.

"What?" He had lost himself momentarily in her twinkling jade eyes, and could not think.

"I have heard that it is huge—Canada, I mean—but I cannot fathom it. One country, so very large?"

He reined in his wandering thoughts, and from there, the conversation revolved around him and his journeys. She asked him questions no one since his arrival had ever thought to ask. What did the natives live in? Did they truly wear nothing but feathers? Were they cannibals? Where had he traveled? What had he done? How long was he there? Did he travel the whole time, or did he settle and live somewhere for a while? Were there any cities? What did he think would happen to Canada in the future? Would America ever try to take it over again?

He was by turns amused, perplexed, and tantalized by glimpses of a questing curiosity within her, and he was charmed by how entranced she was by nature. He felt a powerful urge to dress her in breeches and steal her away to Canada. She would love it, he thought, never mind that she had grown up in society. She had the right personality—curious, active, unjudging. She was the first person he had met since he had been back in England who believed what he said about his Ojibway friends, and he longed to take her to see George, and his daughter, Mary Two Feathers. Once she was past her shyness, little Mary had asked him questions, too, about the far-off land he had come from and the ocean journey there, about the terrifying creatures called lords and ladies, and about castles of stone. Put Mary and Miss Swinley together and they would talk nonstop. The picture was so vivid in his mind, he could see it, could see Miss Swinley in breeches, sitting by the fire as Mary asked her about far-off London.

He shook himself out of his reverie. Of course, she was there in London to meet and marry a rich man, was she not? That thought chilled him to the marrow and deadened, for a minute, his pleasure. But he determined to enjoy the moment and let tomorrow take care of itself. What harm could there be in sitting with a pretty girl and talking for a half hour? No harm at all.

The half hour of the dance came and went, and still

they talked. Finding two empty chairs behind a pillar, they sat for the last few minutes. Unconsciously, Marcus reached out and grasped her gloved hand, holding it as they spoke, and she did not grab it back, but smiled at him with a sweet shyness that he found captivating.

But then a shadow fell over them. Miss Swinley looked up and her face paled. She snatched her hand from his grip and stammered, "M—mother, m—may I introduce Mr. Marcus Westhaven?"

"When pretty girls dance in the month of May, tra la, then all the boys will kiss and run away, tra la—" Singing gaily, Arabella descended the stairs of Leathorne House next morning, and headed toward the drawing room. Last night's ball had been wonderful, and even her mother had been much more agreeable to Mr. Westhaven than she would have thought possible. She started into the room but stopped on hearing a raised voice.

"Na, m'lady, t'will never do, you know. I hears that yer gel ain't performin' her duty, an' we'll be forced to reckon with ya 'bout yer debt. Too bad, but an undooti-ful child is the devil's right hand, ya know. So what 'bout this 'ere money ya owes us?"

"I d—don't know where I can get the money. Please, please, just a little longer! I have sold my jewels; I don't know what else I can do."

Her mother's voice was tearful, and Arabella felt her stomach twist in a convulsion of fear. She clutched the doorjamb and listened, putting her cheek against the smooth painted finish and closing her eyes.

"Look, I hates ta put it to ya like this, but if that gel o' yourn ain't betrothen in the next while, I'll be forced to do somethin' right nasty to you or yourn, if ya takes my meanin'. Mornin' m'lady, an' all the best o' the day to ya."

Arabella hastened into an alcove, but saw the character, a man in a drab and shabby coat, leaving through the hall toward the back door. She rushed into the withdrawing room to find her mother sitting with a frozen expression on a sofa. She dropped down beside her. "Oh, Mother, I heard! What did he want?"

"Money," Lady Swinley said, dully. "Always money. Money I do not have."

So it was as bad as her mother had intimated, and maybe even worse.

"Will they wait? If we have nothing, what can they do?"

"They can first force us to get rid of everything in Swinley Manor. It is all given in security. And then . . . oh, Arabella!" She clutched her daughter's hands and she was shaking. "I am afraid they will take Swinley Manor away from me. I will have no home."

Arabella's day turned dark and somber from the bright mood of just minutes earlier, but realist that she was, she knew what she had to do, and without delay. Why had she been avoiding it? Better to have it done with and everything settled than to live on in this hopeful, idiotic dream, a dream of finding congenial companionship at the very least, in marriage.

After all, what did her prospects look like? Bessemere was a nice fellow, but he was young and still under the thumb of his mother. It would take too long to be sure of him, even if she did have a hope of bringing him around. Count Verbrachan had danced with her once or twice, and she felt his interest in her, an interest that did not seem wholly healthy or normal. He had pinched her hard on her arm, leaving a bruise, when she had refused to walk out on the terrace with him at the Connolly ball. His demeanor terrified her. Better to be bored and repulsed than frightened and cowed, Arabella decided.

And so, Lord Pelimore would be it.

Over the next week Arabella tried her best to find Lord Pelimore alone, but she swiftly realized that he had been offended by her disappearing with Westhaven, for he pointedly ignored her and paid court to another girl, one of the giggling seventeen-year-olds he had so disparaged. She was terrified that her one chance at marriage was slipping away; and to think she had deliberately put him off! Was she mad? Finally she managed a few moments alone with him, only to find that Westhaven was there, too, watching and listening. She had refused to walk with him—though in truth she longed to—and had fled each time he appeared ready to approach her. She felt a dull ache in her chest, for she had never enjoyed a half hour so well as when they had sat together talking.

He was outside of her experience, an adventurer, bold and wild like the land he spoke of. And yet he had listened to her prosaic stories of a childhood spent mostly at school and in Cornwall with every appearance of enjoyment. He had laughed and gazed into her eyes with . . . well, it almost looked like affection, the emotion that warmed his gray eyes to the color of smoke. And always his nearness made her tingle. The merest caress of a ringlet left her breathless! But she could not afford to whistle a fortune down the wind for mere tingling. Her mother needed her, and she would not desert her in this, her hour of need.

With renewed determination she set herself to the task at hand. She could not let Westhaven's nearness stop her from what she was there to do; did it matter what he thought of her, after all? So in the few seconds she had as they met in the crowded ballroom, stalled near the chaperone chairs by the thick crowd around them, she went to work. Smiling demurely at Lord Pelimore and fluttering her lashes, she said, "You will have me thinking that I offended you in some way, my lord, if you do not sit this next dance out with me. In truth, I am fatigued, and you would be doing me the greatest of favors."

Westhaven was watching her, an incredulous look in his stormy eyes.

Pelimore squinted at her and grimaced. "Well, if you put it that way, I'll do you the *favor*, m'girl. Truth to tell, I kind of got the idea you and that young wanderer, Westhaven, had something goin'."

"Westhaven?" She arched her brows in surprise as she gracefully took a seat beside him. With the merest hint of malicious satisfaction, she said, knowing he was listening, "That young pup? Why he is not nearly . . . well, *mature* enough to interest a girl like me, if you know what I mean." She leaned close to Pelimore, and he goggled down her low bodice. "A girl likes to feel secure with a man, you know, and one would always think he would be taking off on some adventure or another; no stability, you know." Arabella tried her best, but a hint of wistfulness *would* creep into her voice. She could think of nothing more exciting than going off adventuring with such a man as Westhaven. Luckily, Lord Pelimore was not sensitive to things like that.

"True. Glad you realize it. Older man is what a girl your age needs. Gettin' on yerself; need some stability in your life."

She glanced sideways at Westhaven, so tall and handsome, lounging nearby. He had overheard Lord Pelimore, she knew it by his smirk. Getting on, really! One would think she was in her dotage rather than just three-and-twenty. Were all men insensitive boors? She could not bear to say another word with Marcus—she had begun to think of him thus, as Marcus—close enough to hear, and so she fell silent and let Pelimore bore her with stories of his rakish youth back in the far reaches of the latter half of the last century. Unfortunately, though, the man did not come to the point with a proposal.

And it was the same the next night, at the Beloir literary evening—how did Westhaven get invitations to all of these things, she wondered?—and at the Sanderson musical afternoon the next day after that. Westhaven was always there, always watching and listening as she did her best to lure a marriage proposal from the elderly baron.

And now Westhaven had gathered his own court of fascinated women, who oohed and aahed over his stories of derring-do and dashing adventure, and Arabella gritted her teeth over it all, and lost her concentration every time she thought she was getting somewhere. Pelimore was proving to be surprisingly sensitive, and if her attention was not wholly on him he became huffy and left. Men! She longed to say good-bye to the whole sex and join a nunnery. Of course, the Church of England did not have nunneries, and so she would have to convert to Catholicism, but—oh, it sounded lovely! Nothing to do all day but contemplate and pray.

Eveleen was off visiting in Dover, so she did not even have her best friend's company as comfort, though it was probably best. Eveleen O'Clannahan, sensible spinster with decidedly odd notions, was yet proving to have a surprising romantic turn to her personality that was jarring from so rational a woman. How could a woman as intelligent as Arabella had always thought Eve, believe in such discordant and disjointed things as the freedom of women from the tyranny of men *and* romantic love?

But Arabella must do what she was there to do. There was no more money left; her mother had told her that when the butcher had sent a hefty fellow to collect. The staff had not been paid, nor the collier, nor the feed bill, nor the milliner. She needed to marry, and she needed the marriage settlements *soon*.

She dressed carefully for the night's entertainment, a recital at the O'Lachlans'. In addition to the amateur performers a soprano had been engaged to sing, and Arabella loved Italian opera. She was a gifted pianist herself, or so everyone told her, and she knew the O'Lachlans would ask her to perform. It was her chance to impress Lord Pelimore, and she would take it.

She dressed in the ice blue silk, again, and went to the soiree alone, with just Annie for company. Her mother claimed a sick headache and said she must stay home in a darkened room. So Arabella went, mingled, and then, when asked, played a Haydn sonata of great emotion. There was applause at the end and the company arose to make their way to the refreshment room before the soprano was scheduled to perform. She looked around to see if Lord Pelimore was suitably impressed. Unfortunately, he was nowhere to be seen, his chair empty, though he had asked to escort her in to dinner. When she inquired she found that he had gone home before her solo, complaining of a stomachache. He had left her his apologies.

All that effort, for nothing.

Alone, she drifted out to the terrace. All this energy expended, and all to capture an old man whom she would have to live with as husband and wife for the rest of her life, or as long as his lasted, anyway. Judging from old Lord Oakmont, that could be another thirty years.

And that was if she was lucky. If she was not lucky she would find no one to marry her, and then she did not know what they were to do. Her mother would not even discuss it, and so she did not know exactly where they stood, if there was any possibility of retrenchment through leasing Swinley Manor, or of selling off some of the land. She just did not know, and her stomach was constantly tied up in knots from worry.

And then if Lord Conroy should come to London, and word of her mother's machinations should make the rounds of the *ton*—it was all too worrisome.

There was a light misty rain coming down, but it had been warm that day and she relished the feel of it on her bare hands, gloveless because she could not wear gloves when she played; she needed the intimate contact with the ivory to truly transmit her feelings through the instrument. The terrace had a deep overhang, so the vaporous rain just barely drifted onto her arms, cooling her heated skin. She used so much energy performing that she was always feverish after.

In the distance she could hear the clop-clop of horses' hooves on the pavement, and the shoosh of carriage wheels in the rain, all mixed with the faint drift of music from the pianist hired to perform during the refreshment break. He was a German fellow, and the piece was melancholy and dramatic.

She had always loved London and the Season. It suited her energetic nature to be always doing something. But the gaiety of previous Seasons was over; now it was time to get down to the serious business of marriage. It was time for her to shoulder her responsibilities to her mother and to her family home.

And there was no illusion now that she could please herself in her choice of a mate. It looked like Lord Pelimore was as good as she could expect. She should have settled her mind before this; she had known it all along hadn't she? But somehow this was the first time it really sank in, what her life had become. An overwhelming sadness burst like a ripened seedpod, scattering sorrow through her heart, and she laid her head down on her arms where they rested on the wrought-iron railing. How would she ever do it? How would she bear to be married to a man she could not even like?

And then the hot tears came and the wrenching sobs, drowned out by the sound of the music.

She had slipped out to the terrace, Marcus thought, following Arabella as if she were leading him on a cord. He couldn't help it. He was furious with her for ignoring him, and unbearably angry that she was throwing herself at that old fraud, Lord Pelimore, but still, he would talk to her, attempt to talk some sense into her, perhaps. He had tried to visit her at her home, but there were always others, always visitors in the drawing room, and she would not heed his signals and meet him alone.

But he would tell her now, by God. He would tell her exactly what he thought of fortune hunting—he slipped out through the double French doors onto the terrace and was arrested by the sound of sobs.

She wept! He stared at her, her slender figure doubled over and her head down on her arms on the wrought-iron railing of the terrace. Pierced to the core by her unhappiness, he was frozen, unable to move. He never imagined that beneath that glittering façade, behind those laughing eyes, such wrenching sadness could exist. He moved forward.

"Arabella," he whispered, as he turned her around roughly. She straightened and tried to pull away, but he enfolded her fiercely in his arms and felt her melt against him, her sobs becoming deeper and wilder.

He let her cry, rocking her gently and talking in hushed tones, nonsense really, but the kind of things men think women need to hear. He told her everything would be all right, that there was nothing in the world worth making her beautiful eyes red over, that he would fix everything.

At that, she tried to pull away again, but he would not let her go. He looked down into her drowned green eyes in the pale light from the music room. The crashing chords of the piano coincided with the heavier rain that poured down outside of the overhang, looking like a silvery curtain. The pain and fear in her eyes were too much, and he lowered his face and gently kissed her mouth, tentatively at first. Any hesitation and he would have released her instantly.

But there was no hesitation; her bare hands stole up around his neck and she pressed herself to him, her unexpectedly passionate response rocking him until he was unsteady on his feet. Her lips were velvety soft and sweet, and he had to fiercely tamp down the rush of desire that raced through his blood. He wanted to pick her up and carry her away, steal into the night with her in his arms. Instead, he would have to be satisfied with this moment, this unbearably perfect moment of bliss.

Arabella was shaken to the core by the abrupt rise from bitter sadness to glorious joy, the sweet fulfillment that his lips seemed to promise. It was like being swept into an inferno, all white-hot fire and brightness, consuming her with a passion she had never experienced before. If it never ended, then she never had to face the truth, never had to admit reality, never had to awaken from a dream of hunger sated and need satisfied . . .

But he broke the contact, just to take a huge, gasping breath, before he tried to capture her lips in another kiss. Too late! Too late. The magic moment had been shattered, and she came to the abrupt realization that if anyone saw, they would delight in retailing the shocking story of Miss Swinley alone on the terrace, kissing that unruly Mr. Westhaven. She would be ruined. And after all, lovemaking with a poor man would not pay their bills, nor save her home, nor rescue her mother from the trouble she was in.

She twisted away from Westhaven. Wiping the tears that remained on her cheeks, she said, "You are a cad, Westhaven, for taking advantage of my . . . my weak moment." Her voice sounded thick and strange in her own ears, but steady enough, she was glad to note.

He tried to take her in his arms again, saying, "Weak moment? Arabella if you are sad—"

"Who gave you permission to call me by my given name, sir?"

"Arabella," he said, grinning. He pulled her into his arms and laid a kiss on her cheek.

She wrenched herself away from him and slapped him, looking fearfully over his shoulder into the music room. People were starting to come back for the soprano's performance.

"What is wrong with you?" he asked, rubbing his cheek. A red mark was going to show. "Why do you respond one minute, then push me away the next?"

"Have you never heard of flirtation?" she asked, coldly. It hurt to do this, but she must, she *must!* He must leave her alone so she could go to her fate, and this was an opportunity to sink herself irrevocably in his eyes. "You are far too sure of your attractions, sir. Can a girl not have a little fun? Gain a little experience? It is harmless enough; people do it all the time."

She was rewarded by a blaze of anger in his stormy gray eyes. "Heartless flirt, jade!" he said. He turned away and retreated to the door. He glanced back with a troubled, puzzled look in his eyes, but then strode away, through the music room and beyond.

Success, and yet all she was left feeling was a great, yawning chasm of emptiness in her heart.

Seven

There was no reason to stay after rejecting Marcus Westhaven, and so Arabella pled a headache that was very nearly real and fled the musicale while the soprano, not so very wonderful after all, screeched and dipped through an aria. She had come alone, accompanied only by Annie, whom she tore away from the party atmosphere of the O'Lachlans' kitchen to leave.

She would never *ever* forget the look of disgust and contempt on Marcus's face when she coldly suggested she was just using him for practice flirtation. But no matter how it hurt to know what he must think of her now, no matter how painful it was to tear apart the fragile, sweet connection they had woven between them, she could not help but feel that she had done the right thing. There was no future for them, and it seemed he would plague her until she put him in his place once and for all time. She had done that now; she doubted if he would bother her again. But in her bed alone, after Annie had left her and she had blown out her candle, it was cold comfort.

She snuggled under the covers in the chilly darkness of a room with no coal fire to heat it—the last of the coal was being conserved for cooking and for heating the main rooms—and contemplated her life. She had often thought about marriage, especially over the three Seasons she had spent in London, ostensibly looking for a husband. She had had many offers, but had never accepted one. There was always something wrong that kept her from accepting a man, and she never felt too pressing an urge to marry until this Season, until her belated knowledge of their financial predicament. She had come close once last Season with a young man whom she genuinely liked and respected, but her mother had refused to countenance the match, and she had sent him away after a nasty scene which had made her believe she had had a lucky escape from matrimony with Lord Sweetan.

And then the previous fall she and her mother had gone to stay at the country home of the Countess and Earl of Leathorne, longtime friends of her mother's. It was expected that she and the son and heir, Lord Drake, would make a match of it. He was rich, and she was in need of a husband, so what was the impediment?

The impediment from her aspect was that she could not love him. They just never seemed to find a common ground on which to build even a friendship, much less the kind of intimacy necessary, she thought, between a man and a woman who intended to wed.

Why? He was rich, he was handsome, he was generally good-natured, though he was at the time suffering from problems brought on by his military service. As well, he was a genuinely good man, and had treated her kindly enough—at least he had when he even remembered her existence. She had even, to her everlasting shame, employed devious means to rid herself of competition for his hand in the form of her cousin, True, although she could see that the two were falling in love with each other.

But in the end love had triumphed. True had married the viscount and Arabella was pleased, truly overjoyed about it! True was her anchor in the world in a way her mother had never been, and to see her happy

was a secret delight that she hugged to herself, for her
mother was so very bitter about the marriage that she
could not even speak about it openly without inspiring
Lady Swinley to streams of vituperation. Arabella might
envy her cousin's good fortune in material matters, for
Drake was wealthy, but those two were meant to be together, and even when she tried she could not work up
any animosity toward either of them, nor their marriage. It was as it was meant to be.

She turned over on her side and stared off into the
darkness. What was wrong with her? Was she incapable
of love that she could not even feel it for so good a man
as her cousin's husband, Lord Drake? As her eyes got
used to the darkness, she saw, glowing in the dark like
a beacon, the small, white bark basket on her bedside
table. She stretched out one hand and traced the rough
texture of the surface. The question drifted through
her mind again; was she incapable of love? She had
begun to think so, until Marcus Westhaven had entered
her life. He was everything she had always pictured in
the perfect beau; tall, handsome, bold, adventurous,
and with an air of wildness that she found enticing and
enthralling.

But were those not all surface attributes? Surely there
was more to love than a handsome face or a pretty figure. This was an unaccustomed train of thought. She
had never thought so before, but she had begun to wonder, after watching her cousin and Lord Drake together,
if there was not something more to love, something she
had never experienced, a bond between two people that
welded them into one.

How did it happen? *When* did that miracle happen;
before marriage, when the couple fell in love, or as they
wed, or after the marriage? She had attended three weddings over the course of the winter and spring; True
had married her wealthy viscount, True's younger sister

Faith had married the brother of her best friend, and the girls' father, an elderly vicar Arabella had always loved as if he were *her* father, *too*, had married the plump, motherly widow, Mrs. Saunders, in a ceremony that was simple, and yet for Arabella, most touching.

Each wedding had had moments of emotion, touching scenes that lived on in her memory. But of the three, the one that stayed with her was the vicar's. He was in his late sixties and the widow in her fifties, but the love that shone from their eyes as they were joined in wedlock was a stunning surprise to Arabella. Love, at *their* age? But yes, it was love, as fervent and real as any pair of mooning twenty-year-olds, and perhaps more fast and steady for their age.

So what was love? She rolled over on her back and stared at the ceiling, pulling the soft covers up under her chin and drawing her feet up out of the chilly regions of the bed.

The feelings that had coursed through her the moment Marcus had taken her in his arms had been powerful and new. But they were physical; thrumming blood, a thrill down her spine, and tingling in her toes. Was that love, then? Is that what the vicar and the widow felt that made them want to marry? It seemed ludicrous, but was it?

Restlessly she rolled over on her side again, eyes wide open in the dark, the blackness like a velvet blanket around her, except for a faint brightening of the window through the heavy drapes, and the white blur on her sidetable that was the basket Marcus Westhaven had given her. Love had to be something more than just tingling and thrumming and thrilling. It *had* to be! So what she felt for Marcus Westhaven was just a passing fancy and it would not, as her darkest fears would have her believe, plague her for the rest of her life with regrets and fearsome longings.

Arabella closed her eyes against the darkness, but try as she might she could not rid herself of the sensation of lips firmly pressed to her own and hands that trailed down her back, leaving alternately icy and burning traces on her skin under her gown. It was not love!

But whatever it was, it kept her awake until the early morning sun brightened the eastern sky.

Reading was not far from London, not even a full day's ride for a young man on a horse. So when the message came that the old man was conscious, it had not taken long to respond. Marcus sat at the bedside trying not to inhale the scent of old man, bed linens in need of washing, and a lingering smell of imminent death. He gazed down at the man on the bed and examined the blue veins that traced a path across the temple and into the sparse hairline. It had been so many years. He didn't recognize this frail body, this figure that barely made an impression in the bed, as the man he remembered from his childhood, the old man who smelled of tobacco and horehound and stable, and whose voice boomed out in a commanding bass. Suddenly the man's eyes fluttered open.

"It's you, eh? Don't know why you bothered comin' to see me. Lawyer says you're the one, all right. Gonna get it all; don't have to make up to an old man after all, y'know."

Smiling, Marcus relaxed at the familiar tone of brusque impatience and said, "I hope I am as cussedly ornery as you when I reach your age, Uncle."

"Won't reach my age; nobody does!" The crabbed hands plucked at the covers irritably. He eyed Marcus with something like resentment. "Wouldn't have recognized you myself, you know. Last time I saw you, you was just a little lad—a little bugger if I recall—always askin' questions and wantin' to ride the horses."

"I haven't changed that much. I'm still always asking questions and wanting to ride the horses. As for the other part—I suppose I'm not so little, but I might still be a bugger!"

The old man cackled and then yelped, "Call m'man and tell him I want to go downstairs today. Hate being in bed all the time! Nothing to do, nothing to look at. If I'm gonna die, might as well see somethin' besides this room. So, you been gallivanting around enjoying the Season? Making up to all the pretty gels? They do still make pretty gels don't they?"

"They do, at that. One in particular is very pretty, like some kind of a . . . an angel. But a calculating wench. Kissed me, then told me it was just for practice! She's planning on marrying a man of sixty and some odd years!" Marcus sat back in his chair, stretched his legs out in front of him, and said, "Disgusting, I say."

"Good for him, *I* say," the old man retorted. "If I was ten years younger I'd be giving him a run for his money, if she's as pretty as you say. What's she look like?"

Marcus closed his eyes. "Blond hair, bright, like spun gold. Eyes the color of oriental jade, the finest kind. Lips like rubies, only soft as velvet and honey mead sweet."

The man cackled again, and then coughed, his thin shoulders hunching as he hacked and wheezed. Marcus sat up straight, alarmed, but his uncle's valet came running and lifted the old man to a sitting position, pounding on his back.

As the cough subsided and he caught his breath, the old man rested back against the pillows propped up on the massive headboard for him. "Realize you described the gel in terms of gold, jade, and rubies?" the old man said, as his valet fussed around him, straightening the bedlinens. "No wonder she's a fortune hunter! Got to keep up with her looks!"

Marcus laughed. "I hadn't looked at it that way."

"So is it just her looks that keep ya comin' back to her?"

"I didn't say I kept coming back to her," Marcus said, examining his uncle's surprisingly shrewd eyes. But it was true. He had followed Miss Arabella Swinley for a number of days before the embrace on the terrace. He knew he was fouling up her plans for tempting Lord Pelimore into a proposal, and took a strangely savage delight in disconcerting her. Ruthless little wench. "It's just—well, I don't want to see her throw her life away."

"Liar. There is something else there that you're not tellin' me."

"Maybe," Marcus said, abruptly, moodily. "But that is my business." He recovered his good humor, not wanting to upset his uncle. Who knew how long they would have to talk? The doctor said he could go anytime. This last coma that he had just emerged from had been longer and deeper than any other. He was very sick—dying, in fact—and he knew it. "But it is true as far as it goes. She is a brilliant diamond, about to be set in dullest pewter. It is not good enough for her. She . . . I suppose I think she deserves something better."

"Then marry her yourself!"

With a grin, Marcus said, "She wants a rich man, and I am very poor, in her eyes."

"I'm sure you could convince her. You're a handsome devil, I'll give you that. Women like that kind of thing, almost as much as they like money. See if you can't tempt her into makin' a disastrous alliance!" He cackled again, but it died to a wheezy cough, the sound a harsh rattle in his chest.

The valet held a glass up to the old man's lips; he drank a little of the pale liquid, but then sputtered, "I want to go downstairs, you bacon-brained idjit! Damned if I'll spend the rest of my life in this bed. M'nephew will take me for a walk in that damned Bath chair I used to use, b'fore I got bedridden."

Marcus was a little alarmed at the thought of being in charge of the old man's movements in such a way. He wondered if he was helping his uncle feel better, or hastening his demise. He hoped it was the former and not the latter. The doctor said the old man had not done so much as sit up for many months before Marcus's arrival home. The last few weeks had been spent in a coma, and he had just emerged within the last couple of days. "Sir, you are hardly strong enough—"

"Don't tell me what I am," he said and struggled to a sitting position again. The bed was huge and it dwarfed the frail man at its center, but it could not swallow up his personality, which still dominated the room. He glared up at his patient valet, and said, "Ain't gettin' any younger while you shilly-shally around like an old woman. I am going to get dressed and come down to lunch with my nephew like a real man, and then he shall take me for a walk in the garden in my Bath chair. And that is that." He cast a sideways glance at his visitor, then, and said, in a more uncertain tone, "That is, if I am not keeping you from more exciting events?"

Marcus stood and gazed down at his uncle. He had not seen the old man in almost thirty years. Unbeknownst to him, he had been presumed dead years ago when no more letters came to family members. But it had seemed pointless after the death of his mother and father to keep writing to aunts and uncles who never answered, so he had stopped. And in the interim many had died, resulting in the present turn of events. "I would be delighted to stay to lunch with you, if you will let me tell you more about the delightful, tantalizing, maddening Miss Arabella Swinley. Maybe you can give me some ideas as to how to handle her. She slapped my cheek, you know, and after *inviting* my kisses."

"Slapped you, eh?" He cackled and slapped the bed-covers. "I like her already. Feisty—no milk-and-water miss like they make nowadays. I'll give you the benefit of my wisdom, boy. I don't imagine women have changed all that much over the years. The devil knows men have not."

"I'll wait for you downstairs, then, sir, and we shall walk in the garden." Marcus glanced out the window at the brilliant sunny day, and hoped it was not too cold out. He did not want to be accused of helping the old fellow get pneumonia. There would be many who would assume it was purposeful, no doubt, not that he cared what a bunch of society snobs thought. But he did care, he found, to his surprise, about his uncle, and would not hasten his demise even accidentally. "Perhaps after that we can come in and you will let me beat you at whist."

"No more hesitation, my girl. You get a proposal from Lord Pelimore tonight! I have arranged with Olivia Howland to have you sit next to him at dinner, so make the most of it!"

This was hissed in Arabella's ear by her mother, just as they entered the Howlands' fashionable Bruton Street residence for a dinner party. She did not need the warning. Just that morning the butcher, who had become increasingly importunate, as they had apparently not paid him a penny since they had come to town, had threatened that since they were staying at the earl and countess's house, that perhaps *they* would be approached. Arabella had been appalled. She did not want their personal insolvency to be bruited about the streets, especially after that awful Conroy incident, which she was sure would come back to haunt her somehow. And it was unbearably humiliating to think of the Earl of Leathorne, her cousin's father-in-law, being approached for the money.

So she was determined that the end of this night would see Lord Pelimore asking to visit the next morning with an interesting question. But on entering the drawing room where the party was gathered before going in to dine, who should she see but Marcus Westhaven, sitting and grinning up at her from a sofa, which he shared with the very pretty matron, Mrs. Olivia Howland.

What was he doing there? She had not seen him since that awful scene on the terrace at the O'Lachlans', and had been glad to hear he was out of town again. But now here he was, as large as life, a broad smile displaying square, white teeth.

A streak of jealously raged through her at the way Mrs. Howland, sans husband, flirted outrageously with Westhaven. She laid her pretty delicate hand on his arm and snuggled close to his sizable frame, gazing up at him with a simpering expression on her lovely face. And he, the devil, was flirting back, smiling down into her exquisite eyes.

Arabella sniffed, put her nose up, and headed for Lord Pelimore, who was sitting with Lady Jacobs, a buxom, fortyish widow who had reportedly cut a wide swatch through the ranks of *tonnish* men of a certain age. It was well known that she and the aging baron were intimate, and Arabella thought that it might be good if he had that outlet even after marriage. Anything that would lessen his need for her as companion was to be considered a good thing.

Lady Jacobs looked her over assessingly. "Miss Swin-

ley, how comely you look. I believe I remember that
gown from last year; quite one of the prettiest of your
wardrobe."

Arabella fought the urge to snipe back after that
snide remark. It would not do to appear petty in front
of her future bridegroom. A wave of revulsion shook
her, but she determinedly suppressed it and sat down
next to Lord Pelimore. "As always, Lady Jacobs, you are
the picture of refinement."

The woman frowned and looked as though she was
trying to find the expected malicious retort in that, but
finding none, remained silent.

"I am so very grateful to see you better, my lord, after
your recent indisposition!" Arabella laid her hand on
the man's arm in a daring show of familiarity, then
glanced over at Westhaven. The elderly baron started.
But Arabella could not afford to waste time. His lordship
had been absent from the social scene for three days,
unfortunately the same amount of time Marcus Westhaven had been missing as well. Unfortunate because
without Westhaven's presence she could have made up
for lost time. Arabella was determined, though, not to
let Westhaven interfere with her plans anymore. She
would ignore him and devote herself to Lord Pelimore.

The company was small, just twelve gentlemen and
twelve ladies. When the butler came to the door, bowed,
and announced dinner was ready, Olivia Howland
jumped to her feet in a swift movement and organized
the procession to the dinner table according to her seating plan. Arabella found herself on Lord Pelimore's
arm, just as her mother had said. But when she sat down
at the table, she found that on her left was Marcus Westhaven. And his gray eyes were alight with mischief.

"What good fortune, Miss Swinley," he said, with a
smirk on his face, "that I should have the opportunity

to apologize for my shocking misbehavior a few nights ago."

"If you were so intent on apologizing," Arabella said, in frigid tones, "I have been home every day, and at balls and the opera every night. You did not see fit to make an effort to apologize, so I cannot believe that you were so very concerned."

He gazed at her steadily. "It sounds as if you are quizzing me as to my whereabouts, young lady. Bad *ton.* Very bad *ton.*"

Oooh! Outrageous man! As if he would know bad *ton* from good *ton.* She ignored him.

"I was visiting relatives, if you *must* have an explanation for my absence. I have been out of the country so long that most of them thought I was dead, it appears."

"What a disappointment to them when you appeared alive and so very healthy." She was being rude, she knew, but she did not care. Lord Pelimore, on her right, was just being served and she waited while his soup plate was placed before him.

"Mmmph, real turtle," he exclaimed as he took a mouthful.

Arabella, who had been about to speak to him, decided it was better to let him eat first, she supposed, since he was so intent on his dinner.

"Do you accept my apology?"

Westhaven's voice was a whisper in her ear, and the small hairs on the back of her neck stood up. Reluctantly she turned back to him. What a pity he was so handsome. That, she had decided, lay at the back of her undeniable attraction to him. That must be all it was. Olivia Howland at the end of the table was trying to get his attention, probably wanting to make sheep's eyes at him, Arabella thought acidly. It was well known that she was bored by her husband, a minor diplomat attached to the War Office, so it was no wonder she was drawn to Marcus Westhaven. He looked, in the elegant surroundings of the dining room, like a wolf in the midst of a flock of helpless sheep. The other men's finished appearances looked effete and pallid next to his rugged, lupine vigor.

"I . . . I accept your apology, sir, now leave me alone, please!" Where the plea had come from, Arabella did not know, but it was heartfelt. She could not concentrate with him next to her. He radiated some force that held her helpless and confused in the face of it, but she could not allow it to interfere any longer in her pursuit of Lord Pelimore. It was imperative that she sew up this betrothal with no more delay.

There was silence, and she darted a look at Westhaven. He was gazing at her with indecision in his hooded gray eyes. He started to say something, then stopped. On her right, she could hear Lord Pelimore scraping the bottom of his soup plate with his spoon. She had not touched her own soup and could not bear to even think about it at that moment. There was something in the air between her and Westhaven, something hanging unsaid, something important.

"What is it?" she whispered, looking into his eyes. The gray of them was dark, with coal flecks in their depths and a coal ring around the iris.

"Arabella, I want to tell you—"

"Miss Swinley, what is all the whisperin' about?" Lord Pelimore chose that moment to be attentive to his dinner partner. They were between courses, so that explained it.

But Arabella could not afford to miss the opportunity, nor could she let him get the wrong impression about her and Westhaven. "We were not whispering, sir; Mr. Westhaven was just informing me that—that I had a curl amiss."

"Mr. Westhaven should keep his 'informing' to himself," Lord Pelimore said, testily.

"It was kindly meant, sir. A lady must always wish to know when her appearance is not . . . not up to scratch." She was scrabbling for conversation and sounded hen-witted at best, she thought.

The baron stared at her. "Can't see anything wrong with your hair, young lady. You look perfect, as always."

"Why thank you, sir."

"Lord Pelimore has found something upon which we concur," Westhaven said, dryly. "You *always* look perfect, Miss Swinley."

"I suppose your colonial ladies have no time for such nonsense as pretty dresses and bonnets," Arabella said, responding swiftly to what she fancied was some kind of implied criticism. Somehow, even a compliment from him sounded like fault-finding.

"On the contrary; maidens will always be maidens, wherever they reside. There are some remarkably pretty girls in the Canadas, Miss Swinley."

Somehow the answer did not please her as she supposed it ought. It promised to be a long, awkward evening. "I'm sure there are," she retorted. "And I am sure you have flirted with every one of them."

Eight

After dinner, as the gentlemen sat smoking cigars and drinking port, Pelimore gazed steadily at Westhaven through a cloud of smoke. Under cover of a rather loud political discussion taking place at the other end of the table, concerning the Luddite threat and what to do about it, the baron said, "What's your interest in Miss Swinley?"

Marcus, startled, blew out a mouthful of smoke and said, "Interest? I have no interest in Miss Swinley."

"Good. Because just between you an' me, man to man, as it were, I intend to offer for the gel."

Staring at the much older man, his black dinner coat covered in a fine layer of gray ash, Marcus was surprised at the wave of revulsion and anger that swept through him. It really wasn't any of his business, since Miss Swinley appeared determined to have him, too. But he couldn't help himself. "Is she not—pardon me, sir, but is she not a little young for your tastes?"

Complacently flicking ash off the end of his cigar, Pelimore said, "Need a young'un. Got to breed an heir. Can't abide m'nephew, an' he's set to inherit since my Jamie died last year. So, I'll just get another heir before I pop off."

Sprawled at his ease, no one but those who knew him intimately would have recognized the coiled tension in Marcus. He felt it in himself, felt the anger that roiled through his belly at the casual assumption of right to Arabella's body, as though she would be this man's chattel, to breed and then forget. Lord, but he had been living in a freer society for too long! He had forgotten the arrogant assumptions made by those with any sort of power. Not that it did not happen in the colonies, but then he had not spent much time in York, the largest center of society in upper Canada. Most of his time was spent in a canoe charting waterways. His ideas had become positively radical, it seemed, while he had been away. Though he always did think differently from those around him. That was what had sent him away from home in the first place, his inability to conform his thoughts and beliefs to those of the people around him.

But he must remember that just because they did not see eye to eye on much, did not mean that Lord Pelimore was without any human feeling. And so he would give this man a chance to profess some caring for Arabella, some decent pretense of affection. "What about Miss Swinley? Why her?"

Lord Pelimore, face red from too much port, waved his hand around and said, "Look at her, man! She's a diamond! If I gotta bed a young one, it's gonna be a diamond, not some wizen-faced little spinster girl, like all the old dragons have been throwing at me lately. My money's gonna buy quality, not shabby castoffs. Can't believe some young buck hasn't snatched her up." He rubbed his hands together. "But she'll take me. She's bin making up to me for a while now, and pretty soon I'll let her know it's worked. She can have me an' m'money s'long as she gets me an heir. I'll enjoy the gettin', too." Pelimore winked at Marcus. "Man of the world to man of the world," he said, jabbing at Marcus with the lit end of the cigar. "I don't mind telling you, I will *enjoy* the gettin'. Bin a long time since I had a virgin."

A slash of hot anger coursed through Marcus. If the

man hadn't been old enough to be his father, Marcus would have challenged him for such disrespectful language toward a lady. Worse than disrespectful; filthy and degenerate! But who was he to talk? He who had grabbed at her like she was some doxy to be had for a shilling or a pint of gin!

But it was not right that a blooming girl like Arabella should wed this man, this cretinous old aristocratic lout. He refused to believe she held him in any affection. No, she was going for the biggest money pot she could find. And he did not know why he cared. If she was as money-grubbing as all that, then he should just abandon her to her fate.

But he couldn't. And he wouldn't. Whether she liked it or not, she had a champion. He would save her from herself, and from making a mess of her life, if he could.

The Season was progressing nicely, everyone solemnly declared. It was that most glorious of Seasons, spring in London, with not just one, but two royal weddings to look forward to. Princess Charlotte, the Regent's well-loved daughter, was set to marry a handsome young man, Prince Leopold of Saxe-Coburg on May 2, so 1816 would go down in history as a most propitious time for marriage. And it was a love match, everyone said.

And then, two months later there would be another rare spectacle, for Princess Mary, one of the King and Queen's middle-aged daughters, was set to marry her cousin and longtime intended husband, the Duke of Gloucester. Perhaps not a love match, but appropriate and long overdue, nonetheless.

There seemed to be an added sparkle of life to London society; every ball was pronounced a capital success, every girl was a diamond, every young gent a fine buck.

And yet there was definitely something missing for Arabella. For her the Season seemed solemn and dark and desperately wanting in joy, one long, tedious worry session.

Except when Marcus Westhaven was around, which he seemed to be more and more. She should be cutting him; she knew it, and yet she could not do it. No matter how maddening he was, he was also charming, handsome, good-humored, and since he had learned the new steps, a wonderful dancer. Desperately in need of merriment, Arabella could not help but respond. He always seemed to know just what to say, just what to do to make her laugh. She missed him terribly during his mysterious absences, but after a few days gone, he would turn up in London again with some small gift for her, or a posy of country flowers to brighten her day.

April, with its brilliant sunshine, drenching rain, and glorious bursts of flowers came, and the first ball of the month was the Hartford ball. She was feeling sprightly because her mother had obtained some money from their steward, enough to put off the wolves at the door, though not nearly enough to pay all their outstanding bills.

And she was wearing a new gown fashioned from a bolt of cloth her mother said she had obtained for nearly nothing. It was sea green, close in color to her eyes, and it had a shimmer of gold through it. With some rescued lace from a dress that was hopelessly out of fashion and could not be worn, she felt like a new woman. She and her mother drew up to the Hartford residence that night in the Leathornes' elegant carriage, both in reasonably good spirits. As she often did, her mother disappeared immediately as they entered.

Arabella stood on the landing above the ballroom and glanced around looking for some acquaintance, hopefully Eveleen, who was supposed to be back in town any day now. But the first person she saw was Marcus Westhaven. He approached her and she saw the admiration in his eyes. It gave her a thrill down her spine to see the way his gaze lingered, and the fire that flared deep within the charcoal of his eyes. Ever since the dinner at the Howlands' he had been attentive and courteous, still always there, but with a supportive smile and a compliment. He walked with her and talked with her, almost as if he were courting her. She could become accustomed to such treatment. His small gifts were never out of keeping with their friendship, his conversation was never distressing. For the moment the friction that had seemed a natural part of their relationship was absent.

Her mind wandered for just a moment. What would it be like to have a husband like Marcus? Would he always be this attentive, or would their marriage devolve into the sullen frigidity she had observed between some couples? But no, she must not ponder such topics as marriage to Marcus Westhaven. She would just enjoy the days and evenings of freedom, while Lord Pelimore, forced to return to his country manor to solve some problem or another that he had explained in protracted detail in a note he had sent to Arabella along with an enormous bouquet of flowers, was absent. Her mother would not plague her until her prospective husband was back.

"You look like a spring morning," Westhaven said, taking her hand and holding her away from him as he gazed admiringly at her. "That green is lovely, but not nearly as beautiful as you are."

How was it that a young lady as experienced in town flattery as she, should be so flustered every time Westhaven said something kind? Arabella felt her cheeks flame. "Thank you, sir. May I say that you look very handsome yourself." And he did. For so poverty-stricken a gentleman, he always appeared "bang up to the mark," as cant would say it. Of course, a man only needed one good evening suit and he was set for the Season, but still . . . She eyed him curiously, noting his snowy white linens and perfect mathematical. "Your valet is to be congratulated."

He chuckled. "I shall take the compliment on myself, as I have no valet. A poor man must fend for himself. And my hotel does my laundry."

Why was it that she always hoped some circumstance had changed, that he had found out his inheritance was going to be wealth beyond his wildest dreams rather than a few hundred pounds? Wishful thinking she supposed. Silly, really, because even if he had been wealthy and titled, he was not to be trusted, at least not for her needs. Marcus Westhaven did *not* play by the rules. She required a beau she could count on to marry her, not just flirt with her, and for her purposes Lord Pelimore was that man. She sighed and took Mr. Westhaven's proffered arm, and they descended the steps into the ballroom.

Just enjoy the moment, she repeated to herself. *Just enjoy the moment.*

Another squeeze, Marcus thought disparagingly. What was it about the upper crust that they relished being packed together like seamen at a mess table? The Hartford ball, to which he had been invited because of one of his invaluable letters of introduction—he could have played upon his family name and antecedents, which were very good indeed, but this way was quicker and less complicated—was one of the premier occasions of the Season, and he had known Arabella would attend. In that he was not disappointed.

He had waited in a fever of anticipation near the

door, lingering out of sight until the mother disappeared, and then approached her. This last week or so had been enlightening. Never had he wholly given himself up to pleasure and gaiety for so long a time, and never had he enjoyed dissipation more. He began to see how addictive it could be, devoting oneself to dancing, drinking, playing cards, and escorting pretty women.

In fact, Marcus found it surprisingly easy to play the beau for Arabella Swinley, even though he had precious little experience. She brought out some latent gallantry in him, some wish to make her eyes smile and her lips curve up into that delightful bow when he presented her with a posy or a poem. He had only had one London Season when he was a cub of just nineteen, before he disappointed his parents' hopes and left for the Canadas. He had never been back since, not even when news finally reached him that his parents were dead, lost at sea in a shipwreck. What had been the point? By then they had been gone for seven months; that is how long it took for the letter from the family solicitor to reach him in the far-flung wilds of upper Canada.

And the letter merely stated that there was no money. What little there had been was required to settle up the estate of his parents. His father had lost a lot in speculating on a canal venture that had gone badly; if he had lived, it would only have been to go to debtor's prison or worse. So there had never been anything to come home for. Even this last bit of news, that he was his uncle's sole heir, would not have touched him if he had not felt a certain curiosity to see the old sod again.

But still, no matter how enjoyable this time was, it was just one brief episode in a life that must have more meaning than that of a mere London beau. He did not intend to stay. He would be heading back to Canada as soon as his business allowed, though he supposed that was a callous way to look at the impending death of his uncle. He had, through his recent visits, conceived a certain fondness for his uncle that was unexpected, given the old man's irascibility.

And a certain fortune-hunting beauty would not change his mind about leaving England. No matter how her eyes sparkled when they danced, or how she fit into his arms like she was meant to be there, and despite how her laughter made his stomach clench into a knot, or how her image stayed with him long into the night, in the darkness of his room at the Fontaine.

He should not be enjoying her company so much, knowing who and what she was. What place did a scheming fortune-hunter have in his life? But still, it was gratifying to dance with her and talk with her, and know she was the most beautiful girl in the room, even if all the other men were swooning over this year's diamond, Lady Cynthia Walkerton, a girl to whom he had been introduced. She was well enough in her own way, he supposed. She was certainly beautiful, and she knew all the little tricks that were designed to make him feel manly and strong, the languishing glances, the trembling smile, but never did she talk freely, laugh like Arabella did, or touch his heart in ways he could not explain and did not want to examine too closely.

He led Arabella into the first dance of the Hartford ball, a waltz, relishing the feel of her small waist under his hand. He gazed down into her eyes, brilliant in the chandelier-lit ballroom. What had turned her into a mercenary little schemer, when he would have said she was made for finer things? She was not wanting in sense, nor intelligence. She was as smart as any woman, or any man for that matter, that he had ever met. It made him angry that she would waste her brilliance, her exquisite fire on an old poseur like Pelimore.

"I wish I were rich," he said, casually, gazing down

at the gentle curve of her cheek and the swan-like extension of her lovely white neck. She was gazing over her shoulder, scanning the crowd at the edge of the ballroom floor, and he had a feeling he knew what, or rather whom, she was looking for.

He got the response he wanted. Her head snapped around and she looked up at him with a shocked expression.

"W—why?"

Suspicion hardened into certainty. "Because I can tell that even now, dancing with me to this wonderful music, you so beautiful, and me handsome, as you claim, you are scanning the room to see what wealthy game there is for you to hunt tonight. I would wish your eyes were on me, instead. If I were instantly in possession of a hundred thousand pounds, you would be gazing with rapt attention into my eyes."

"I thought you had left off teasing me," she said, disappointment coloring her voice.

"I am not teasing, Arabella. I am merely stating the truth. You are looking all around to see if you can find better game, someone richer than Lord Pelimore, perhaps?" His anger had grown as he spoke. He didn't know why, but he wanted to hurt her, to get under that perfect, smooth social skin she wore like armor. He wanted to see the real Arabella, as he had seen her on the terrace the night he had kissed her. He clutched her waist tighter.

"You are imagining things, Mr. Westhaven." Her voice was icy.

"And why is that young man near the steps staring at you? He has not taken his eyes off you since we took to the dance floor."

She followed the direction of his nod, and he could see the widening of her eyes and feel the tightening of her hand on his shoulder. She made a slight misstep, and he pulled her closer, helping her regain her footing and relishing the feel of her lithe body skimming close to his.

"Who is that?" he repeated. It was some man she was dangling on her string, he thought, another man as obsessed with her as he was. Was he rich? He certainly was well dressed, and he wore an assortment of gold fobs and quizzing glasses at his waist. Perhaps while Marcus had been away visiting his uncle at Reading, she had been pursuing other fish.

"It . . . it is just an acquaintance from last Season." Arabella turned her gaze away. It was Lord Sweetan, her most eager beau from the previous Season. She had liked him and had given him every reason to think that a proposal from him would be most welcome, but he was not rich enough to suit her mother and she had turned him down. It had been an unhappy moment; he had not taken it well at all. But she had thought when she heard the news that he was engaged, he would forget about her "betrayal," as he had put it in that last, distressing interview. From his expression—bitter and angry, it looked, even at this distance—she would imagine that was not so.

"More than an acquaintance, I would hazard a guess."

Westhaven's voice was hard, and she glanced up at him in puzzlement. Men were so very unaccountable. What was wrong with him that he now sounded so bitter, when the evening had started out on such an even keel? Her chin went up. "You are right. He offered for me, and I refused him."

"Not rich enough for you?"

What was wrong with him, this incessant harping on money? With a savage delight, she said, "That is right. I need much more money than poor Daniel has before I will consider a man. A hundred thousand pounds is my price." The joy was gone from the evening anyway, she thought. If he was going to act this way, then he could just sulk somewhere else. And stay away from her.

His hand tightened around her waist even harder, his grip like iron, and she gasped. "Mercenary little witch, aren't you?" he growled, pulling her closer, his gray eyes stormy.

"Didn't you know all women are, Marcus?" She fought the intense thrill that his closeness created within her. She would not give him the satisfaction of enjoying this friction between them. "Money is the only thing we look for in a man."

"Not all women, Miss Swinley. You do not know this, but I was engaged once, in Canada. Moira had not an avaricious bone in her body."

The music ended, and he pulled her arm into his and marched her over to her mother.

"I'll bet she left you for a man with more money," Arabella said, bitterly, in a low tone that her mother could not hear. "That was why you did not marry her."

"No. She died before we could wed." He turned on his heel and left her.

How had that gone so wrong so fast, Marcus wondered as he prowled the edge of the ballroom, listening to the gay laughter and flirtation all around him. It was just that he had seen her scanning the edge of the ball-room, and had known instantly that she was looking for wealthier game than he. It had hurt his *amour propre*, he supposed, though he had not thought that he had any to be hurt.

He still didn't know if she was serious when she told him her requirements in a man, or whether she was deliberately baiting him. That was a distinct possibility.

He became aware of a buzz of conversation behind

him, and realized it was because he had heard Miss Arabella Swinley's name mentioned.

A female voice, petulant and with a grating whine in the upper register, said, "—and I said I found it shocking that a young lady would lead a man on so, and then only to refuse his proposal—"

The voice faded out again for a moment, and Marcus turned to see who was speaking. Two young ladies stood together, near the gentleman who had been staring at Arabella with such venom in his gaze.

The girl glanced at the young gentleman and moved away from him and toward Marcus. She lowered her voice, and said to her companion, "I have heard that she is the most shocking fortune hunter. She only rejected my poor fiancé because she had richer game in sight. She dragged her poor mother to Lord Conroy's home last autumn, and stayed and stayed until poor Lady Farmington—Lord Conroy's mother, you know—thought she would go mad, poor old dear. It ended with the most shocking scene imaginable."

Marcus had edged forward, despising himself for listening to gossip, but unable to restrain himself. Everything about Arabella Swinley interested him, unfortunately, and that was clearly who the object of this conversation was.

"What happened?" the other girl asked, in a breathless whisper.

Marcus edged even closer, and the first girl glanced up and saw his eyes upon them. She straightened, eyes wide, and moved away, saying, "That is that adventurer, Mr. Westhaven. He is the most frightful hanger-on at every event, and—" Her voice trailed off as she moved back toward Arabella's former beau.

The mystery deepened. Marcus gazed across the ballroom at Arabella, who was standing with her friend,

Eveleen O'Clannahan, in the midst of a circle of young men.

Who was she? The cold, calculating fortune hunter or the sweet, laughter-filled enchantress? Or both?

She caught his gaze and even at a distance he could see the sweep of pink that mantled her cheeks. She shook back her blond curls and determinedly turned away, taking the arm of a very young, very green gentleman. Grinding his teeth, he turned to leave, but found Lady Cynthia Walkerton at his elbow. "My lady," he said, bowing to her, "Would you care to dance?"

Smiling up at him, she said, "I would be delighted, Mr. Westhaven. It just so happens the gentleman I was supposed to dance with was called away, otherwise you would not be so fortunate as to find me without a partner."

The last was said with an arch look, and he realized that without intending to, he had come close to insulting her with his casual assumption that she would be free. He hastened to repair the damage. "I knew that such an accident of fate was my only chance at such a rare opportunity." He took her into his arms and was gratified to sweep past Arabella Swinley, returning her cool look with a bold stare. Let her make of that what she would.

Nine

"I am so glad you agreed to come on this picnic," Eveleen said, glancing over at her younger friend with a sly grin.

Arabella gazed at Eveleen with new suspicion. It was a brilliant April morning and they were already on the road out of London, going for an impromptu picnic to Richmond. Eveleen's regimental friend, Captain Harris, and his friend, Captain James, were accompanying them, but on horseback. They could not abide the poky rate of travel afforded by the carriage, so they had ridden ahead to bespeak tea at an inn on the road. A carriage loaded with servants and baskets of comestibles followed.

"I would almost think you had some devious scheme in mind," Arabella said, slowly.

"Me?" Eveleen's lightly freckled countenance was the very picture of innocence. She angled her parasol to keep the sun off her pale skin. "I have nothing in mind but a marvelous day of picnicking and a lovely carriage drive in the country."

"All right, I will not question you for now." Arabella tried to relax and enjoy the day. This was what she needed to take her mind off the vexatious problem of Mr. Marcus Westhaven. No! She would not even think his name. She would forget she had ever known such an annoying creature, no matter if her conscience

pricked her at the words she had last spoken to him.
"Tell me how your visit to Dover was? Did you enjoy it?
And how badly I missed you!"

Giving her a swift hug, Eveleen satisfied her curiosity
on all counts, then both fell silent, as they enjoyed the
sparkling sunshine and the burgeoning green of the
countryside. The air held a tang of freshness that could
be found in no quarter of the city at any Season. Arabella thought that London was all very well, but perhaps
it was not quite the center of the earth, as its inhabitants
seemed to find it. This was a shocking train of thought,
for she had always loved the city. Why, then, was she
suddenly so weary of it? It did not bear thinking about.
Another day.

Soon, they could see ahead of them the roadside tavern the gentlemen had been headed toward, not grand
enough to be called an inn, really, though it clearly had
rooms above. Eve was acting strangely excited, Arabella
thought, as her friend bounced up in the seat and cried,
"Look, there are Captains Harris and James."

"And which one is your beau, Eve?" Arabella teased.
"Captain Harris seems particularly attached to you."

"Ah, that is because he knows I have no intention of
marrying him. He is . . . amusing. And physically he is
such a handsome specimen, do you not think?"

A little shocked, Arabella glanced at her friend. "I . . .
I do not think I have noticed."

"Oh, come, Arabella! What woman does not notice
a spectacular set of shoulders, and muscular legs
and . . . and other things? Only the unfortunate blind,
my dear. Even the prudish see it, even if they do not
know why it makes their hearts palpitate and a glow rise
to their cheeks."

"Eveleen!"

"Oh, pish-tush, my girl. Do you mean to say that you
have not noticed that Mr. Westhaven is most impres-

sively well-endowed in all of the previously mentioned areas, plus a few that were *not* mentioned?" She giggled at her friend's shocked expression. "Come, admit it!"

"Well—" Arabella remembered the rainy night on the terrace and the feel of strong arms wrapped around her. Yes, his strength had been duly noted and cataloged along with his powerful arms, his height, and his broad shoulders. And she had not failed to notice long, muscular legs and an aura of coiled strength that radiated from him in dizzying waves. "I must say that he kisses divinely," she admitted, with a giggle. She put her hand over her mouth and stifled her laughter.

Eveleen gave a mock look of scandalized shock. "You have kissed him? Oh, Arabella, that is as good as betrothed."

But there, Arabella became serious. "I only wish that were possible, though I must say he is the most infuriating, rudest man on occasion. Men say women are unaccountable, but at the Hartford ball the other evening we were dancing. I was looking around the room for you—I knew you were back, and I was hoping to see you, which I did, but by then I couldn't tell you all that had happened, you know—when he accused me of being on the lookout for a richer man than even Lord Pelimore! What right, I ask you, does he have to be so rude to me? And especially after he has been so pleasant lately! Naturally, I told him that of course I was on the lookout for a man with a hundred thousand at the very least, and then—oh, I should not bore you with my petty disagreements with that maddening man."

Eveleen waved at the two gentlemen ahead, but then turned back to her friend. "No, say on! I am always interested in petty disagreements. What happened then?"

Arabella told her the whole conversation, and about Lord Sweetan staring, and Westhaven being so nasty about it. Eveleen nodded and mm-hmmed through it all. "I saw him that evening. He seemed thoroughly put out, even though he was dancing with that little cat, Cynthia Walkerton. I wondered what had happened to make him look like a storm cloud and act like a rudesby. We spoke for a few minutes, but he seemed . . . angry. He spoke of going out of town, which is why he has not been sighted in the last couple of days, I suppose. Are you sure you did not fight about anything else?"

"I . . . I said something unforgivable to him, Eve," Arabella admitted, shame-faced. She looked down at her hands, pulling at her gloves and patting at her pretty spencer. "I don't know what got into me, but he spoke of . . . of a fiancée. He was engaged once! And I said she probably left him for a wealthier man, and then he told me that no, she died. I was so mortified! But he walked away before I could apologize and now he will likely never speak to me again. Not that I want him to!"

"Of course. Not that you want him to." Eveleen's voice was distracted.

They had arrived at the tavern, and their groom let down the step and the captains rushed forward to take each lady's hand as they jumped down to the stableyard.

"Fancy this, Eve," Captain Harris said, familiarly. He put his arm around her shoulders. "I have met a fellow I know from the Canadas, from the war with America. Attached to our regiment as a hydrographer, don't you know."

"Well, how about that," Eveleen said, casting Arabella a guilty look.

Arabella gaped at her, appalled. Could it be—but no. Surely it could not.

"Strangest thing," Harris continued. "Turns out he's living in London right now, and has even been to the same balls as I, but I didn't recognize him. He had a ragged-looking beard then, in Canada—a great long one! And he dressed like a native, you see, and was shockingly brown. Would have taken him for a brave without the beard, that's how brown he was."

Fanning herself, Arabella knew what was coming.

"What is this fellow's name?" Eveleen asked.

"Marcus . . . Marcus Westhaven."

Arabella wanted to stay in the carriage, but Eveleen tweaked her for her cowardice, and if there was one thing she prided herself on not being, it was a coward. So together they entered the inn. Since Captain Harris had already asked if the party could join Mr. Westhaven, they walked over to him and Harris introduced his friend, Captain James.

They drank tea and ate biscuits. Arabella did not know how it was, but her vaunted courage deserted her, and she could not meet his eyes through the whole meal. Eveleen was in her usual fine form, and with three gentlemen to entertain was at her witty best. But occasionally she would throw looks Arabella's way, trying to draw her in. Suspicion darted through her brain that Eveleen had somehow arranged this, and she wondered if Marcus had had a hand in it, too.

Finally, as the table was cleared and it was time to move on if they intended to go the rest of the way to Richmond, Eveleen said, "Mr. Westhaven, are you spoken for today? Do you have important business that cannot possibly be put off for one afternoon?"

"Not at all, Miss O'Clannahan. As I said the other night when we spoke, I have taken to stopping at this inn overnight when I am traveling. I am not overfond of London, and there are sights around here I remember from my childhood. What is your fondest wish?"

Arabella sucked in her breath. So, Eveleen had likely known he would be at this inn! It was all a setup; her friend's romantic streak was at work in this scheme.

Never had Eveleen's liveliness and managing ways been more poorly timed.

"I wish you to accompany us to Richmond," Eveleen said. "I see you have that magnificent Arabian outside, and like all the Irish I am a fine judge of horseflesh. I would see you put her through her paces opposite Captain Harris's bay hack. I have been trying to tell him this age that he—the horse, not Harris, you understand—is a poor animal, but he denies me. A race on Richmond's open parkland will decide the matter."

Marcus looked undecided. Then he gazed directly at Arabella and said, "Miss Swinley, may I have a moment of your time in private conversation?"

Stunned, she stuttered, "Y—yes, certainly."

He drew her away from the table to an inglenook by the fire, not lit on this warm April day. He knelt beside her and forced her to look into his eyes. His were dark and concerned, and his face was marked by an expression of doubt. "Miss Swinley, I cannot help but notice that you have been avoiding me today. I know why. I made myself abhorrent to you the other evening with my unwonted accusations. I had no business treating you in that manner, and I most humbly apologize. I could not answer your friend until I found out whether my presence would be repugnant to you. I never want to cause you discomfort, and if comfort can only be purchased by my absence, I will leave your party this minute."

It was a handsome apology, almost as handsome as the petitioner, Arabella thought, gazing down at Westhaven where he knelt before her. She had a sudden, absurd vision of herself and him in just such a position, only he had just asked for her hand in marriage. She could feel it, the sweet blossom of joy that would bloom in her heart and the giddy sense of the world shifting finally into place. She would scarcely know how to con-

tain her exultation, so she would let it burst forth and
throw her arms around his neck and cry *Yes; yes Marcus
I will marry*—

"Miss Swinley? Must I take your silence as proof that
I have offended you beyond all reconciling?"

"No," she said, quietly. Her voice strengthening, she
repeated, "No, Mr. Westhaven." She could almost hear
her cousin, True's, voice in her head, guiding her. Always True was there when her conscience plagued her
and she knew she had done wrong. She thought of her
cousin as her good angel, but she suddenly realized that
what True would advise her to do was not only what was
right, but what she *wanted* to do. It was not going to be
a chore; it was the opportunity to redeem her character
just a little in his eyes, and more important, to make
peace with the part of her heart that whispered she had
been cruel and thoughtless.

"In fact, since you have so handsomely apologized,"
she continued, "I will confess that what kept me from
meeting your eyes was the knowledge that I have been
the one to offend unforgivably." She met his eyes steadily now, and was caught off guard by the gentle light in
his smoky eyes. "I did not mean . . . I did not want to—"
She stopped, unaccustomed to begging forgiveness, but
determined to do the deed properly, she started again.
"I spoke slightingly of your . . . your fiancée and I have
not forgiven myself for such an inexcusable offense
against your feelings. I am so very sorry for your pain,
and I most humbly apologize."

There was silence for a minute as his eyes gazed deep
into hers, searching, probing down to her very soul.
Arabella, a calm sureness that she had finally done the
right thing filling her heart, felt her lips curve up in a
smile. No matter how deep he looked, he would only
find sincerity.

"Then we shall both admit that we have been hasty

and impolite and can be in charity with each other once more," he said, grinning and standing. He held out his hand and said, "May we cry friends, then? Please?"

She gave him her hand, and felt his curl around the soft kid of her gloved fingers as he pulled her to her feet. They stood together in the dim light of the small dining room, gazing at each other with foolish smiles on their faces. "Friends, Mr. Westhaven. Good friends."

The party advanced to Richmond, a drive of another hour and a half, to a spot Eveleen appeared to know well, parkland beside a pond. They settled on blankets on a sloping green, and the gentlemen eyed each other's horses while servants set out their repast. The day had the freshness of April without the bite of a spring wind that occasionally mars such a day.

Eveleen drew her knees up and set her chin on them, watching Harris and Westhaven setting the rules of the race they were to run. "Now, are you not glad we met Mr. Westhaven?"

Watching her friend, Arabella knew her suspicions were correct. "You arranged this," she said. "You spoke to him at the Hartford ball, knew he would be at that inn today, and arranged this." It was an accusation, but she could not say she was unhappy with the results, so her voice betrayed no anger.

Eveleen shrugged. "Westhaven knew nothing, I promise you, Bella. I wanted to go on this picnic anyway, and there was every chance we might have missed him, you know. He only mentioned that he often stopped at that inn on his way back to London, and that he would be away for three days this time. And it is just happy coincidence that Harris knows him." She glanced over at her friend, opened her mouth to speak, but then shut it again. She was silent for a moment, but finally said, "My dear, I know you feel you must marry wealth to rescue your mother and yourself from poverty, but I would that you had the opportunity for a little . . . romance, first."

Shaking her head in dismay, Arabella lightly replied, "Sometimes I do not understand you! You talk about women being chattel and marriage being bondage and all that, and then you talk about romance like the mooniest seventeen-year-old! At times I think you hate men, and at others—Eveleen O'Clannahan, I just do not understand you!"

Cocking her head to one side, her feathered bonnet giving her a charmingly fey look, Eveleen said, "That is because I am a study in contradictions. It is my Irish blood, my dear, a little tempestuousness in my otherwise perfectly refined nature. Oh, Bella, look now!" she cried, pointing. "Look at the gentlemen! Your young man has cast off his jacket and is bending over examining the withers of Harris's hack. Are his buttocks not stupendous?"

Appalled and crimson with embarrassment, Arabella said, "Eveleen!"

Her friend gazed at her frankly, brilliant blue eyes wide and knowing. "*Look* at him! It will not turn you to stone, you know, to think of all the things men and women do in private. You will have to do that to get an heir with rickety old Pelimore, why not do it first with a man such as Westhaven?"

Deeply shocked and shaken, Arabella swallowed. She could hardly speak, but felt compelled to say, "Are—" She swallowed again, her throat dry as dust. "Eve, are you counseling me to . . . to *bed* Marcus?"

"Aha! Marcus, is it? We are on first-name terms, are we? How shockingly imprudent! Your mother would be appalled; she would shut you up in your room for a month and feed you bread and water!"

Her mockery had a savage edge to it, and Arabella looked into her friend's blue eyes, noting an expression of . . . of what? Despair? Pain? Deeply felt hurt? She laid her hand over her friend's, where it was, bare, on the blanket. "Eve, what is it? I don't understand you."

"I am only saying, take your pleasure, my friend, before they sentence you to a life of being some man's chattel." Her voice was thick, but her air was one of forced gaiety. "I am not always going to be here to encourage you; you must recognize that you are only young once—feel it, live it, breathe it! Marcus Westhaven is a good man, even if he is not rich. He would make your first time a delight, rather than torture."

Arabella, troubled by her friend's demeanor, was silent. How could Eveleen talk that way? It was beyond any boundaries of decency, and she ought to censure her for it, but she was disturbed more by her friend's tone than by her words. What was wrong with Eveleen, and why would she not share what was disturbing her?

"Eve, what is wrong? What—"

"Oh, don't mind me," Eveleen said, rising abruptly. "I am always a little broody this time of month. Or would be if—"

She strode away and joined the discussion over the hack, leaving Arabella to watch and wonder. The day suddenly seemed not so very bright. Something was terribly wrong with Eve, and yet as close friends as Arabella believed them to be, she still did not feel right in questioning her any further. Only time would reveal the problem, perhaps. She stood and shook out her skirts, feeling a chill despite the bright sunshine.

Ten

If a cloud seemed to shroud the sun for a while, it soon disappeared as Eveleen returned to her customary bright demeanor. The two ladies stood on the green with Captain James, and cheered as Harris and Westhaven raced down the long green sward, around a distant pond, and back.

Arabella's heart pounded as she watched Westhaven's magnificent frame bent low over his Arabian's neck. What a splendid horseman he proved to be! The clear victor, he was already off his mount before Harris sped to join them. The captain flung himself from his saddle and clasped Westhaven's hand in a firm grip, pumping it enthusiastically.

"Told you that bay was a broken-down gasper, Harris," Eveleen crowed.

"So you did, Eve." He panted, leaning over, hands on his knees, to catch his breath. He straightened and said, "Splendid match, Westhaven. Want a rematch sometime." Harris mopped the sweat from his neck and then dug in his coat pocket. Laughing breathlessly, he let a stream of gold slip into Westhaven's hand.

"Name the time and place, Harris, and I will oblige," Westhaven said, counting out the money. "Or p'raps we will have a canoe race down the Serpentine!"

Both men shouted with laughter and clapped each other on the back, and Arabella concluded it was some private joke from their time in Canada. When they all retreated to the blankets and Westhaven flopped inelegantly down by her side, she said, "What is a canoe? You have mentioned such a vessel before, but I cannot picture it."

While they ate, Westhaven described the elegant dimensions and design of the native boat, and Arabella pictured him, brown and bearded, making his way through the Canadian wilderness with his Ojibway—Marcus had explained that Ojibway was a tribal name—friend and guide, George Two Feathers. She turned to ask Eveleen what she thought of what Westhaven had been saying, but the words died on her lips. Harris lay with his head in Eveleen's lap, and she fed him grapes. His teeth nipped at her fingers and she kissed his nose, nibbling at it as he had her fingers. The intimacy between them was unmistakable; they seemed more like a married couple than merely courting.

As she watched the pair, Arabella could not get out of her mind Eveleen's startling advice, and though she had no intention of taking it, it plagued her with powerful and dark images of two lovers entwined in the shadows, one with Marcus's face and one with—yes, with hers. She turned away from both the image and her friend's shockingly free behavior with her beau. She had never seen such intimacy between two people, and it left her feeling oddly as if she had eavesdropped on a private conversation. Westhaven watched her and smiled with what looked like understanding.

And so she resolutely banished all gloom. This was not a day for worry, nor for dejection; it was far too beautiful, and she was truly enjoying the company too much. Even Eveleen seemed completely recovered from her fit of moodiness. The real world of obligation and formality seemed far removed from this sunny park and it was not to be wondered at if their behavior became a little freer, a little heedless. Harris's friend had brought his fishing rod and announced his intention of throwing a line in for a few hours. Harris took Eveleen's hand and the two disappeared into a shady copse, but not before she threw a mischievous look over her shoulder, and said, "Do not come looking for us, you two!"

Arabella's cheeks flamed as inevitably she wondered what they were up to. She decided she did not want to know. This was a new side to her friend, one she had not suspected; morally, Eveleen had always seemed most circumspect, at least in London company. Marcus diplomatically ignored Eveleen's parting words and suggested that Arabella might like to take a stroll.

"Alone at last." He chuckled as he took her arm and they walked toward a copse of trees, in the opposite direction from their friends.

Arabella glanced up at him, a little alarmed at his ambiguous words, but he was looking off into the distance and seemed to have nothing in particular on his mind. They strolled in silence for a few minutes, both lost in their own thoughts.

"Do you intend to go back to Canada?" she asked, apropos of those thoughts.

"Yes. I cannot imagine staying here in England forever. I miss Canada already."

"Will you return to your work?"

He nodded. Unself-consciously, he put his arm around her shoulders as they strolled into the shade of the copse of trees. There was a dry path that wandered through, and Arabella inhaled deeply the fragrance of last year's dead leaves and the biting fragrance that overlaid it from the needles around the occasional pine. She loved the scent, and it took her back to childhood days wandering the woods with True and Faith. She should shrug off his arm, she supposed, but it felt comforting, like a warm shawl over her.

"I think, though, that I will be traveling west when I get back, west to the mountains. There is so much of the continent not yet opened up. What Lewis and Clark have done for the American West, I wish to do for the Canadian west. There is so much to see, Arabella, so much to do!"

His voice held passion and excitement. Arabella had never heard a man talk as he did. Most of the young men she had met in London through the Season had only displayed passion when talking of hunting or sport of some kind. Marcus Westhaven seemed to feel that genuine passion for life itself, and would not be held back from what he wanted. For the first time Arabella began to wonder if this was what Eveleen had spoken of, this ability to do as one wanted, go where one wished, that women were cheated of merely because of their sex. This was what men experienced all the time. What would it be like?

If only she were a man, she would accompany Marcus—leave England behind and explore the world! She was enthralled with his future plans, and a vision of wide vistas, huge mountains, rushing, tumbling cataracts crowded her brain. "Tell me more about Canada, Marcus," she pled, slipping her arm around his waist and feeling a thrill at the unaccustomed sensation of muscles flexing under her fingers through the fine fabric of his shirt. Somehow, they had fallen into first-naming each other, but it felt as natural as his arm around her, and she had no wish to go all missish on him.

"Let's see, what shall I tell you? My first real sight of Canada—I do not count the eastern area as Canada, not *my* Canada, anyway—was Montreal Harbor, and a dirtier, more disease-ridden place you have never seen! Our vessel was quarantined for a week, and all I could do was gaze at the shore and wish I could leave that rocking, boring jail of the ship. When I finally did, I made my way immediately out of the town and into the wilderness. I was so young—only nineteen. It called to me, Arabella, like the Siren songs the sailors used to hear, and I responded by falling deeply in love."

They walked and talked for an hour, and then finally sat on a log near the other end of the pond from Captain James, who they could still see casting his line. They gazed out across the calm pond; the sky, a brilliant blue, almost sapphire, with tiny clouds puffing across it like sails on a lake, was reflected like a mirror, and a swallow swooped low and shot straight up into the azure heights. Arabella was content for the first time in a long time and yet she did not understand why. Her problems were still what they were. The moment Lord Pelimore was back in town her mother would be plaguing her again, though she had seemed mysteriously distracted lately. And this interlude with Marcus was just that, a pause before the final, serious push to attach Baron Pelimore began.

"Tell me more, Marcus. Tell me more." She laid her head against his shoulder and closed her eyes.

Marcus almost couldn't breathe and his heart beat a rapid tattoo, though he concealed this from Arabella. He talked on as she laid her head on his shoulder. He could smell her lilac woman scent—her soft blond hair was tickling his nose, and he wanted to kiss her. The desire was so suffocating that he could not take in a breath without shuddering, and he did not want to alarm her with his need.

Was it truly pure physical need that he felt, as he had been telling himself? Or was there something more between them? He would never forget her eyes as she begged for forgiveness in the inn on the way to Richmond. In that moment, he felt like he could see through her clear down to her heart, and could see the goodness that dwelt within her, the tender side of a fiery and feisty woman. He felt a sudden urge to take her in his arms, kiss her, and ask her to marry him, and the thought shook him to the core. It was the first time the thought of marriage had ever occurred to him spontaneously like that. He did not intend to marry, ever, and was heading back to Canada as soon as this sad business with his uncle was over. There was no room in his life for a permanent woman.

Of course, there had been Moira, but she had fit into the rugged frontier life he lived. When he had asked her to marry him—circumstances had dictated that proposal, not his own wishes—he was all of twenty-one and she was twenty-seven. They had planned to marry and settle on some land down near Lake Erie, land she owned from her father's involvement on the British side of the American Revolutionary war. When she died, he had returned to the nomadic life of the army, and then the war had broken out. Since then he had decided that marriage was too much of a burden when a man liked his life adventurous.

And a woman like Arabella, pampered and used to all of the best in life, would never fit in among his friends. *Look at her now,* he thought, gazing fondly down at her. Dressed for a day in the country, she still wore gloves, a walking dress of some pretty shiny material, a Spencer, and a ridiculous, tiny hat perched on her blond ringlets, which, as always, were perfectly coiled.

Moira had been a rugged Scotswoman. She was beautiful in her way, but her hair was simply pulled back on her neck, her dress was of sprigged cotton, handmade and well-worn, and her perfume was rainwater. And she was not afraid of hard labor, having worked her father's farm her whole life. She knew how to muck out stables, make candles, boil maple sap for sugar, collect wild rice in the native way, chop wood—and still, as much as she fit into the land he loved, he would not have asked her to marry him, but they found out she was with child, *his* child. He turned away from the dark memory of the months leading up to her death. Even with all her hardiness she had died before childbirth from some mysterious illness connected with the pregnancy.

No. No man had a right to expect any woman to live like that, and he could not give up his dream of going back to Canada. The sweet flower he held in his arms was a cultivated plant; she would wilt and die in the wilderness.

She opened her eyes and turned her face up to him. "You have stopped talking. Why?"

For an answer, against all his common sense, against all of his sensible resolutions, he covered her lips with his own and felt her immediate surrender to his kiss. Fire and ice raced up and down his spine, and he felt the swift pulse of desire, followed by the throb of arousal. He plundered her mouth for a moment longer, then put her away from him, angry at himself for letting his passions overpower his reason. He felt a sureness within him that she was absolutely innocent of experience. She may have kissed before, but not in this way, not with the wanton disregard of propriety that he had led her to with his own lust.

Her eyes were dazed and shadowed with desire, the green deepened to an olive of incredible hue. Her lips were moist still, and he licked his own lips and took in a deep shuddering breath. What he would give to have her, just once, to love her as a woman should be loved!

But no one knew it would never be, better than himself. He could not—*must* not—forget her destiny, a rich man's treasure.

"Marcus?" Her voice was sweet and thick, as though she held a mouthful of Devonshire cream and honey. She moved closer to him on the log and threaded her arms under his, around his waist.

He pushed her away, gently, though it was the last thing he wanted to do. "I always seem to be apologizing to you for my behavior," he said, ruefully. "It is getting annoying."

She sat straight, pulling away from him, and the haze disappeared from her eyes. "Then don't do it," she said, tartly, and lifted her chin, shaking back her mussed curls. She took a deep breath and swallowed. "Tell me of George and Mary Two Feathers, instead."

After a silent moment, they returned to the safety of neutral subjects.

"You seem so very fond of Mary," Arabella said, after he described her, her fawn dark eyes and glossy black hair, and how she called him "Père Marc."

"She is about the age my—" He stopped and looked away, struggling with his emotion, then continued. "She is so very easy to be fond of. She is bright and engaging and smart as a whip. She dances at the lodge meetings in an outfit her mother made her, all buckskin and feathers and little bells obtained by trading with the English; I have been privileged to be named her second father. It is an honor." He stared straight ahead of him and spoke woodenly.

Arabella could feel some curious hurt within him. "Do you ever want children?"

She saw him flinch as if she had slapped him, and an idea stole into her brain. But how to ask? "Did you . . . did you have a child once?" she said, as gently as she could.

"Almost," he said, brokenly.

"Moira?"

"Yes."

There was silence but for the trill of a lark. A light breeze had sprung up and it rustled through the brush that crowded the pond edge and created dancing ripples on the surface.

"I am so, so sorry, Marcus," Arabella said, gently, and laid her hand over his. "You must have loved her very much. And to lose not only her, but the life she carried—" Inevitable pain streaked through her, but she abandoned it as an unworthy emotion. He had loved and lost, and she regarded him with a kind of awe she reserved for deep suffering.

"I . . . I suppose I did," he said. He covered his eyes with his hands for a moment, then took a deep breath and shook his head, smiling. "Moira was truly wonderful. Brave, resourceful, tough. Those don't sound like womanly traits, but I admired her for them, more than I can say."

Arabella thought how her mother would criticize to hear a woman spoken of in such terms. In her mind men wanted women to be fragile, frail, a delicate ivy needing the strong oak of the male to cling to, so she could wind herself around him and live off his strength. But in her own experience she had seen that the men she had most admired, and that included her cousin True's husband, Lord Drake, appreciated strong women, women who were themselves. Was there something in that then? Did she not have to pretend to be something she was not for her whole life?

But no, she was going to marry Lord Pelimore, and she had seen how he criticized the girls who seemed too independent. He derisively called them "boys," and said they would never marry, for no man would want them. She would be doomed, then, to play the clinging vine her whole life, or live in disharmony with her husband.

She turned her thoughts away from London. "Would

you like to have more children?" It was out before she could bite it back, and so she watched Marcus curiously, wondering what his answer would be.

He frowned and laced his fingers together. They both watched his long, strong fingers create a pattern as he threaded them through each other. "The idea has its charm. When I see Mary and George, I think I would. But—" He shook his head. "I think that part of my life, that *possibility* in my life, is over. I belong in Canada, and the moment my inheritance is out of the way, I will return."

Disappointed, Arabella said, "It is only a couple of hundred pounds. Can they not send it to you?"

Unaccountably, he looked uncomfortable and stood. He took her hand and pulled her to her feet. "There are . . . details to be worked out, paperwork to be signed."

"Ah." That was men for you; they went all mysterious whenever financial matters came under discussion. And of course she, a mere woman, could never understand.

They walked, but some of the comfort between them had disappeared. He held her hand, though, and they walked back through the woods to their picnic area, which had been tidied by the servants—the groom, two drivers, and a maidservant—who now sat a ways off having their own lunch.

Arabella and Marcus were just sitting back down on the blanket when Harris and Eveleen came out of the far copse. Eveleen had a grin on her face, and when she got nearer, Arabella could see twigs and leaves clinging to her hair and dress.

Harris collapsed on another blanket, yawned, and said, "I am sleepy. Going to take a nap, children." He closed his eyes and drifted to sleep rapidly.

Eveleen sat down beside her friend and took a bottle of lemonade out of the basket that anchored one corner. "I am so thirsty," she said. She took a long drink and corked the bottle again, sighing with satisfaction. "What have you two been up to?" she asked, brightly, looking from Arabella to Marcus.

Assailed by suspicions of what her friend had been doing, flustered and confused that she would even think such a thing, Arabella was unable to answer. Marcus jumped in and retailed parts of their conversation, leaving out the kiss.

"How well behaved you two are."

She seemed her usual bright self, but Arabella detected a hint of dissatisfaction, or edginess in her friend, she couldn't decide exactly what it was. It irritated her, this distance between them, this secrecy on Eveleen's part.

Nettled, she replied, "Better well behaved than misbehaved."

"Better misbehaved than bored!" Eveleen's smile had turned sour, and her voice had a bite of tartness to it.

"Better bored than with child," Arabella blurted pointedly, glaring, and then was immediately sorry. Especially when Eveleen's eyes drifted shut and she fainted.

Eleven

There was shocked silence for one moment, and then Marcus flung himself into action, kneeling beside Eveleen on the soft blanket and checking her head to make sure she did not bump it.

"Here, you," he called to Eveleen's maid, a tiny girl named Molly. He beckoned to her. "Smelling salts! Bring smelling salts."

Molly dithered and fluttered, but in the end it turned out that she did not carry that necessity, Miss O'Clannahan never having had an ill moment in her life before this one. Arabella's Annie was not with her, or she would have been so equipped. One of the manservants brought a bottle of water and a cloth, and Marcus hastily poured some of the chilled liquid over it and held the damp cloth to Eveleen's pale brow.

Arabella was shocked to the core and near tears that her nastiness should have had such an outcome. What had she been thinking? How could she be so bitter, so spiteful? And even now it was Marcus, virtually a stranger to them, who was holding her limp friend, and tenderly administering to her. Finally finding the use of her limbs, Arabella knelt beside them and took one of Eveleen's hands. "Eve, Eve?" she said gently. "Awaken, my dear."

Glancing at her with a question in his tormented eyes, Marcus said, "Is there something here that I do not know about? You do not need to tell me what it is, if it is a secret."

Arabella gazed at him blankly for a moment, and then remembered her mean-spirited remark and what it might seem to imply, and further, what that implication would mean to Marcus. Shame engulfed her. What had overtaken her? She had reacted to Eveleen's tweaking her on her innocence with such a monstrous barb! Monumental bad judgment, and this was the result. Calmly, she looked Marcus in the eye and said, "No, there is nothing there, believe me. It was merest chance that what I said—horrible, mean, and impolite as it was—should have this outcome."

At least so she believed. Or was there something there? Arabella shook her head as Marcus, satisfied with her answer, had gone back to his nursing. Watching him, she wondered if he had performed this service for his beloved Moira before her demise. A streak of jealousy chased by remorse coursed through her. He was unlike anyone she had ever met, she thought as she watched Eveleen's eyes flutter open. He was unlike anyone she was ever likely to meet again. He was everything that a man should be, and more.

"What . . . what is wrong?" Eveleen sat up, then held one delicate, freckled hand to her head. Her maid dithered around in the background, offering up prayers for her mistress's recovery.

"You . . . the heat overcame you for a moment," Arabella said, awkwardly.

Eveleen's eyes widened. "The heat? Oh. Yes. The heat. Molly, do stop that moaning, I am perfectly all right, as you can see."

Harris, oblivious to the commotion, snorted and turned over, settled himself once again, and slept on.

"Are you sure that you are all right now, Miss O'Clannahan?" Marcus asked, squeezing out the rag and handing it back to the manservant who stood nearby, ready to offer assistance.

"I am fine," she said. "I just—it was just a passing faintness. How odd! I have never felt that way in my life."

"Eve, I think we should be going home, don't you?" Arabella watched her friend with worry nagging at her. She wished a certain suspicion had not entered her brain; once there, it would not be calmed. But how could she ask? What could she say?

The drive back to London was long and quiet.

The next morning Arabella was handed a note by a footman as she sat down to breakfast. It was brief and to the point; Eveleen was going away for a while. She and Sheltie were traveling to a distant relative's home on the Isle of Wight.

Stunned and disbelieving, Arabella read the last few lines. *"Do not worry about me, my dearest friend. I will tell you all about my decision to leave London, but only when the time is right. Just trust me that I am fine. For yourself, forget some of my disastrous advice and heed only this; Marcus Westhaven loves you and you love him. I can see it in both your eyes when you look at each other. Marry him, even if you have to break with convention and ask him yourself! Good-bye, my dear, and I hope to see you in the not-too-distant future."*

"What is that, my dear?" Lady Swinley asked as she entered the breakfast room.

"A note." Arabella frowned down at it and chewed her lip. So much of Eveleen's life was a mystery to her, and so much of her character, too. She was like a placid lake with a mirror surface that teemed with life and tumultuous activity underneath. Who was the real woman? And what did the note mean?

Lady Swinley's dark eyes sharpened and she snatched

the paper from her daughter's hand. "From Pelimore? Is it from Pelimore? Is he finally securing your hand? I cannot believe he has been content to be away from London for a whole week on business! Business! His business this Season is getting a wife, and he should be more attentive to it. It would serve him right if you found another wealthier beau while he is frittering his time away on his estates."

Arabella snatched back the letter, desperate to keep her mother from reading it. Lady Swinley had enough to say about Marcus Westhaven, all of it bad; she did not need to see Eveleen's mysterious advice. "No, Mother, it is just a note from Eveleen saying she has gone out of town for the rest of the Season. And as far as Lord Pelimore goes, you know as well as I do that he is with Lady Jacobs, his mistress, this week. *That* is what detains him."

Her mother hissed with shock, the sound whistling through her gapped teeth. She gripped the curved mahogany back of a dining room chair so hard her knuckles turned white. "Arabella Swinley, I never thought to hear you say such an indelicate thing! That is what comes of consorting with the likes of Eveleen O'Clannahan. No daughter of mine—"

"Do not disparage Eveleen to me; she is my friend!" Arabella clutched the note to her bosom.

"And I have never been sure that she was a healthy, moral influence. But regardless, no daughter of mine will ever say or think such coarse, vulgar . . ."

Arabella failed to listen to what no daughter of Lady Swinley's would ever do, say, or think. She read the note again, and worried over Eveleen's sudden disappearance. The Isle of Wight? Though she had never been there, she had heard tales of that island off the south shore of England, and they were stories of pirates and smuggling and sundry illegal and dangerous activities.

She had not known Eveleen had relatives there. But as her friend was already gone and had not left an address for Arabella to write to her, she supposed there was nothing for it but to pray for her, wait for another letter, and hope that her suspicions were not true. She hoped that Eveleen was not with child and alone.

At the Vaile ball that evening, Arabella stood alone and missed Eveleen. She kept thinking what Eve would say about that dress, or what witticism Eve would come up with on the occasion of a certain couple's engagement. Was that all their friendship had amounted to? A social liaison, a pairing of two sarcastic spinsters? She hoped not. She truly loved Eve and felt that they had woven a friendship over the last few London Seasons. The note had been so brief; Arabella truly hoped that her friend was not in trouble.

Standing there at the edge of the ballroom floor, watching the groups of young girls stroll by, their heads together as they giggled and gossiped, Arabella realized that she had not really made a lot of friends in London. Hundreds of acquaintances, many valuable social contacts, but few friends. Why was that, she wondered?

Perhaps she knew, and just did not want to admit it to herself. She had noticed in herself in recent months a few mannerisms that were startlingly like her mother's. She almost sounded like her mother sometimes—judgmental, snobbish, fault-finding, harsh. Had she driven people away with her shrewish manner? Look at how cruel a barb she had leveled at Eve, her best friend! That was the action of a harpy. She was lucky Eve seemed to have forgiven her, or perhaps had forgotten her words.

Is that what she did to others, though? Drove them away with her sharp tongue? Had there been opportunities for friendship that she had caused to wither and die with her caustic remarks, or her cool demeanor?

And yet Eveleen had become a steadfast friend. She did not think she had been any different with her than with anyone. And she had *tried* to drive away Marcus Westhaven and it had not worked for some reason.

As the music started with a screech of bow across violin strings, and couples took to the dance floor, her thoughts drifted inconsequentially to the past, and her occasional opportunities to observe her parents' marriage. Lady Swinley let no opportunity for fault-finding pass. She belittled her husband in private and in public, complaining constantly about his weaknesses even in personal areas that should not be canvassed in company. Her behavior had undermined what could never have been a strong marital bond, until Lord Swinley frankly loathed his wife, from what Arabella had observed on her rare visits home.

And yet Lady Swinley accused her daughter of being vulgar, for merely stating the truth, that Lord Pelimore was visiting his mistress? It was ludicrous in the extreme. Was it not more vulgar to air in public personal grievances with one's husband?

Did she want to be like that? When she married would she treat her husband like that, hold him up for public ridicule in that manner? Her two choices were to marry a man above reproach or learn to hold her tongue. Since the first was highly unlikely, she would have to start practicing the second.

"Tuppence for your thoughts."

The voice in her ear made her jump, and her heart leap. "Marcus!" She whirled to find him grinning down at her. She had a strange urge to throw her arms around him and thank him for not abandoning her despite her occasional sharp tongue. If nothing else came of this Season, she was learning the value of friends. Instead of greeting him in such a wildly inappropriate manner, she smiled up at him and said, "I'm glad you're here."

His gray eyes widened and he cocked her a comical grin. "You do me honor, madam!" He swept her a deep bow, and she giggled.

"But what is the most beautiful girl in the room doing standing alone and not dancing?"

"I . . . I—" Arabella frowned. Now that she thought of it, why *was* she alone? Surely at least one of her beaux should have approached her by now? Her court had been thinning of late—most had defected to throng around Lady Cynthia—but surely some of her more devoted admirers—

Then, through a clearing in the crowd she spotted Daniel, Lord Sweetan, his fiancée, and the Snowdales. The Snowdales! In a second all the humiliation of her snubbing at their hands returned to her, and she wanted to slink out of the ballroom. They had been silent until now, and she had believed the danger from that quarter was past, but what if they had decided to tell what they knew? What if even now they were telling Daniel? After her rejection of him the previous Season he had been extremely angry; he would feed upon that black mark on her character and would doubtless show no compunction in retailing it abroad. Marcus followed her gaze.

"That is that wretched couple who cut you in the store the first time I met you. And they are with—"

Arabella's mouth trembled and she finished his phrase. "They are with the man I rejected. And they have likely told him all of the details of that dreadful day at Lord Conroy's family home—" She felt Marcus's curious gaze settle on her as her words trailed off.

"What exactly happened that they felt they should snub you?" he asked, stooping slightly to catch her eyes.

"It doesn't matter," Arabella said, hastily. She

glanced around the ballroom, looking for an escape route, wondering if she should send for Annie. "I must leave, before—"

"Before what, another snubbing? You survived the first one very well, I think. Surely you can brazen this one out, too."

Worse than snubbed, she would be ostracized and she would be laughed at! And all of her hopes, all of her schemes would die in the face of society's ridicule. She would never be able to hold her head up in London again, and would have to retire . . . somewhere! Where, she did not know, for Swinley Manor would be given up to the moneylenders if she did not manage to marry Lord Pelimore.

"You do not understand," she said, turning on him. "You have no idea! This is not the backwoods and these are not painted savages! Their opinions matter; they could destroy me—my position in society, my future plans—with one well-placed *bon mot*—"

"No they are not 'painted savages,' they are a good deal less civilized!" Westhaven retorted, his voice low and fierce. "Cruelty has no gender, nor any particular culture attached, Arabella. I don't know what you have done to earn their ire." He frowned and gazed down at her, then reached out one hand and touched her arm. It was a small gesture, but it comforted her a tiny bit.

"I cannot imagine it was such a very big solecism," he continued. "I know you, Arabella; you are thoughtless on occasion, sometimes you speak before you think, but you would never deliberately hurt someone, so I can only believe you have offended some arbitrary social rule—wore pink on a Sunday or something ridiculous like that."

She turned tragic eyes on him. How little he really knew of her! And how kind of him to say such a sweet thing when she had been rude to him just moments before. "If only it were something so simple! If only. But I am afraid—I fear—"

He gazed steadily at her. "I don't believe you. I think you have much more courage than you give yourself credit for—pluck to the backbone is the phrase, I believe. Buck up, my dear one; if all the world should crumble around you, I will still be your friend."

They were magical words, magical and inspirational. How had she managed to inspire such friendship in a man like Marcus Westhaven? He was as steadfast as a rock, and she felt she could trust him. She gazed into his dark gray eyes and saw in them courage that had faced a thousand challenges. Was she such a wet goose as to turn tail and run from a bunch of cork-brained, thin-blooded aristos? No, she was better than that, and better than *them!*

If she was ruined, if no one in London would look at her and talk to her anymore, well, then, she would go to join Eveleen on the Isle of Wight, or she would run away to Canada with Marcus. A thrill of wild hope ran through her. She would be free. No one would blame her for leaving—they would expect her to! And she would no longer be responsible for helping her mother out of her predicament; she would not be able to, after all. No rich, well-positioned man would marry a girl who had done what she had been accused of doing at the Farmington home. If she was ostracized, she could forget marriage to Pelimore or anyone else, for that matter.

Marcus was watching her. He nodded with satisfaction, reading the resolution on her face. "That's better. Now, take my arm. We are going to stroll over there, and you are going to say hello to the frightening Lord Sweetan and the terrifying Lord and Lady Snowdale and you are going to introduce me."

Arabella giggled. That would be a challenge after the

Snowdales' last run-in with Mr. Marcus Westhaven! She
felt a strange lightheartedness at a moment when she
should be feeling a dark dread. If they all snubbed her,
if the story of the debacle at the Farmington home had
gotten out, then she was ruined in London society for
a very long time. She would be damned as a schemer
and an unprincipled trollop. She would not even have
a chance to explain the unexplainable; perhaps even
Marcus would turn away from her when he learned what
she was accused of—but no. She did not believe Marcus
would turn from her then. She looked up at him as
they crossed the broad ballroom floor; he seemed so
big and sturdy at her side. She almost thought she
caught a glimpse of his burnished steel armor!

She turned her eyes to the gathered lords and ladies,
searching for signs of hostility, looking for the coldness
that would inevitably descend like a curtain if they saw
her as an encroaching schemer. It did not matter. If
every other person in the world turned away from her,
she was safe in the friendship of Marcus Westhaven.

Marcus glanced down at Arabella. He felt her trem-
ble, and wondered again what she had done that was
so very horrible? It was some social faux pas, of that he
was certain. He looked back up and examined the
group they were approaching. Lord Sweetan. That was
the fellow who had asked her to marry him. She rejected him because he was not rich enough. He shook
his head in puzzlement, still not able to reconcile the
two halves of Arabella. There was no doubt that she was
mercenary and on the husband hunt for a rich man.

But on the other hand, she was warm and lively and
smart and beautiful—the list was far too long. They had
talked over the weeks, often and at length, and she had
spoken mostly about her family, about her cousins Truelove and Faithful, and their father, the vicar. The tone
of her voice was loving and warm and tender. There

was so much in her that contradicted the notion that
she was money-hungry and grasping, and yet, and yet—

She was a puzzle, no doubt about that.

Her friend, Eveleen, had damned the mother for the
changes in Arabella, and he saw no reason to doubt
that it was the maternal influence that was responsible
for the scheming side of the girl on his arm. If only—
But he would not let himself think of all the "if onlys."
His future was back in Canada. He longed for the open
spaces, the howl of the wolf, the companionship of his
friend George. The minute the dreadful business with
his poor uncle was over he would shake the cloying,
fetid muck of England from his boots and head west
across the sea, west to Canada.

Leaving behind this beautiful English rose to bloom
in peace. He looked down at the trembling curls that
bobbed near her smooth cheek and felt a tug at his
heart. It was not just her beauty that affected him so
deeply. He watched her chin go up as they approached
the crowd around the Snowdales and Lord Sweetan.
She was mustering all her courage for what must seem
a battle to her. There was something piquant and dear
in her that beckoned to him; twining tendrils from the
fair flower at his side threatened to wind round his heart
and take root, but he must not let that happen. Where
he was going she could not follow. Twining tendrils had
no more place in Canada than hothouse blossoms.

"Steady, my girl," he said as he felt her quiver slightly.
"Steady. Picture them without their clothing."

She giggled, but there was an edge of hysteria in her
laugh. He pressed her arm tightly to his side.

"Miss Swinley," he said as they reached the crowd,
"will you do me the honor of introducing me to your
friends, so I might offer them an apology for my rude-
ness in the store that day a few weeks ago?"

Twelve

Arabella glanced up at Westhaven. What nerve! But then, he had nothing to lose, not like her. The Snowdales gazed at him with identical expressions of indecision on their faces. Either they were not used to such audacity, or they were not sure how to treat this encroaching colonialist.

She felt Westhaven squeeze her arm again, and she said, "Lord and Lady Snowdale, may I introduce to you Mr. Marcus Westhaven?"

He bowed and took Lady Snowdale's hand in his. "May I say, my lady, that I have craved this introduction for some time just to abase myself at your feet. I had no right to presume you in the wrong, that day, when you so clearly are a leading arbiter of faultless social manners. I have indeed spent far too much time in the wilds, alone, fighting the forces of nature, and would have lost my way in this social climate if not for the kindness of such leaders of the *ton* as yourself."

Lady Snowdale's irritable expression melted to one of complacence, and then sharpened to interest. Arabella was fascinated by how easily he had won her approval, and how cynically he had manipulated her. She never would have suspected it of him; he always seemed to hold himself separate from hypocrisy, and yet in this instance he was emptying the butter boat over Lady Snowdale without a blink to suggest he was engaging in blatant sycophancy. He may have been out of the social milieu for some time but he was a quick learner, that was clear. He knew just how to appeal to a social snob like Lady Snowdale, flattering her with the suggestion that she and her husband were leaders of London society when they were in reality just small players in the grand spectacle; too, he clearly saw that winning Lord Snowdale was a matter of winning Lady Snowdale first. The viscount was guided in everything by his wife.

A ripple of whispered conversation fluttered through the crowd around them, and Arabella turned to Daniel, Lord Sweetan. They had not been cut, so perhaps the Snowdales had not been telling all they knew or had heard about the horrible episode at the Farmington manor house, but Daniel still had cause to be angry with her, or fancied he did, anyway. She had led him to believe she would look favorably on his suit, but that was because she *had* looked favorably upon his suit until her mother had shown her that it would not do. Sweetan was a younger son, and she had, at the time, Viscount Drake in the wings if she wanted him . . . she thought, anyway.

Looking at Daniel now, she could not imagine marrying him. His usual expression was one of self-satisfaction, but it had soured since last year. His little fiancée was at his side, jealously looking over Arabella's dress, her jewels, her fan, in short, everything about her "rival," as she must fancy her. She was glad she had worn her new green gown.

"Lord Sweetan, what a pleasure to see you and have the honor of wishing you happy. I understand congratulations are in order?"

He nodded, his lips compressed into a thin line.

"May I make known to you Mr. Westhaven?"

Marcus stuck out his hand, but Daniel only gave him the tips of his fingers. It was an insult. It quite clearly said "You are not worth the whole hand of someone so above you as I." Arabella felt rage boil up in her. Of all the stiff-necked, boorish, stuffy maw-worms! Marcus was worth ten of him. And yet . . . had she not frozen out mushrooms and social climbers in much the same way? She had, indeed. Daniel was behaving with what he felt was his perfect right.

But still . . . fury burned through her at the deliberate nature of the insult.

Marcus felt her anger. What a puzzling mix of spitfire and snob she was! As if he gave a damn what this weak-chinned fribble thought of him. But the man was now drawing forth his little fiancée, the girl who had supposedly replaced Arabella in his affections—the girl who had gossiped about Arabella with such ferocity.

"Lydia, my dearest heart, this is Mr. Westhaven, and may I introduce you to the Honorable Miss Arabella Swinley?"

To her credit, Marcus thought, despite her anger at her would-be suitor, Arabella was very kind, taking the girl's hand and looking down at her—she was a tiny squab of a thing with none of Arabella's elegant height and even less of her address—and saying, "How lucky Sweetan is! I hope you will be very happy."

With the introductions over, conversation turned to general things, and eventually to the talk of the *ton;* who the mysterious heir to the Oakmont earldom was.

"I have heard," Lady Snowdale said, glancing around her, "that he is—"

The music started again, just then, and Marcus drew Arabella away from the crowd.

"Marcus, I was interested in that conversation!" she said, looking back over her shoulder at the small group.

"Why? Do you care who this nabob is?"

Arabella gazed up at him in puzzlement. He had such an odd tone to his voice. What on earth was wrong with him? Slowly, she said, "I am as interested as anyone. We all want to know who the mystery man is. He could have joined society as the next Earl of Oakmont, but instead has chosen to shun the *ton*. It is a puzzle and I dearly love a puzzle."

"And that is your only reason?"

Arabella looked away from his piercing gaze, remembering her own thoughts, her musing that if he happened to be young and attractive as well as rich, or even merely middle-aged and relatively agreeable, that she would perhaps consider him a good substitute for Lord Pelimore. Just the memory of the elderly baron was enough to cast a shadow on an evening that had turned out to be more pleasant than she had expected. She had not been shunned, and though she was grateful to escape that scene it also left things where they were; she must marry Lord Pelimore.

She said good-bye to her silly dreams of running away to Canada or the Isle of Wight, and reassumed her responsibilities. There was only one answer and she still knew it. She must make every effort to attract an offer from Pelimore. This brief interlude had been a halcyon period of joy and nothing more. She gazed at Marcus, his handsome face, his square jaw, his stormy eyes.

"Of course it is my only reason." He was angry, or close to it, anyway, and once more she found herself not understanding him. What could turn him, in the space of seconds, from a congenial companion into a sulking, grim-faced bear? She opened her mouth to tell him that if he was going to grimace so unpleasantly, then he could do it elsewhere, but for the first time she thought twice. Did she really want this conversation to devolve into one of the petty squabbles they seemed to fall into so readily? No, she didn't. She wanted him to hold her as close as propriety would allow, and waltz for the half hour allotted them in society.

If only she had the time to learn all his moods, to softly soothe the angry lines on his face that drew his mouth down and wrinkled his forehead. New thoughts for her, she mused. She thought of Eveleen's words in her letter. In love with Marcus? No, she would not allow that she was in love with him, but she could *fall* in love with him very easily, she thought, and yet could not allow herself that luxury. A strong mind would be required, but she was equal to the task.

After all, she had never even been this close to falling in love before; surely she could back away from the edge of the precipice now that she knew it was there.

Keeping her voice purposely light and smiling up at Marcus, she said, touching his arm, "Are you going to look like a thundercloud all evening and chase away every potential partner I might have, or are you going to ask me to dance yourself?"

It was later. Marcus, recovered from his mysterious bad mood and with a hint of mischief in his eyes, had told her he was going to ask Sweetan's fiancée to dance. He did, and a little dazzled, the girl said yes. Really, it was unfair of Marcus, Arabella thought. Daniel could not hold a candle to the older man for address, looks, manner, or anything else, though he was the superior in birth and finances. Marcus Westhaven was quite the best-looking man in London this Season, Arabella brooded, despite his casually loose clothing and his longish hair. Or maybe *because* he stood out in a crowd. Again, she was faced with the knowledge that she had never met anyone quite like him.

She thought back to the scene earlier, and her fears that the Conroy debacle had gotten about. If it told her one thing, it said that she must not delay a second longer. When Pelimore came back to London she *must* elicit a proposal out of him. He had been close once and she was a little fool to have put him off. No, her future was settled. She would marry the baron, bear him an heir, and then, with his wealth and the security it offered, she would enjoy living in London. Pelimore could continue with his mistress, and she . . . well, she would think about that when the time came. It would be enough not to have to worry about her mother anymore, or where they were going to live, or how.

Any day Conroy or his parents could come to London, and then it would be all over. She had been exceedingly lucky so far, but that would not hold forever.

"May I have this dance?"

It was Marcus again, and she smiled up at him. "Well, I do not know, sir. Two dances in one evening . . . I would not want to look fast."

"Then just walk with me. The terrace is beautiful."

"Ah, and have you already escorted a lady out there, sir?" She arched her eyebrows and looked him over, haughtily.

"I have," he said, laughing. "Miss Lydia Chancery was horrified, and yet, if I am not mistaken, just a little thrilled to find herself out on the terrace being spoken to quite improperly by the 'Wolf of London,' as I have heard myself referred to."

Arabella gasped. "Marcus, you didn't! You didn't tempt that poor girl to misbehavior, did you? It could ruin her engagement, you know, if she was caught doing anything improper."

It was Marcus's turn to look shocked. "Do you really think I would harm that poor little dabchick? No, I just whispered in her ear—nonsense, you know—and stole a kiss on her downy cheek."

"I don't believe you! If Daniel saw that it would be enough for him to call off the engagement and call you out!"

"As if he could do me any damage!" The scorn in Marcus's voice was evident.

How little he knew, Arabella thought. Not every London book could be judged by its elegant cover. "Do not underestimate him, Marcus. He is certainly not as powerful as you physically, but like all gentlemen, he has spent much time learning to shoot and fence. He is accounted a fair marksman and an even better swordsman. How could you do it?"

"Kiss her?"

He gazed down at her, his dark eyes holding an intense look, and she felt a shiver race through her. Really, how could gray eyes look so warm? "Yes, how could you k—kiss her?"

"I pretended she was you," he said, his tone silky, caressing.

She stared into his eyes, speechless. What could she say to that?

They drifted outside. The night air was warm, the breeze like a caress on bare skin. The terrace was, of course, not like that of a country home, but was large by London standards and lit by the moon, hanging like a guinea in the sky, golden and lovely. Arabella thought about his words; they were a sweet balm to her soul. Pretended Miss Chancery was her? Empty flattery, likely, and it just proved how good he was at Spanish coin.

Or *was* it just flattery? He had long showed a preference for her company; Eveleen seemed to think he loved her. But then she thought that Arabella loved *him*, and that was not so. They were just two people attracted to each other, but with no future. He would go back to his colonies with his couple of hundred pounds clutched in his purse, and she . . . she would marry Pelimore and bear him an heir. Soon if she was lucky, so she could get on with the business of her life.

She leaned her bare arms on the wrought-iron railing

and stared out at the small walled garden, some variety of early white flowers gleaming among the dark green of the foliage, touched by moonlight. For the first time she realized that his "heir" would be her baby, her son! A child of her own. Would she love it . . . him? And what if she had a girl? Would she then be expected to keep bearing children until a boy was born?

She shuddered. Women died in childbirth much too frequently. Granted, wealth bought you better care and a better diet; the death rate for wealthy women was not so high as for the poor, but still. And children! She still could not get over that they would be the children of her own body, not just separate little entities that she could bear and then forget. Could she?

Mothers did all the time; look at her own upbringing. She had been a disappointment to her father because she was not the male heir he needed to carry on the title. Perhaps that explained his attitude toward her, one of bemused tolerance. But shouldn't her mother have cared more?

Marcus put his arm around her shoulders, and she started and gazed up at him. "I am afraid to ask for your thoughts right now, my little shrew. I never know what you are thinking. I used to, when I was very young, believe that women had simple minds, that all they thought about was clothing and such fripperies. Moira taught me the error of my thinking, but it left me with a void." He chuckled, raised his eyebrows, and continued. "I shall be brave after all. What were you thinking?"

"Of children," she blurted out.

"Any particular children?"

"Mine. My . . . my future children when I marry."

He removed his arm from around her shoulders. "Ah, yes, the heir and spare you will provide . . . who? That old fraud, Pelimore? What a waste of your beauty." His tone was cold and ironic.

"Is that all you can say?" she cried, disappointed. "Is that all it is wasting?" She was piqued that all he thought about was her looks, just like any man. She had thought him deeper, but clearly he was as shallow as any of the aristocrats he disdained.

"No, that is not all." He took her shoulders in his hands and turned her to face him, pressing her back against the railing. He glared down at her and across his face flitted a succession of emotions. Finally he said, "It is a waste of your life, your vivacity, the warmth you so desperately try to subdue so you can appear as chilly and frivolous as everyone else here in London."

He enclosed her in his arms and sought her mouth. She felt it moving over hers and she was stunned by the ferocity of his embrace. What had she done—what had she said?

For one brief moment he released her mouth. She gasped and tried to pull away as he said, "Why do you try so hard to hide who you really are, Bella, why?" Then he claimed her mouth again and savaged it, drawing on her lips and parting them with his probing tongue.

She pushed him away and wiped her mouth with a shaking hand, furious and confused and trembling. "Don't *ever* do that again. I don't like it! I hate it! It is disgusting—*you* are disgusting! You have no right—" She was shaking and could not continue.

"No, I have no right, but soon a man will. Pelimore. How will you feel when he does that, and then when he pulls at your clothes and climbs on top of you and pierces you with his own body; will you like it then, my little honey-pot?" His voice was savage in its intensity, throbbing with feeling.

She slapped him hard, as hard as she could. He was insufferable and he deserved to be run through for saying such a crude and horrible thing. "Now you have insulted me past all endurance," she spat, her voice low and filled with loathing. "Leave me. Now."

His eyes hooded but still blazing with dark passion, he seemed to swallow back some of the emotion that governed his actions, and he said, his voice choked, "I apologize. What I said was absolutely unforgivable, but, Arabella, listen to me—"

Furious and shaking, Arabella hugged herself, wrapping her slender arms around her shoulders. She cried, "No, I will *not* listen to you. What I do with my life is none of your business. I will marry whom I please, and what I do with my husband is m—my business, too. I am sure Pelimore will treat me as the lady I am, unlike you."

Westhaven snorted and drew himself up to his full, towering height. He gazed down at her steadily, and said, "Then you do not know men, my dear, for all I described is merely fact." He stabbed the air for emphasis on each telling point, his finger jabbing at her. "I have known men like Pelimore, and he will use you as his brood mare and find his pleasure with someone else. And so he will not think one moment about *your* pleasure or needs. Prepare to be bred like any prized livestock."

Thirteen

Hateful beastly man! Arabella pounded her pillow and flopped onto her side. She had stormed away from Marcus after slapping him again, even harder, and had not seen him again for the entire evening. What more was there to say, after telling him she found him disgusting? She hoped his face was bruised! How dare he say such ugly, despicable, filthy . . . truthful things.

Truthful? Reluctantly she faced her worst fears and admitted them. Every instinct told her that she could not expect tender wooing, or elegant lovemaking from Lord Pelimore after they were wed. Had she not been thinking that she hoped he kept his mistress? It would be embarrassing if the man professed tenderness toward her. This was a marriage of convenience, after all, that she was pursuing. She needed security and Pelimore needed an heir.

But Marcus made it sound so ugly, so brutal, so animalistic, calling her a brood mare! Was that the way it was between men and women? Surely some men—but then, even *his* kisses had been hard and savage. Not . . . not all of them, perhaps. Last night's had, but there had been that other time—She thought back to their first kiss. That time on the terrace, when he came upon her crying, his caresses had been full of sweet compassion and care then, his kiss gentle and healing, proving he was capable of tenderness. But this time he had claimed her mouth with a savagery that astonished her. What did it mean?

He was a puzzle, that was certainly true. He had those *terrible* moods. She would say or do something innocuous, and he would look like a thundercloud! And he plagued her constantly about her need to marry a wealthy man. What was wrong with him? Did he not understand the most commonplace facts of life?

The plain truth was, a woman could not marry without security. No amount of "romance" in the world made up for that one tedious fact of life.

Arabella pulled the covers up under her chin, wishing they had enough coal to heat her room before bed. The spring air was still chilly at night, and her room felt like a tomb. When she was rich she would never be cold again, nor would she ever worry about the butcher and the chandler's bills, or about how to keep up appearances with no money.

Money. Gold, filthy lucre, blunt, brass, sovereigns, *guineas.* The ugly truth was without it one could starve, or end up in the poorhouse, or just go on in tedious poverty forever, never knowing a moment's respite, never having the peace that came with sufficiency. She had known a girl who had married a poor man because she "loved" him. That love had not survived a year of having to live in a hovel in an unspeakable part of town. Her husband was a solicitor's assistant, and had wooed her, Arabella was sure, because she was from a moderately wealthy family. He had not counted on the family's quite proper refusal to see their daughter after the marriage, nor to help them in any way financially. They had cast her aside—she had openly defied them, after all— and would not see her even when she was with child.

Arabella had gone to visit her once, but it was too painful and she was not tempted to repeat the visit. Poor Lizzie tried to put on a good front, but it was clear

that she did not even have the wherewithal to keep a
maid of all work. She was forced to make the tea herself,
and then Arabella feared it was tea that she could ill
spare. Arabella was tempted to try to help her—was
even on the point of offering money—but could see
that her friend's pride would not allow her to accept
help, for that would mean admitting that she was in
desperate need. There was a look in her eye that plainly
said any offer of money would have been an insult. Being poor was a failure in some unexplainable way.

Once the baby was born, Arabella heard that Lizzie
could not stand it anymore and went home, disavowing
her husband and living in retirement with their child,
dependent on the charity of her family, their purse open
once she left her husband, as they had wanted. She
would never be able to divorce, and so would be tied
to her solicitor husband forever. Not a pretty ending to
a "romantic" story of love eternal and wedded bliss.

Arabella shivered under the covers. Little did she
know then that she would soon be poor, too. It was all
very well to sneer at a calculated effort to marry a
wealthy man, but Marcus Westhaven had no idea what
he was talking about. His Moira was likely moving *up*
the social ladder by marrying him, and she was used to
hard work. But *she*, the Honorable Miss Arabella Swinley, could never marry someone like Marcus, without a
groat to his name—

What was she saying? Arabella pounded her pillow
again and turned over. First, he had never asked her to
marry him, nor had he ever implied any feeling for her
other than . . . well, other than the sort that makes a
man kiss a girl. And second, she could not believe she
was even thinking of what marriage to him would be
like! It had been a kind of madness for a few moments
in the ballroom at the Vaile House, when she had contemplated social ruin and running away to Canada. It

sounded very romantic, but it would be nothing but misery, she was sure. Nothing but unadulterated, horrid, miserable work and labor, and for what? Just for the way his lips felt on hers? Just for the feelings that trembled through her body when he held her close?

For even when she was pushing him away and telling him that he was horrid and that she did not like his kisses, she had been lying. Necessary lies, but still lies. When he claimed her lips and kissed her with a kind of mad and desperate need, she had felt a thrill begin in her toes and work through her body until she felt as though she were aflame. Arabella stared into the dark. Is that what had made Lizzie run away with her solicitor's assistant? That physical hunger? That all-consuming desire?

She shivered. It was a good thing she had been so rude and had hit him so hard. Marcus would likely never bother her again, and she should—she *must* be grateful. How long would she be proof against that kind of persuasion? Not that he had asked her to be his, but Eveleen's insidious words had worked into her brain like a worm. She would give her innocence to an old man who only wanted her for her childbearing capabilities, and it seemed such a dreadful waste when now she had a faint suspicion of the kind of sweetness that lay beyond reckless abandonment with a man like Marcus Westhaven.

Yes, it was a very good thing that she had slapped him and sent him away from her. She turned over and tried to sleep. But there was one last thing she had to do. She slipped from the bed, took the little bark basket that Marcus had given her from her bedside table and shoved it in a drawer. She did not want to see it when she awoke. Or ever again.

She nipped back under the covers, only to dream endlessly of the wilderness, a pine forest, the whistling

wind, and a snug cabin by a silvery, rushing river, with
Marcus Westhaven holding her close all through the
long cold nights. She clutched her pillow to her and
slumbered, a smile finally curving her bow lips as she
drifted into the deepest of repose.

A sleepless night was mild punishment for his crime,
Marcus thought as he strolled the streets of London. It
was early, yet, and all he saw were servants sweeping
front steps and bustling about their other chores. Whatever had possessed him the evening before? What mag-
got had crawled into his brain and spawned such
reprehensible cruelty? He had been unspeakably rude
to Arabella, vicious even, and she had done nothing to
deserve it. He was not normally a moody person. He
did not understand himself lately. It seemed that he was
always tottering on the edge of rage; he was jealous of
every man Arabella looked at and furious with her for
her cold-blooded acceptance that she would wed a man
like Pelimore. He was even jealous of this so-called nabob who was Oakmont's heir! Now if that was not the
height of absurdity, he did not know what was.

He wanted her for himself. He could no longer ignore the feelings that stormed through his blood-
stream, and yet he could not imagine how he had come
to such a pass. He supposed he had loved Moira, but
really, would he have asked her to marry him if she had
not been carrying his child? Likely not. He was young
then, and only thought of making his fortune. Moira
had caused him to change his plans, but only because
he cared for her deeply and would not see her bear
their child without the protection of his name.

But after she died, making his fortune had not
seemed as important as just living for the moment. He
had drifted for many years—apart from his work during

the war, that is—until he got the letter from England, the letter that had sought him out in the wilds of Upper Canada, up near Hudson's Bay. He considered ignoring it and going on with his life, but there must have been a part of him that was ready to go home, curious, perhaps about what a decade or more had done to England.

Marcus looked up and realized that he was in front of the Mayfair town home that was Arabella's abode this Season. Maddening minx! Was he blinded by lust? Did he just imagine that there was some fine core to her, some fiery, beautiful inner light that was tamped down by convention? He frowned and tapped his foot on the flagstone paving.

It was a little early for morning calls, but he hoped to find her alone. *Needed* to find her alone. He had that to say which could not be said with other visitors. His apology must be detailed and complete, or he could not rest. He was admitted, and waited in a morning parlor, a sunny room on the south side overlooking a fenced garden across the street, dimly seen through lacy curtains. He stood staring with his hat in hand; he did not think he would be there long enough to give it up. She might even refuse to see him, or she might have him thrown from the premises. He wouldn't have blamed her if that was the case.

He heard a rustle of skirts and turned. She stood framed by the door, her lovely blond hair down and back in a simple bun. Gowned in a simple muslin morning dress of a moss green color, she wore no adornments: no jewels, no lace, no ribbon. She looked enchanting, the prettiest he had ever seen her and that was saying a lot, for she was a beautiful woman. There was an expression of uncertainty on her pale face and she did not advance into the room. She looked like a fawn about to flee if he became intemperate.

"Please, Arabella, come and sit." He waved his hat at a brocaded fainting couch that lined a wall.

She entered and sat primly, eyes down on her folded hands. Needing to see her eyes, Marcus knelt at her side and she looked up, startled, her green eyes glowing in the sunny room.

"I came to apologize," he said, hoping he sounded as humble as he felt. He did not have much experience with apologizing, though he was getting into the habit with this young woman..

"That was not necessary, sir. I believe you apologized last night." Her voice was brittle but politely toned.

"Not properly. Not for everything." Damn, she was staring down at her hands again, twining her slender fingers around each other. For a moment he was caught by those hands, and how different they were from Moira's. His fiancée's had been work-roughened and brown. These delicate hands could no more milk a cow, haul water, plant vegetables, and saddle a horse, than he could net a purse.

He cleared his throat, able to see in his mind's eye only too well what they *could* do, given the opportunity. Maybe this madness, this fire in his blood, *was* just lust, passion, yearning. He had never been one to avail himself of casual liaisons, but perhaps he would be more fit for a lady's company if he had.

She looked up, a question in her eyes, and he was in that single moment sure of one thing. This longing was *not* just an indiscriminate desire for womanly flesh. It was Arabella. He wanted her in ways he had wanted no other woman; he wanted to claim her as his own and give himself to her in return. There was something about her, some indefinable sweetness, unbearably endearing, and yet fiercely denied by herself. It was that that he loved as much as anything. He knew how vulnerable she was, and how much she hated that yielding, tender part of her, perhaps to the point of disavowal.

Keeping his voice gentle, he said, "I must apologize again, Arabella, for the awful things I said last night. I had no right to treat you that way, nor to use you so roughly. I am so very sorry, both for what I said—my hasty temper—and the uncivil manner in which I handled you. Forgive me."

Her expression softened. She worried her lip with white teeth, but then said, "You *were* horrible, Marcus. I don't understand you when you are like that. I should punish you longer for your treatment of me, but I find I can't."

He gazed into her green eyes with hope. He had expected resentment and anger; perhaps it was a good sign that he was to be treated with neither. "It's just that I wish you would give up this scheme to marry Pelimore."

Her face froze. "Marcus, stay out of business that does not concern you," Arabella said.

There was a warning, but there was also a kind of sadness in her voice. Maybe there was still time to dissuade her—he could not let it go, not while there was a chance. "Just consider, my dear, what marriage means. You will become his wife, 'flesh of his flesh.' Marriage means uniting in every way possible, not just legally! Do not do this without love, or . . . or at least respect! Affection!"

She turned her face away and gazed out the window. Her voice was tight when she said, "Do you think I do not know what marriage means? That I am not prepared? I am not a silly little green girl, Marcus. I know what I am doing."

A spurt of irritation flared in Marcus. His fists clenched. "Do you really? Do you know what he will expect of you?"

"Marcus, don't."

Her voice was tired and her expression set. He swallowed his anger. What was it about her that tantalized and irritated him at the same time? He could ask himself questions forever and never learn the answers. He must accept that she knew what she was doing. Or did he have to accept it? Did he dare say the word, make the move, ask the question that would change everything? Did he dare tell her she need not throw her life away as she was prepared to do?

He reached out to her. "Arabella, I want to tell you—"

At that moment Lady Swinley erupted into the room, took one look at him knelt in front of Arabella in the act of taking her hands in his, and screeched, "Get out! Get out, you interloper. You have no business here. Albert! Albert, show this gentleman out!"

Well, she had never liked him, but this was beyond the pale. He stood. "Lady Swinley, I do not think this is necess—"

"I said get out, you swine!" Her pinched face was pale with fury.

"Arabella," he said, turning.

She had stood and was going to her mother. "Mother, calm yourself! Mr. Westhaven was just—"

"I don't care what he was doing, he must leave! It is too early for callers! You are not dressed properly yet. He should not have come so early!"

Arabella's green eyes were wide with alarm as a string of spittle flew from Lady Swinley's mouth. "Marcus," she said, turning. "Maybe you had better go. I will talk to you later. Mother is just a little . . . is just not herself this morning."

"She is exactly herself," he said, grimly, picking his hat up off the floor where he had laid it while talking to Arabella. "But I will go." He touched her shoulder, rubbing his thumb against her fabric-covered arm. "Will I see you later at the Moorehouse ball?"

She nodded, her eyes wide and full of some unreadable expression, and he moved toward the door. He looked back, but she was administering to her mother, patting her back and speaking in a soothing whisper. He left. After all, he would see her later. And in the meantime he could think about what had occurred to him as he knelt in front of her. Should he or shouldn't he?

Fourteen

Arabella knew that part—or even most—of her mother's anger was because she had misinterpreted that scene between her and Marcus, whom Lady Swinley had always disliked and damned as a mushroom. They had spoken on occasion, and always, Lady Swinley had found something to criticize about his manner, or his antecedents, or even his looks. It must have appeared, posed as he was, that he was asking for her hand in marriage, and that would be enough to send her mother into hysterics. Of course it was not that. No, that was something that would never happen.

But it took the better part of the morning and into the afternoon to calm Lady Swinley down. She told Arabella that she had had another visit that very morning from "that horrid man" as she called the moneylender, and it left her feeling faint and afraid. She would not rest, she said, could never be comfortable again until she knew her daughter had Lord Pelimore sewn up as her intended; then and only then could she relax in the knowledge that their future was secure.

But Arabella could not put out of her mind what Marcus had said. Affection. Respect. He named those two qualities as important in a marriage, even if love was lacking. As she gazed ahead into the long years of bearing and raising children, living with one man, his

lover, his nurse should he fall ill, did she care enough
about Lord Pelimore to do all of that?

Well, no. She wasn't sure she even liked him as a
person. He was abrupt and rude and didn't seem to
care about her at all other than as a sort of trophy. The
thought of being his lover made her stomach queasy,
and the unavoidably intimate nature of being his nurse
could only be worse. Affection and respect were definitely not among the emotions she experienced when
she thought of her prospective groom-to-be.

Knowing how she felt about the man, would she love
the children they created together? She supposed she
would. Was that not a mother's job? Did it not come
naturally to women?

But Lord Pelimore himself—good Lord, she did not
even know his given name. It was at that moment, just
hours after the scene with Marcus and her mother, as
Arabella contemplated her future life, that Lord Pelimore, the unnamed gentleman, was announced.

Lady Swinley sailed into the parlor behind him, completely recovered from her earlier indisposition. "My
good sir," she said, curtsying deeply before him as if he
were royalty. "How welcome you are in our home once
more."

She was using the voice Arabella privately called her
"baroness" voice. It was cultured and perfectly modu-
lated, unlike her usual "mother" voice, which was by
turns badgering and whiny. The "mother" voice had
always grated on Arabella's nerves, but she dismissed
the thought as unworthy.

Pelimore cleared his throat, handed his cane to Lady
Swinley, and said, "Quite, quite. Mind if I have a few
moments alone with your gel?"

Lady Swinley's dark eyes glistened like obsidian. "Oh,
yes, my lord, yes. Take all the time you need. I shall
be . . . oh, around somewhere should you need to speak

to me." With that she backed from the room, closing the door behind her.

So this was how her fate was to be sealed, Arabella thought, stiffening her spine. She would be betrothed before he left the room; she was sure that was what he came for. It was in the fusty frock coat from a previous decade and his formal manner. It was in the determined set to his beetling brow—oh, horrors! She had never truly noticed that particular part of his face before. Would her son have that same obstinate, overhanging brow? Best not to worry about that. After all, looks were only a small part of a man's person. And she would endeavor to ignore Pelimore's shortcomings, concentrating instead on her thankfulness to him for helping her mother and her out of their predicament. Surely gratitude was not a bad place to start a marriage?

She sat down calmly on the couch, the same one Marcus had knelt in front of hours before. This time she would not put the baron off. If it was to be done, it was best done quickly and gotten over with. Was that not a paraphrase from Macbeth? Not good luck to think it even, perhaps, but then—

"Ehem, Miss Swinley, it cannot have escaped your attention—"

A quick surge of panic rose within her like floodwater. "Lord Pelimore," she said, hastily, "would you care for refreshments? Wine? Tea?" Despite her resolution, it would be impolite to not offer him something.

"No. As I was saying, Miss Swinley, it cannot have escaped your attention that I have bin most assiduous in my atten—"

"Or a plate of cakes. Cook is a master baker and produces the lightest, most delicate—"

"Now see here, Miss Swinley, let me have my say. All well and good to be modest, but I thought, you bein' older, I wouldn't have to put up with none of this girlish nonsense."

Silenced, Arabella nodded.

"Now, where was I?" He frowned, stared down at his shoes for a minute, and then looked up again, a relieved expression on his face. He scratched his nose and harrumphed once, then said, "Miss Swinley, it cannot have escaped your attention that I have bin most assiduous in my attentions . . . attentions, yes. I am looking for a wife; you are looking for a husband. Seems to me we oughta hitch our teams together and make a go of it. What do you say?" He stuck out his hand. "Shall we call it a deal and shake on it?"

So that was it. That was to be the proposal she would accept after having rejected ones where the gentleman poured out his heart, swore undying love, offered to lay down his life for the fair Arabella. One of her devoted swains had even penned sonnets which he read aloud to her in a flowery arbor one May day three years before.

But they had all been rejected for reasons as frivolous as their hair color, or some trivial annoyance they caused her, good men, some of them. Worthy men. Men with whom she could have found, perhaps, some modicum of happiness if she had been less haughty, more accommodating, sweeter-natured. And now, as punishment, she would take the only proposal she was likely to elicit this Season. She would wed a man who spoke as if she were a horse to hitch up with. He wanted to shake on their proposal! If she should have a daughter, and that daughter said, "Mama, how did Papa ask you to marry him?" would she tell her the truth? Arabella shuddered. Better to lie, she supposed.

"What do you say, Miss Swinley?" Pelimore broke into her thoughts, his voice querulous. He dropped his hand and stared down at her.

Rebellion stirred in her heart. "No. *No,* I cannot m— marry you, sir. I am sorry, but I cannot!" She twisted her hands on her lap and swallowed hard.

Her voice and words startled even her, but Pelimore was apoplectic. *"No?"* he roared. *"No?"*

Arabella stiffened her backbone and raised her chin. Her voice more settled, she met his eyes and said, "I am sorry, sir, if I have caused you any pain, but I do not think we should suit."

"Now see here, m'girl, if you think to get a better settlement—"

Arabella rose. "I am sorry sir, but I must repeat, I just do not think we would suit."

Pelimore gazed at her suspiciously. "I understood you and yer ma were cleaned out. She gave me to understand you were at low tides and in need of a pretty purse."

Coloring, Arabella realized that her mother had been stage-managing the whole affair, from beginning to end. She was being sold to the highest bidder, as it were, no different than a piece of horseflesh at Tattersall's. It shouldn't have surprised her, but it did; it left her mortified and saddened. Marcus's words came back to her. "He will use you as a brood mare." How right he was. There *had* to be another way. She would find another way!

"You misunderstood, sir. I thank you most sincerely for your kindness but still say no. I will bid you good day." Chin up, Arabella sailed from the room as regally as her mother ever would and headed upstairs immediately to her own chamber.

Mere minutes later the door to her room burst open and her mother stormed in.

"Annie, leave us!" Lady Swinley, panting and red-faced, ordered away the maid, who was preparing Arabella's hair for the Moorehouse ball. The girl scurried away, closing the door behind her.

Arabella had known this was coming, had known Lady Swinley would not leave this matter alone to her own discretion. But she would just explain to her mother that she could not, after all, marry without at least some affection for her future husband. It was too much to ask. She was still young, attractive, and the Season was not done yet. Surely someone would want to marry her, someone who would make her feel something other than distaste, someone she could come to love?

But instead of the screaming and hysterics she expected from her mother, there was nothing. She turned in her chair and gazed up at the woman who had given her life. Lady Swinley stood staring down at the floor and tears were streaming down her seamed face.

This was unexpected and Arabella felt a jolt to the heart. "M—mother? What—"

"I cannot believe," Lady Swinley said, slowly, her voice breaking, "that, knowing our situation, understanding it as you must, *still* you will not take a kind, generous offer when it is made—one that would have brought us around and made life worth living again. What have I done that you hate me so?" The last word was sobbed rather than spoken.

"I don't hate you Mother; whatever can you mean?" Arabella stood and held out one hand, appealingly, to her mother.

" 'How sharper than a serpent's tooth it is to have a thankless child!' " Lady Swinley cried, and slapped her daughter's outstretched hand.

From Macbeth to Lear, Arabella thought, dryly, slumping down in her chair once again. They really were in a Shakespearean mode that day. But then her conscience smote her at the real signs of distress on her mother's face. The tears ran in rivulets along the fine net of wrinkles under Lady Swinley's dark eyes and her nose was red from emotion.

"Mother, please," she pleaded, clutching the soft fabric of her dress in her fists. "Hear me out. I . . . I just want a chance to find a husband I can respect, someone I can hold in a little affection. Lord Pelimore is, well, repugnant to me, and I—"

"Repugnant? How is he repugnant?" Lady Swinley's voice had risen to a screech and she paced back and forth, pausing to glare down at her daughter every few steps. "He has thirty thousand pounds a year! He has three homes and a town house! He would have settled all of our debts and allowed me to keep Swinley Manor! And you call him repugnant?" She finally stopped and stood in front of Arabella. "Foolish, wicked child!" she hissed, the gap in her teeth creating a sibilant whistle. "What have I done that you hate me so much? What have I ever done that you want to see me old and poor and thrown out of my only home of thirty-five years? Why do you hate me?"

Later, Arabella would remember her mother's words—how well she knew the baron's financial situation and what the man would be prepared to do for them should he and Arabella marry—and came to understand that the first approach had been made to Lady Swinley. Lord Pelimore was taking no chances on a rejection, it seemed. He had secured the mother's agreement in a coldly businesslike transaction.

But at that moment all Arabella thought of was her mother's words and the pain in her voice. She took her mother's hands in her own and rubbed them. "Mama, please! All I want is to be able to like my husband, to come to care for him in time. I do not see that happening with Lord Pelimore. He just—I just don't."

"It is that Westhaven ruffian, isn't it," Lady Swinley

snarled, her tone venomous. "I've seen you dance with him, stars in your foolish eyes! I heard he took you out to the terrace at the Vaile ball; it was quickly retailed to me exactly how long you stayed out there, you may be sure, my girl! He has been romancing you and turned your head. You risked your reputation, and for what? He does not have tuppence to his name! I have looked into it, and he does not have a single feather to fly on; nobody is even sure where he came from! His parents, if they are the Westhavens people think they are, died debtors! He is nothing and nobody—an insignificant son of an inferior family! Have you been making imprudent mistakes with that pandering knave?"

Arabella started to deny her mother's accusations, but found the words would not leave her mouth. Her refusal to marry Pelimore *was* because of Marcus, if not in quite the way her mother suspected. What did she feel when she thought of him? Surely amidst all the fury he engendered, and the confusion, there was a growing tenderness along with treacherous desire. When she thought of him it was with a warm glow suspiciously like love in the region of her long-dormant heart. He said unforgivable things sometimes, but he also told her home truths, and made her think. Her rejection of Pelimore was because of what he had said about affection and respect for one's mate. Was that such a bad thing, this contemplation she had been forced into?

"What have you done?" Lady Swinley whispered, after a long silence.

Arabella looked at her mother and saw with shock that the woman's face had bleached to a snowy white. "Mother, what is it?"

"What have you done with that jackanapes? I know you met him once, away from London. You were seen coming back into London with Eveleen O'Clannahan and that . . . that infamous hedgebird was riding beside your carriage. You planned a little rendezvous where I could not see, eh? What did you do with him? Have you made yourself unmarriageable?"

"How can you ask me something like that?" Arabella gasped, shocked and chilled that her mother could say . . . could even *think* something like that about her.

"Well, have you?"

Arabella was tempted—sorely tempted—to say yes, that she had lain with Mr. Marcus Westhaven and was tainted goods now. But her mouth would not form the lying words.

"I have not," she said, stiffly, hating that she even had to say that to her mother, who should have trusted her not to do anything unseemly.

"Good. I feared your association with Eveleen had perhaps corrupted you. I have heard things—but that is to no end. You will marry Pelimore, if I have to accept for you!"

"I will not! I have already said no to him, and he quite understood me!" Arabella turned from her mother and picked up a shawl that lay across the bed.

"But I spoke to him after."

Arabella turned and gazed in consternation at her mother.

"Do not look at me that way. I am thinking of what is best for you. There is still a chance; you will marry him. If you do *not* marry him, I will set you adrift; you will no longer be my daughter!"

"You cannot disown me! I am your daughter whether you like it or not."

The argument raged on and was not settled even as they left for the Moorehouse ball. Arabella would have preferred to stay home, but she wanted badly to see Westhaven. She *needed* to see him. With Eveleen gone he was the only one she could talk to about this.

She was so very confused. When Pelimore had en-

tered the room she had fully intended to accept his
proposal of marriage, and yet she found herself saying
no without a single thought of what she would do if she
did not marry him. And beyond some vague idea of
finding someone more to her liking, she still did not
know.

Eveleen had said "Marry Westhaven." As if that were
an option! What should she do, propose? And then run
off to Canada with him, leaving her mother for the
moneylenders to deal with? It was ludicrous, and yet—

And yet the picture still held its charm in her mind.
She could see Marcus leading her, holding her hand as
they climbed some high Canadian promontory with the
fresh breeze in their faces. And canoeing! It sounded
thrilling, paddling down a rushing stream in the narrow, swift boat Marcus had described as a native water
craft; how much more exciting would that be than paddling that old punt she had used as a child at the
squire's millpond near the vicarage. Almost she could
see herself, her restless nature finally with enough
movement and activity to give her respite. At the end
of every day she would know what she had done, rather
than wondering what had frittered away the hours.

The carriage pulled up in front of the Moorehouses'
London home, bringing her out of her reverie. It was
a ridiculous dream, anyway. Marcus had not asked her
to run away with him, nor had he shown any sign he
was serious about her in any way. And she certainly
would not be the one to ask him!

What would he say, she wondered, when she told him
tonight that she had rejected her elderly suitor? She
fully intended to apologize for the abrupt manner in
which he was shown the door that morning. Then
maybe they would go out on the terrace, and this time
she would not slap his face. Something had changed;
some part of her wanted to experience again the deeply

passionate kiss that had so startled her the previous evening. She was still afraid, but oh, that fear had an edge of thrilling desire to it!

Lady Swinley, who had been silent since their argument in Arabella's room, disappeared immediately once they entered the Moorehouses' ballroom. Arabella spoke to a few acquaintances, then looked up as someone tapped her arm. She whirled, expecting to see Marcus, but it was Captain Harris.

"Miss Swinley, a delight to see you here tonight. Have you seen Eveleen? Is she here?"

"N—no," Arabella stuttered. Had Eveleen left London without telling her beau? After their behavior at the picnic Arabella had half expected to hear an announcement of some sort from them, despite Eveleen's vehement denial that she ever wanted to marry.

"Can't seem to track her down," Harris said, a frown on his handsome face. "Knocker is down off her door. Where is she, do you think? Has she gone to visit her aunt for a few days again?"

Arabella considered her answer, but saw no way to avoid what she must say. "Captain Harris, I am sorry. I really thought you knew. She and Sheltie have left London for at least the rest of the Season. I understand that they are going to stay with some relations on the Isle of Wight. That is the last I heard, anyway."

It was a troubled and confused Captain Harris who left her a few minutes later and exited the ballroom.

The evening dragged on, and still Marcus did not appear. Arabella danced a few times, she ate, she talked to her acquaintances, and yet always she was watching for Marcus. Madeline Moorehouse, a young woman of not more than five-and-twenty, was the hostess, and she drifted over to Arabella after the midnight repast was over. Lady Cynthia Walkerton was with her.

"I cannot help but notice, my dear," she said, her golden eyes alight with mischief, "that you are looking at the entrance constantly. Are you, mayhap, keeping an eye out for a rather rugged, handsome gentleman newly arrived from the colonies?"

Arabella flushed. "No, I—I—"

Mrs. Moorehouse and Lady Cynthia exchanged a look. "Well, he is not coming tonight. He has disappointed us. Moorehouse had made a special effort to invite him since he has become the fashion—he tells such entertaining stories of the Canadas, you know, and of his savage friends—but he sent a note tonight that he was unexpectedly called out of town and cannot attend. Now what do you suppose was so urgent that he could not wait until the morrow?"

The hint of malice in the young woman's voice was unmistakable, but Arabella was at a loss to understand it, nor did she try. She was far too disappointed.

"I cannot imagine," Arabella said, faintly.

"Well I can," Lady Cynthia said, her lovely eyes wide and her expression concerned. "It is rumored—just rumored, you understand—that he is to wed a country squire's daughter, a girl with ten thousand pounds. Perhaps even now he is pressing his suit. What say you to that?"

Fifteen

What was she going to do? Arabella felt as though the world were on her shoulders, and there was no one in whom she could confide, no one to whom she could turn. She started to write a letter to her cousin, Truelove. True embodied the essence of common sense. She would tell her what was right, what would solve her own dilemma without destroying her mother. She poured her feelings out on paper, all the confusion she felt over her duty to her mother, all the pain of Marcus's desertion just when she needed to talk to him most, all of her fear of the future.

And then she tore it up.

True was in a delicate state, expecting the baby soon, and she would not burden her. She would not have the woman who stood in the stead of a big sister to her, worrying and making herself sick when there was nothing really she could do. The last letter she had received from Truelove had left her troubled and vaguely worried. Her cousin did not quite sound like herself, had seemed depressed in spirits. Adding to her worries would be the height of selfishness. Somehow Arabella would figure things out herself.

Days passed. Marcus had indeed left London; everyone spoke of it and the rumors flew that he was as good as betrothed. Could it be true? Surely no man with an ounce of decency would have kissed her as he did if he was romancing another young lady. Arabella began to wonder if being thrown out by her mother had finished any caring that he might have had for her. He was a man after all, and pride would not allow him to linger where he was clearly not wanted. He may have met a young lady in his travels, and have only returned to her to propose after being tossed from Leathorne House.

Or was that just treacherous vanity speaking?

She continued going to balls and routs, musical evenings and even a lecture or two, but found that without the hope of seeing Marcus there, it all seemed dull. She danced occasionally, flirted very little, and spoke even less. Her mother had not spoken to her since the day she rejected Lord Pelimore's proposal.

It was a strange interval. She had a lot of time to think with both Eveleen and Marcus gone and her mother not speaking to her. She felt like she was growing up—she had been a child her whole life, flitting from one romance to another with no thought to the future and what her responsibilities were, even though she had come to London that spring fully intending to marry for financial reasons. But still, in the back of her mind there had always been the thought that someone would rescue her, some knight in shining armor would ride in and save her from wasting her precious life in a marriage of mere convenience. Surely she was made for better things! What those better things were she had never quite been sure.

But it was not going to happen. No duke was going to see her and instantly fall in love with her. No mysterious prince was going to arrive in London and sweep her off her feet, solving all of her financial problems and giving her a glorious new life.

She wondered if that would have even made her happy. Would she have loved one of them, a duke or a prince, any more than she could love old Lord Pelimore? Even respect and affection were not to be purchased, but arose from a good and true heart.

She had mismanaged her life so far. She had spent her time in fruitless pursuit of admiration, enjoying the young men who languished after her and their pain when she rejected them. Even Lord Sweetan; she had thought it romantic that he was so distraught over losing her, but she had never considered defying her mother's wishes to marry him. In truth, she had never loved him. She had merely enjoyed being loved. She was a useless parasite on society, taking all and never giving back, and she began to feel ashamed of some of her past thoughtless actions, hurtful gossip she had indulged in, insensitive behavior on occasion.

It seemed to her that ever since the first day her mother had brought her to London in preparation for her first Season, her character had been descending a downward spiral that was now ready to hit bottom. And she had no one to blame but herself, really. In her first Season, dazzled by the atmosphere of the *haute ton* and thrilled by the recognition she gained as a diamond of the first water, she supposed it had all gone to her head, making her vain beyond redemption, and she had never looked back. And now was her Season to reap what she had sown.

It had been a week since Marcus had left town. Rumors persisted and grew that he was to become betrothed to the daughter of a country squire. All agreed that it was quite as much as a penniless adventurer, as some named him, could expect. Arabella did not really believe it—or did she?—but it ate away at her a little. How well did she truly know him? He had made no attempt to let her know where he was going, and it was not the first time he had disappeared from London for days, even a week or two at a time. Plenty of time to romance some country debutante in Lyme Regis or

Bath, or one of the other watering holes that were the launching point of many a daughter of the country gentry. It was revealing that not a soul blamed him for his alleged behavior, just as everyone would have congratulated her if she had allowed herself to become betrothed to Lord Pelimore. Self-interest was raised to an art in London, and was respected more than true goodness or altruism ever would be.

But as Arabella began to look around her, she realized that this perception was because she had confined herself to certain circles of London society. There were other circles, ones where goodness was not unusual, and kindness was valued. There were men and women who worked for change in society, who tried to help others, the poor and wretched that abounded in London. If her acquaintances seemed, to a man and woman, to be silly and vain and dull, it was because she had never looked deeper, never attempted to connect with those of more worth, if less glamour. If only she had made friends within those sets instead of being satisfied with the friends and acquaintances her mother pushed her toward.

But it was far too late for fruitless repining. Things would soon be at a desperate pass, and she must decide what she wanted to do with the rest of her life.

It was the evening of the annual ball at the magnificent Duc de la Coursiere's home, traditionally a masquerade of the most refined and acceptable sort. With Annie's help Arabella had fashioned a costume from a hopelessly out-of-date gown of white and gold and went as Diana the Huntress. But something was different. In years gone by—months gone by, even—she would have looked forward to the evening, the looks of admiration from the gentlemen, the teasing and flirtation that would assure her that she had not lost her touch, the conquering of susceptible hearts.

Instead she found that she didn't really care to go, and yet staying home was not the answer. This queer ambivalence was strange and troubling. She felt cut off from everyone and everything she cared about. She was beginning to wonder if she had ever known herself, the way she was seeing life and her part in it now. It all seemed so empty and shallow, a vast wasteland of frivolity in which she had been the most vain and flighty young lady of all.

The ball began as it did every year, with the Duchesse de la Coursiere posed at the top of the stair, announcing in her lovely, liquid French that the ball was to begin. *"Alors, mes enfants, commencez!"* For the very first time Arabella, unattached, watched from the edge of the ball-room as lines of couples formed for a minuet, the traditional first dance of the de la Coursiere ball. The orchestra, concealed in an alcove up in the gallery, played and the music drifted down like mist over the company, glittering in their costumes and dominoes.

Latecomers still streamed in at the door, adding to the crowd and the heat. Shepherdesses, Kings Henry and Richard and Arthur, Queens Cleopatra and Elizabeth and Marie Antoinette, highwaymen and mermaids, all chattered and danced and promenaded while Arabella watched, musing on the grand spectacle that was London society at the height of the Season.

Her mother had decided not to come, sending a message to Arabella through Annie that she had a terrible headache and would not be attending. Arabella suspected that this was merely the second volley of the campaign to force her recalcitrant daughter into agreeing to marry Lord Pelimore after all. She would feign illness, playing upon her daughter's sympathies and worry.

As if attaching the aging baron was any longer a possibility! Lord Pelimore had been told no, and had apparently retreated to the arms of his paramour, or to his country estates. In either case, out of reach of the Swinleys. Arabella was relieved and yet troubled, for she still had no idea how to get her mother and herself out of their financial mire; the situation was becoming increasingly desperate and the debt-holders increasingly importunate. She drifted around the edge of the ballroom while she pondered her situation.

But then, near the door something, some movement or familiar figure, caught her eye. She glanced up and froze in horror. It was . . . it was the end of her Season. It was her doom. It was the one thing she had feared since the beginning of the Season, although recently she had become complacent.

It was Lady Farmington trailed by her faithful son, Lord Nathan Conroy, both wearing only simple dominoes over their normal evening attire, but with the hoods thrown back so there was not even any pretense of concealment.

In that instant, incapable of moving as she was, the ghastly debacle came back to her, the entire episode and her utter humiliation at being thrown from the Farmington country manor on a stark January day.

The whole sordid episode had started innocuously enough the previous autumn. Lord Nathan Conroy, childhood school friend of Lord Drake, her cousin Truelove's new husband, had invited Arabella and her mother to the family home of his parents, Lord and Lady Farmington. It seemed promising. He was clearly taken with Arabella, proving to be much more susceptible to her charms than his friend, Lord Drake.

While not welcomed with open arms at Farmington, they were tolerated—it just was not the done thing to toss out invited guests no matter how unwanted they were—and life at the palatial manse soon settled down into a long visit . . . a *very* long visit. Arabella and Lady

Swinley stayed on through Christmas and into the New
Year, despite Lady Farmington's hints that if they wished
to go, no one was stopping them. There was a houseful
of other guests, some of them lingering, like the Swinleys, because it was better than going home to meager
dinners and cold fireplaces.

One evening during a scavenger hunt got up by Lady
Swinley—all the company had been avid for entertainment in the dour household—Arabella and Lord
Nathan Conroy, teamed up for the game, had followed
a clue into a room that turned out to be a dressing
room with a bed tucked away in the corner for the maid
who slept there sometimes.

They had found the silk-embroidered slipper they
were looking for, but when they tried to leave and rejoin
the hunt, they found that both doors were locked, the
one into the adjoining bedroom and the one leading
to the hall. They tried pounding on the door and shout-
ing, but they were in a remote wing of the mansion and
no one heard them. They were sitting on the bed, talking when Lady Swinley, accompanied by another of the
house guests, "happened" to try the door and walked
right into the dressing room to find the son and heir
of Lord and Lady Farmington sitting together with the
Honorable Miss Arabella Swinley on the bed in the
dressing room.

Lady Swinley had "fainted," after screaming the
house down, bringing dozens of servants and house
guests to view the scene.

Arabella could not bear to think about the aftermath
of that event, the recriminations, the suspicions, the accusations. It appeared that the silk-embroidered slipper
and accompanying hints were not on anyone else's list,
and the woman with Lady Swinley readily agreed that
the door was not locked when they arrived, and thus
Lord Conroy and Arabella had had no reason to be

closeted in the dressing room for something over an
hour, alone, *together.*

Her innocent daughter had been compromised,
Lady Swinley announced, and she demanded a proposal, or *adequate compensation.*

Until that moment and the words "adequate compensation," Arabella had not realized her mother was
behind the scheme. They had become accidentally
locked in, she had thought. But the moment her
mother made her bold demand, she knew it was all a
plot to force Conroy into marriage. And when she
looked into the eyes of Lady Farmington and saw the
distaste and distrust there, she knew that her mother
had vastly underestimated the woman's determination
to keep her son out of the hands of fortune hunters. It
was just a matter of hours before that woman would
find a way to eject them.

Which she did. The countess relied on the consequence of Lord and Lady Farmington winning among
the *ton* over the word of two nobodies from Devon. She
also shrewdly bet that Lady Swinley and the Honorable
Miss Arabella Swinley would not willingly talk of the
event when their plans failed. After all, what mother of
an eligible young man in London would look kindly on
a pair damned as fortune hunters and schemers?

The sad thing about the whole episode, Arabella
thought, was that Lord Conroy's waning interest in her
had revived as they had sat alone in the dressing room
and talked, and their conversation had taken on very
interesting overtones. He had seemed on the point of
a proposal, even. And she had liked him enough to
accept, if he made the offer, and would have considered
herself lucky, even if he was a little hen-led by his
mother. She was strong enough to counter the effects
of motherly interference, she thought.

But Lady Swinley had burst in on them just as Lord

ɔnroy was earnestly beginning to speak of marriage,
ıt before a proposal. And ultimately Conroy had not
ıly allowed his mother to throw them out, he had
ood in the doorway behind her, watching Arabella
ave. She had been weeping—from humiliation and
ɔt sorrow, she now admitted—but he did not so much
; look into her eyes, nor did he try to comfort her.
ʹhat kind of a man was that?

A well-born and powerful one, even if he was a weak
easel. And now he was here, in London at the de la
oursiere ball, with his mother. Arabella turned and
ied to hide behind her mask, her heart thudding and
ıe blood pounding in her ears, overriding the music
ven in its insistent thrum. What was she going to do?
Ier worst fears had been realized; the Farmingtons
ʹere in London, and it was only a matter of time before
hose who knew about it—the Snowdales among
hem—realized where their loyalties lay, and sided with
he powerful, rich Farmingtons against the poor and
elatively obscure Swinleys. If they hadn't quite believed
he story of her supposed iniquity before now, they
ʹould once Lady Farmington spread her side of the
tory among the *ton.*

Where was Marcus when she really needed him? Ev-
:leen, with her caustic wit and fierce friendship, would
ıave been appreciated. Even her mother's brazen atti-
ıude would have helped her through this, her moment
ɔf humiliation. Instead she was alone, and must slink
ıway in obscurity if she was very lucky.

But she was not to be so fortunate. She had started
moving toward the ladies' withdrawing room in order
to retrieve Annie, who would get her cloak, when she
was stopped by a high, fluting voice.

"Why it is Miss Arabella Swinley! Diana the Huntress—what a droll costume for you, Miss Swinley, you
sly thing!"

It was Lady Cynthia Walkerton, this year's diamond,
and she was as determinedly snide and catty as she had
been since learning that Marcus Westhaven, whom she
had apparently decided should be one of her conquests,
had appeared to prefer the "older" woman to her own
sweet self. Arabella stayed silent, longing to race from
the room but unwilling to draw attention of that sort
to herself.

"But where are you going, Miss Swinley?" The young
woman's voice was the clear and carrying sort, even over
the orchestra. "Surely you are not thinking of leaving
us so early, *Miss Swinley?* I have not seen your most determined beau, Mr. Westhaven, lately. Has he deserted
you?"

Arabella gritted her teeth at Lady Cynthia's determined and ill-timed repetition of her name. All of this
occurred on the steps, unfortunately near Lady Farmington and Lord Conroy. Nathan Conroy's face beneath
his plain black mask was bleached to a chalky white.
Arabella muttered something about being indisposed
and tried to slip around the young lady in front of her,
but Lady Cynthia moved slightly, blocking her exit, and
it was too late.

In ringing tones, Lady Farmington, who eschewed a
costume and was therefore extremely recognizable in
her customary plum gown, with her maroon and white
domino thrown back over her shoulders, said, "I think
it infamous that some gels, no better than they should
be, see fit to impose themselves on good society!"

There was silence for a moment. The orchestra and
the movement on the ballroom floor continued, but
the company around the steps all halted and listened
avidly for juicy gossip. One gentleman put up his quizzing glass and followed Lady Farmington's glare directly
to Arabella.

The Snowdales, who were just moving forward to

greet Lady Farmington, looked at each other in consternation. Arabella could almost read their minds. So, they had taken the wrong side. They had been seen to speak with and accept Miss Arabella Swinley, and now it appeared that they should have shunned her as indeed they had originally intended. They had been fooled by her civil manner and her defense of them into thinking her innocuous and perhaps wronged by malicious rumor. They would certainly not make *that* mistake again. Lady Snowdale drew her skirts closer to her body, as if she would catch some taint from Arabella.

Conroy was silent, and Arabella cast him an anguished look. Surely he knew that that last scene at their house was not her fault? She had thought him a gentleman at least, a gentleman who would not stand by and see her utterly destroyed! Would no vestige of kindness within him triumph over his fear of his mother?

She turned and was ready to leave, when Lady Farmington spoke again, at large and apparently to the assembled company.

"Of all creatures, a fortune hunter is to be most despised. One can never trust a thing she says, for she is willing to say anything to gain her point. Is that not true, Nathan, my son?"

He cleared his throat. "I—I concur, Mama, one does never know—uh—"

Arabella thrust her chin up. This was it, the moment she had been dreading since arriving back in London. It was here, and she would be damned if she would go down without a fight. "If you speak of me, Lady Farmington, I would have you address me directly!" She put down her feathered mask and squared her slender shoulders, standing to her full height and gazing up at her enemy.

"I would not pollute my own breath by speaking your name!" Lady Farmington's voice was as bitter as bile.

"Then speak not *of* me, if you have not the courage to speak *to* me!"

The sound of a collective gasp, a throng gathering in its breath all at once, made Arabella look around. In those few seconds the music had stopped and a crowd had gathered, mostly, no doubt, to greet the Farmingtons, who were very rich and very powerful. She had insulted and defamed a woman well known for her resentful personality and was now irrevocably sunk. Not a single person there would dare speak to her again.

"Harlot!" Lady Farmington hissed.

"Harridan!"

"Fortune hunter!"

"Battle-ax!"

Lady Farmington glared at Arabella, but had no more words to respond with. Arabella glanced around at the gathered crowd, and then fixed her stare on Lord Conroy. "Mama's boy," she said, with disgust, and whirled on her heel, marching away up the stairs. She imperiously told the butler to have her maid follow her immediately.

Reaction did not set in until she was home and Annie had undressed her and left her with a candle to go to bed when she wanted. She sat in front of the fire in her room, and felt a shiver of dread race through her. London society was everything to her. She was well and truly in the soup now, for no man would marry a social outcast. And the story of her supposed "trap" for Lord Conroy would even now be making the rounds of the Duc de la Coursiere's ballroom. She would be a pariah, and had nowhere to go. Not even home. What would she do? She circled her drawn-up knees with her arms, laid her head down, and wept.

Sixteen

And that is how her mother found her. It was possible that Annie had spoken to her, but somehow Lady Swinley seemed to know immediately what had happened, for before Arabella was even aware she was in the room, she said, "It has happened, has it not? Lady Farmington and her son are in London."

"Yes," Arabella said, wearily. "I am finished. Lady Farmington has made sure of that by now; if there is anyone who does not know the story by the end of this evening, it will not be due to a lack of diligence on her part."

Lady Swinley sat down heavily in a chair across from Arabella, in front of her small hearth where the rare fire Arabella had felt the need of had burnt down to embers. "If you had only accepted poor William, none of this would have happened."

"William?" Arabella frowned and glanced up.

"Pelimore! William Pelimore!"

"*You* should marry him, Mother. At least you know his given name!"

"Sarcasm will not serve, my girl," Lady Swinley said, harshly. "We have one opportunity left. Lord Pelimore still needs a bride, and he is lazy. If I can assure him that you will agree to marriage without further queer starts, then I believe I can wring another proposal out of him."

"Wring another proposal out of him." What a hum-
bling thought that such a thing should be necessary,
Arabella thought, and yet it was the best that she would
ever get now. All she could do with her life at this point
was help her mother regain some comfort for her old
age and save the family home from the moneylenders.
If she could keep them out of the poorhouse it was not
an ignoble end, perhaps. A dull hopelessness settled
over her, and Arabella nodded. "Very well. I do not
think you will be successful, but I promise, if Lord Pelimore should propose again, I will marry him. I see no
alternative."

It was a meek and quiet Arabella who met the baron
in the parlor the very next morning. Lady Swinley must
have apprised him of her agreement, for he did not *ask*
for her hand at all.

"So," he said, wringing his hands together and
smacking his lips, "we are to marry after all, eh, my
girl? I won't ask what your refusal meant; it is a subject
best left aside between us. What say you to a June wedding?"

Arabella, her heart sinking, looked up. "I . . . I had
rather hoped to go to my cousin for the summer, and
be married in September."

"September? What's the matter with June? Doesn't
every gel want a big June wedding at St. George's at
Hanover Square?"

How to say it? Arabella realized suddenly that Lord
Pelimore had come straight to Leathorne House from
his place in the country, probably in response to a note
from Lady Swinley. He had not heard of her humiliation
at the hands of the *ton*, and did not understand that
she wanted to go away, wanted to be out of the harsh
glare of public disapproval for a while. No doubt her
mother had arranged it this way for a reason; she did
not want Lord Pelimore learning about it and rejecting

Arabella as tainted goods. They would be betrothed this morning and the lawyers would likely have the marriage settlements signed by the afternoon. He could not escape after that, no matter what, and she would be damned forever as a fortune hunter by her own actions, this time.

And yet she could not tell him. Her mouth would not form the words. And did it matter, really? She was still willing to abide by the agreement they were making. She would still bear him an heir, if it was within her physical powers.

"M—my cousin is with child, and I had hoped to be with her at her lying-in. Her sister is newly wed herself and in the same state, and so cannot be there. Would you—" It was her first bitter taste of having to ask her husband's forbearance rather than planning her life as she saw fit, and it choked her. "Would you grant me this one favor? If we marry in autumn, then we will have the whole winter to . . . to get to know each other."

He looked thoughtful for a minute, and suddenly agreed. "All right, Bella. I might as well start calling you by your name now, you know. And you must call me Pelimore. I shall be an indulgent husband this once. We will be married in September."

That day the bells rang out in the city of London, but it was not for the betrothal of Lord William Pelimore to the Honorable Miss Arabella Swinley. It was May 2, 1816, and the Prince Regent's daughter, Princess Charlotte, was married to Prince Leopold of Saxe-Coburg, a love match, to all of London's satisfaction. Lord Pelimore was heard to congratulate himself at White's that evening on gaining the hand of the beautiful Miss Swinley on that very propitious day, only to learn from a friend of Lord Conroy's of the scene at the de la Coursiere ball the night before.

To his credit, he defended his fiancée's honor as well

as a man of little intelligence and less wit could. If he was privately furious, he was at least crafty enough not to appear so in public. Better to look like her noble savior than her dupe.

And indeed he was well and truly caught, for just as Arabella had expected, knowing her mother's shrewd and grasping nature, the marriage settlements were signed and sealed. That they were very favorable did not surprise Arabella either. What satisfaction she would derive from the marriage must come from knowing that she was doing her duty; her mother's future and that of Swinley Manor were secure.

May fifth. It was that very day several years before, Marcus Westhaven thought, as he strode out to the hotel stables, that his parents had perished. It was a mournful anniversary, but many years had passed and it was only chance—random chance that he had heard someone mention the date—that he had happened to remember it. Newly arrived back in London, he rode out early, just as the sun sent its first beaming rays over the treetops, to exercise his restive Arabian in the freshest part of the day. He had gotten back to his rooms at the Fontaine late the previous night, but from old habits he did not need much sleep and was an early riser.

He would not be long in London, he thought. Just long enough to see Arabella and talk to her—explain his sudden disappearance, if he could—and then he would head back to Reading. His uncle was sinking fast, he feared, which was why he had stayed so long in the country this time, after an urgent message had come before the Moorehouse ball that he was needed at Reading. The old man had had a bad turn, and had asked for Marcus. He was often sleeping now, a laudanum-induced sleep designed to ease his pain, but when awake he liked sitting with Marcus and playing at piquet or whist.

It was little enough to do for the man, and the doctor seemed to think it was the sole reason he was still living. Marcus had only come back to London on a flying visit because he had a presentiment—he who did not believe in such nonsense—that Arabella was in trouble. How he would find out whether he was right or not when he clearly was not welcome at Leathorne House he did not know, but perhaps some of his acquaintances could tell him what entertainments the lady was rumored to be attending and he could see for himself that she was well. The need to talk to her was so strong it felt like a physical ache in his belly.

He rode his glossy, prancing mount through Hyde Park toward the Serpentine, pondering his day's business. He had to see a London solicitor at his uncle's insistence, to deliver a message from the old man, but then the day was his own. He was startled out of his reverie by the pounding of hooves behind him. He turned in the saddle to see a horse thundering toward him, apparently out of control.

He bolted into action, riding alongside the snorting, heaving beast and catching the reins, to find that it was Lady Cynthia Walkerton, her eyes wide and frightened and her handsome bosom heaving just as much as her steed's.

"Oh, thank you, Mr. Westhaven, thank you! I . . . I don't know what happened. One minute she was walking steadily, and then she must have been frightened by a rabbit or something. How will I ever repay you?"

Marcus leaped to the ground and helped her down from her mount, noting that in such a frightening moment Lady Cynthia's dashing little shako had not come dislodged from her perfectly coiffed hair. She held on to his arm for just a fraction of a moment too long and looked up at him from under the tiny veil that draped cunningly over her hat brim, and he knew as sure as he lived that the horse had been made to run, and that Lady Cynthia, rumored to be a superb horsewoman, had not lost control for a single second.

He released her and stepped back, saying, "Think nothing of it, my lady." He was puzzled as to what her game was—she was the acknowledged diamond of the London Season—but he had been aware for some time that she was pursuing him. He was known to be poor, and he was certainly not the picture of one of her *tonnish* beaux, the gentlemen who crowded around her like bees around the sweetest and prettiest flower in the garden.

"My, but it is so fortunate that you happened to be here, sir. I might have come to serious harm," she said, her voice breaking. "How ever can I repay you?"

That was the second time she had mentioned repayment in as many minutes. He bowed. "Lady Cynthia, you must know that no gentleman would ever demand repayment where no debt exists. I would be a cur to insist upon one."

She dimpled and peeked up from under her veil again. "Still, you have but to command me," she replied, with a breathless quaver in her voice.

"There is one favor you can do me," he said, turning her horse and walking with her and her snuffling mount back to the safety of the public thoroughfare near the Serpentine. Her footman awaited in the distance, clearly not having been worried at all about his mistress's whereabouts or safety.

"Just name it." Her voice was breathless still, and little-girlish; she laid her gloved hand on his upper arm. "I will do anything."

"Can you tell me what entertainment Miss Arabella Swinley attends this evening? I just ask, because I remember you being near often when I was talking to her, and I thought you might be one of her special friends." He turned just in time to see her lip curl a little.

"I am not a friend of hers, sir, and I doubt that you will be when you learn all there is to know about the . . . the lady."

It was deliberately said, and deliberately insulting to Arabella's character.

"What do you mean?" Marcus said harshly.

"I mean that things have come out—tell me, sir, have you ever heard mention of a Lord Nathan Conroy?"

Marcus's blood ran cold. What was it that the Snowdales had said when he had first seen them? He could not remember, but they had whispered something back and forth about Arabella and it concerned a Lord Conroy, he was almost sure.

"I can see by your expression that you know something of what I am about to say. Well, Miss Swinley had the misfortune of being at the de la Coursiere masquerade ball four nights ago, when who should arrive but Lord Conroy and his mother, Lady Farmington. One could see the stricken look on Miss Swinley's face. I almost pitied her, but it would have been misplaced sympathy." Her breathy voice held the vinegar of malice, and her mouth twisted into a spiteful smile. "It all came out then, how she tricked Lord Conroy into a room, pretended the door was locked, and then had her mother find them thus. The mother—Miss Swinley's mother, I mean—of course screamed compromise, and demanded the poor man marry her daughter. Nothing but fortune hunters, the pair of them."

Marcus felt a jolt of revulsion, but swiftly put away his first thought, that Arabella was even more scheming than he had thought, and staunchly defended his friend. "I do not believe it. It was all Lady Swinley's doing, I do not doubt."

Lady Cynthia gave him a pitying look. "Sir, Miss Swinley would hardly go into a room alone with a man and then pretend to find the door locked, if she did not intend to trap him into marriage."

"There must be some other explanation," Marcus said, stubbornly.

Ignoring his obstinate defense of Arabella, she continued. "And when accosted by Lady Farmington about it she was incredibly rude to the countess, one of the most respected peeresses in the realm!"

"Arabella must have had good reason," Marcus said, teeth gritted. He would not let such unworthy doubt creep into him. Arabella had her faults, but he would not believe her capable of such ugly intrigue.

Maliciousness in her expression, Lady Cynthia said, "Well, if you do not believe that, then how about *this?*" She leaned toward Marcus and toyed with his loosely tied cravat, straightening the knot with her delicate hands, then laying them flat on his chest. "The very day after that confrontation, it is announced that Miss Swinley is to marry Lord Pelimore!" She watched his eyes avidly. "She was, no doubt, holding out for something better, but the moment she and her scheming mother realized they were ruined, they sealed the deal with that old relic."

Marcus was stunned. She was to marry that grotty, grubby old peer after all? How could she? What was she thinking? No, he would not believe it; not until he heard it from her own lips.

Lost in his own thoughts, he strode away from Lady Cynthia without a backward glance.

The early afternoon sun was obscured by the leafy fronds of beech and alder tree, and even more so by a deep-rimmed chip straw bonnet Arabella wore as she strolled around the small garden that was opposite the Leathornes' magnificent town house. She uneasily glanced up every time she heard footsteps. She was not looking forward to the interview she was there to conduct. The tone of Marcus's note, delivered through Annie, who had obtained it from a footman, was abrupt and commanding. It was clear he had heard something, but whether it was about her betrothal or that awful scene at the de la Coursiere ball, she could not say. She wasn't even sure which she wished it was.

She heard a quick step behind her on the crushed limestone walk, and turned. It was him, and he was clearly furious, holding on to his anger tightly as though if he let go he might be capable of anything. She composed herself with an effort and smiled.

"Marcus, how good to see you. I feared I would never—"

"Cut line, Arabella." He stood in front of her and looked down at her, his hands working at his sides. "Are you quite mad? Of all the addle-brained, featherheaded, imbecilic—what are you thinking? You will be tied to that grubby old dullard for life; you will have to let him paw you and slobber all over you until he gets you with child, if he even can! He is marrying you for nothing more than—"

"Enough! Be silent. I know why he is marrying me," Arabella said, her voice icy. She was in no mood to be abused, and by Marcus Westhaven! She held her head high and leveled a challenging look at him. "He is marrying me for the same reason all men marry; so they can secure their inheritance and be sure any child they conceive is their own. I am not so shatter-brained as to believe that any man marries for love, or if they do they are usually mooncalves sighing after their first infatuation."

"Ah, but you choose to marry for money. Much nobler!"

"I have no *choice!*"

"You *do* have a choice! If there was any chance you had a scrap of affection or even respect for the old pustule I would not be saying this, but you cannot even like him!"

"M—my affections are none of your business, sir!" Arabella fiercely blinked away the tears that rose into her eyes. She would not let him see her cry, not if he was going to be so cruel about her fate. Did he not understand that she had no choice?

"Arabella! Do anything rather than marry without that affection. You must see that it will not do." He grasped her shoulders and stared down into her eyes.

She gazed at him for a moment, but the expression in his storm gray eyes confused her and she stared down at the gravel instead. His eyes seemed to search her soul, and she was not sure she would hold up well under the examination. "You have no idea what you are talking about!" she said, wearily.

"I do know what I am talking about—your future!" He shook her lightly. "You need not marry at all. What is wrong with living life as a spinster?"

"On what? Pins? Buttons? How am I supposed to live?" She wrenched her shoulders out of his powerful grip and stared up at him, misery clutching at her heart. "It is all very well for you to talk. Men can take a profession, make their own way in the world, but without money I—we, my mother and I, will be out on the street. I had no choice!"

He seemed to take that in for a moment. "You . . . you are lacking in funds?" His mouth tightened. "You could take employment," he said.

"As what? A governess? If you look around you, Marcus, you will see," she said, her voice trembling, "how few governesses there are who are tall, slim, moderately attractive daughters of barons. Such as I do not get hired as governesses; we are too tempting a target for the licentiousness of our employers' husbands and sons and even their servants. Even if I could—even if, by some *miracle*, someone was willing to hire me, what do you propose I do with my mother? We have no relation to whom she can go. And she would not live as a poor relation anyway; it would kill her. She is my mother, *my* responsibility!"

He was silent, and Arabella's fury built at his obstinate obtuseness. "What do you know of a woman's lot in life, you having been off in the wilds of Canada? *What do you know?*"

He was silent, and his expression gave away nothing of what he thought. Arabella stared at him and it came upon her in a rush what it would cost her to marry Pelimore. She had done the unthinkable. She had fallen in love with a poor man. Damn him! Damn Marcus Westhaven for not being wealthy!

And more than that, damn him for not even thinking to ask her to marry him himself, for she would be seriously tempted, despite everything, despite her obligation to her mother, despite Swinley Manor. She would be tempted to run away with him. She had never felt this all-consuming need to be near someone, the fire in the depths of her being that flared every time she looked at him, maddening as he was.

And she was going to cry. She would *not* let him see her cry! She turned and started to walk away. She heard his exclamation of exasperation, then his quick steps, but still she was not prepared for the sudden jolt as he swiftly turned her around and pulled her into his arms.

His lips claimed hers, and she surrendered to the overpowering urge to be held and kissed and made love to. After the first angry crushing of his mouth against hers, his kiss softened and swept her away on a tide of sweet sensation. While he kissed her like that, she could forget everything, could forget the iniquities of life, the sordid reality of it. She wound her arms around his neck and felt his sinewy arms surround her, holding her tight against his body.

But then she conquered her desires and pushed him away, holding her gloved fingers against her lips for one second.

"Good-bye, Marcus," she said, hoping the sob that was in her heart did not sound in her trembling voice. "I wish you well on your journey back to Canada, whenever it shall be."

She turned and swiftly left the small park, through the gate and back across the street to Leathorne House.

"Arabella, wait! Listen to me! I must tell you—"

She broke into a run then, and did not stop until she was inside. And when Marcus tried to call at Leathorne House, she had the butler turn him away. There was nothing he could say to her now that would change a thing.

Seventeen

"The garden is so beautiful," Arabella said. She looked up at her cousin's home, Thorne House, and then over at Truelove, who strolled with her along a gravel walkway bordered by lush gardens, holding the tiny baby girl she had borne just one month before.

"Thanks to you, my darling cousin! It is my first summer here; there are a thousand things I want to do, and yet I still feel so weak. I cannot find the energy for even one. If it were not for you and your boundless energy, it would all still be a mass of weeds."

Arabella impulsively put her arm around her smaller cousin's shoulders, touched the baby's downy head, and said, "Hardly that. Drake would have hired the best of gardeners, you know, if he knew what you wanted. My dear, we are lucky you are"—she paused and swallowed, then continued in a determinedly calm voice—"are well enough to even *walk* in the garden. You had a very rough time of it." She carefully watched her tone, determinedly not letting her voice break, though it was wont to, even now, a month after True's ordeal. She tried not to remind her cousin of the fact that she had come far too close to dying in childbirth and would likely be weak for a good while to come.

Drake, her husband, in the depths of his fear, had sworn that this child would be their only one. He would not risk losing the woman he loved more than life itself just to secure an heir. Arabella had been deeply touched, and though she and her cousin-in-law Drake did not get along, she felt humbled by his love. For that reason she had done her best to be civil to him, and to remain on the good terms they had come to during True's illness.

In that spirit, she said, "I am fortunate that Drake allowed me to do this work instead of hiring someone. I would have felt at loose ends, else."

As she and True strolled in the July sunshine, she pondered fate, and how providence had stepped in to take a hand over the last year or so. Lord Drake was the very man both her and his mother, the Ladies Swinley and Leathorne, had schemed to match her with! It was laughable. They would have hated each other before long, she and Drake, but there was never any question really, whom he would marry. He had adored Truelove from the very first moment of setting eyes on her, Arabella thought, and mishearing her name, calling her "Miss Truelove Beckons." It had been a prophetic mistake.

And oddly enough, she and Drake had despised each other, for some strange reason that she still did not fully understand, for she acknowledged that he was a good man, and a worthy one. She supposed that was providence keeping both of them from drifting into an arranged marriage; that *could* have happened if there had been less antipathy between them. Love was apparently a powerful, unstoppable force.

Even now, almost a year later, the only thing that they agreed on was that Truelove was perfect, the baby was adorable, and that they were lucky both had survived. Their love for Truelove and Sarah bound them as nothing else in the world ever could. Other than that, they tended to avoid being together too much, for they fought over the most petty of things, their discord seeming to stem from a complete lack of understanding of each other's character. Arabella had a feeling he thought her superficial; she knew that she thought him overbearing and tediously serious.

Lady Truelove Drake, formerly Miss Truelove Becket, watched her cousin closely. Arabella had, two months before, expressed her desire to come to True for the lying-in period, and True had been glad to have her. Arabella was more sensible than anyone gave her credit for being—not to mention stronger—and her rational behavior was a relief after the way her mother-in-law worried and her husband fretted. She loved them both dearly, but it was Arabella to whom she turned, pouring out her fears and anxieties. Dear Bella never overreacted, never panicked, never told her she was being a goose. She always responded with calm and comforting sense.

But after the baby was born and True had time to observe her younger cousin at close quarters, she saw that Arabella was not herself. It was not just that she was quieter than normal, or that she appeared beaten down by life. There was a new thoughtfulness to her that should be a welcome relief in one who was always a little feckless. And True would have welcomed it if Bella would have shared a little of what her thoughts were, but she did not. It worried her.

Later that warm July evening, as the clock in the hall-way chimed eleven, she and her husband stood in the dim nursery watching baby Sarah sleep. True said, "Wy, Arabella is still not happy. I don't know what I expected—she is making a marriage of convenience after all, not one of love—but I did expect that she would look forward to having her own establishment, and to being Lady Pelimore. All she ever seemed to want out of marriage was wealth and position, and she is gaining both. But she won't even talk about her wedding or her marriage or after her marriage, or *anything*. I am so worried."

Lord Drake, Wy to his wife, cuddled her close to his body. "You, my darling, are not to worry about anyone or anything. Arabella is quite capable of looking after herself. The girl has raised self-interest to an art form."

"Drake, you are unkind," she said. "But I suppose, in some measure, you are right. She is an adult, not a child. Oh, look, Wy, she is smiling!" True cried, staring down at their baby girl. They both gazed down with awe at the little creature they had created together. The baby burped, and they cooed adoringly, bending over the cradle and gazing in mutual rapture.

"She is the most beautiful creature in the world," Drake whispered. "Next to her mother, of course," he added, squeezing his wife's waist. They stared in silence for a minute, and then straightened.

"As I said, I suppose in your own way you're right about Bella," True went on, once the moment of parental delirium was over. "I know she is strong and self-reliant. But it is just that she hasn't got her old fire, her old spirit. She seems . . . oh, listless, somehow. Resigned rather than happy."

"No one forced Arabella into this engagement; you know that, my dear. She told you so herself. She is a realist. She does not have your warm heart and sweet nature, my love, and you must not expect her to be as tenderhearted as you. She has accepted this marriage to poor old Pelimore as the most palatable way to go on."

Privately, Truelove thought that "poor old Pelimore" was getting the best end of the bargain, a young, beautiful, intelligent wife, but she did not say so to her husband. Their only arguments so far had been over Arabella, and it had taken some convincing—and pleading—to elicit anything more than grudging approval to have her come for the summer. Uneasy peace reigned at the moment, but there was always tension between Wy and Bella. They just did not see eye to eye on anything, though it seemed to have improved for a while after Sarah's birth. "Still," True said, stubbornly, "there is something she is not telling me, something she is unhappy about. I will get it out of her somehow."

Drake chuckled and caressed her shoulder. "Come to bed, my darling busybody. You must not get tired, and you have been up for too long today."

The morning breeze drifted in from the rose garden outside of the breakfast room window, carrying in the intoxicating perfume of a hundred flowers. There was silence around the table as Drake read one paper and True read another. Arabella absently spread butter on a muffin as she stared out at the cloud-strewn sky.

"Listen to this, Arabella," True said. "It says here that Lady Cynthia Walkerton will marry Lord Bessemere, heir to the Haliburton title and fortune. Is that a good match?"

"Brilliant," Arabella said, quietly, setting her muffin aside on the pretty floral breakfast plate, untasted. "Haliburton is a duke, and richer than the royal dukes. And a cannier businessman there has not been in Britain—at least not among the aristocracy. Bessemere will have millions when his father dies. He is a dear young fellow; I am afraid Lady Cynthia will eat him alive."

True glanced over at her cousin with a worried frown. "You know Lord Bessemere?"

"Oh, yes. Bookish fellow. Quiet, but quite charming when drawn out of himself."

"Did you . . . did you spend much time with him?"

Arabella took a sip of her coffee, and indicated to the footman that she would like a refill. "A little . . . not much," she said, stirring sugar into her cup. "I danced with him a few times. But his mother was on the lookout for a fortune—money seeks money, you know."

"Did you . . . was he a favorite of yours?"

Arabella's gaze sharpened and she laughed, but there was little happiness in her expression. "Oh, True, stop fishing. I am not in love with Bessemere, nor am I eating my heart out for him, or . . . or any man! I am perfectly content, so just stop your fussing and take care of your husband, whose coffee cup is empty, if I am not mistaken."

The footman leaped forward at that comment, and True, glancing over the table with a housewife's practiced gaze, said, "Could you ask Cook if there are any more popovers, Albert? Lord Drake is especially fond of popovers and we seem to have run out of them." Laying aside her paper for a moment, she said, "Bella, would you like to go into the village with me later? I have a longing for some new books, and I thought we would look in the drapers for ribbons to go with that pink sarcenet for your trousseau."

"If you like," Arabella said, without enthusiasm. "As long as it will not overtire you, my dear. We can easily leave it to another day."

True glanced over at her husband, but he was still lost in the paper. He had become the complete farming gentleman since they had come to live at Thorne House after the wedding, and she could not be more contented with that. The relatively modest mansion had felt like home the instant she had seen it the previous spring, and she never wanted to leave.

But he showed precious little interest in anything beyond his books, the estate, his wife, and his new daughter, and she worried that his concerns were becoming too narrowly focused. Even the trade school he had set up for injured and out-of-work former soldiers was go-

ing on with little of his direction now. Not that it needed
him. His former batman, Horace Cooper, was very ably
managing it.

True did wish he would stir himself to help her with
Arabella, though, at least, but he was of no assistance
at all. He tolerated her because she was his wife's cousin,
but he showed less interest in her than he did in the
dullest book on new farming techniques!

Brightly, True tried to animate the conversation with
Arabella. "Where will you and Lord Pelimore live once
you are married; in London or at his house in the country?"

"I don't know," Arabella said, pulling apart the muffin and leaving it in crumbs on her plate. She sipped
her coffee again, but still did not eat any of the crumbs
of muffin.

"Will you travel?"

"Perhaps. Whatever Pelimore wants."

Exasperated with her cousin's lack of interest in anything to do with her marriage, or anything else for that
matter, True went back to her paper, desperate to find
any morsel of news that would make Arabella take some
notice. She went through a few more pieces of society
gossip without any luck, then read out loud, "The
fourth Earl of Oakmont has died at the age of ninety-
five, one day after his birthday, at his country home
near Reading."

Arabella looked up. "Really? So the poor old fellow
died at last."

True's eyes widened and she quickly said, "Do you
know him?"

"Oh, no, I know *of* him. He is a recluse . . . was, I
should say. He was ninety-four, after all. But it was the
talk of London who his heir is. It is a mystery and had
all of London agog. Apparently the heir is some nabob
recently come back from India, or something."

It was the most she had said at one time about the Season just past, and True hurriedly looked down at the paper and read out loud, "The claimant for the title of fifth Earl of Oakmont came forward to the solicitors sometime ago, and had been verified as the real and true heir even before Lord Oakmont passed. This step was necessary because the claimant was long thought to be dead, since his parents had died tragically many years before and all contact had ceased from the young man. It can now be told that he was visiting his uncle while his identity was being verified and was present at the earl's passing."

"I have always wondered why the fellow did not declare himself to London society," Arabella mused. "He would have been the toast of the town; I hear he is a bachelor, and that alone would have guaranteed him instant success. He would certainly have been the most popular man in London. I daresay he would not have had to dine alone for months."

"There's your answer," Drake said, his voice dry as he shook his paper out and folded it. "He knew the minute he said who he was he would be pursued by money-hungry harpies wanting to marry him."

Arabella did not respond, though she must have known the barb was aimed at her. True darted a quelling glance at her husband. "It says here he is the heir to several estate houses, hunting boxes, and the main family seat, Lakelands, up in Cumbria."

Arabella appeared to have lost interest again, and True said, a little desperately, "Did you ever meet a gentleman by the name of Westhaven?"

Arabella looked up again. "W—Westhaven? Marcus Westhaven?"

True glanced down at the paper again and found the piece. "Yes, that is the name here."

"Why? Where? Is he m—married or engaged or—"

"No, silly, he is the heir, the one I was just speaking of. Were you not paying attention?" True looked at her cousin's stunned face, wondering why Arabella's voice had taken on a choked sound. "Marcus Westhaven is the fifth Earl of Oakmont."

Eighteen

August was in its full-blown glory. Marcus galloped along a country road, for the moment at peace with himself and his surroundings. It would not last, he knew, but while he felt it he would revel in it. He was on his way to Hampshire and free, for once, of his new-found consequence. It did not sit well on his shoulders and he hoped he was riding away from it.

The house near Reading—his uncle's favored home and where the old man had died just a month before—while comfortable, was a little too formal for Marcus's tastes. If he was honest, he would say it was a *lot* too formal. Gorgeous Turkish carpets woven with the Oakmont seal in the border, Waterford crystal, heavy Georgian furnishings from the middle of the last century, landscaping by Capability Brown—the best and most ornate of everything. Marcus found it suffocating and stultifying. He almost could not breathe in the heavy atmosphere of the mansion.

And worse, there was nothing to do!

For the last fifteen years of his life the fourth Earl of Oakmont had not been healthy physically, though his mind had functioned as well as it ever had. As a result, the estate had been managed from his bed much of the time. By now the steward knew his work far better than Marcus ever would if he studied it from now until he crept into his grave. It was all so well taken care of and

ran so smoothly that there was not a thing for a man
of energy and youth to do but ride every day and receive
the torrent of visitors that insisted on descending upon
the new Earl of Oakmont. This, for a man used to the
wilds of Canada and new sights every day, was irksome
in the extreme. He longed for new vistas and a little
nature.

Even more irritating than the lack of anything to do,
though, was the difficulty Marcus was having getting
used to his new status. He was surrounded by dozens
of servants, bowing every time they saw him and calling
him "my lord" and "Lord Oakmont." And even worse,
every person of consequence, and many more of no
consequence, who had flooded back into the country
from the London Season, deigned to visit him and sub-
tly congratulate him on his coup. As the fifth Earl of
Oakmont he had many more "friends" than would have
even spoken to him in London when he was merely
Marcus Westhaven. What had happened to Marcus
Westhaven, for heaven's sake? Where was the poor fellow? Buried in fine linens and harried by impeccably
mannered servants, that was where he was. He had pen-
sioned off the servants he could, but there were still far
too many for his liking.

Brooding one fine, sunny day, he had suddenly realized that there was not a thing keeping him there. He
was confined, by his period of mourning for his uncle—
though he did not follow many of society's dictates, his
respect for the old man commanded him in this—to
no public entertainments and a black armband on his
sober-colored coat, but no one could tell him where to
go. Among his new acquisitions—and that was another
thing that troubled him; how would he ever get back
to Canada with all of these new responsibilities and literally hundreds of employees depending on his active
management of the several and various estates now in

his possession?—there was a hunting box down in Hampshire. It was a little too early for hunting, if he remembered right, but he would go anyway. A hunting box would not retain the staff of his main seat, nor would anyone there be expecting him. They would be less likely, surely, to make a fuss and bother over him.

And didn't an old crony of his say to look up a friend from the army down in Hampshire? Was there not a Major-General Prescott who lived down that way? He found the note from his friend and stored it in the one bag he was taking with him to Hampshire. He felt so cut off from society now; everywhere he went people treated him differently because of his new title. But Greyling had said that this Prescott fellow was down-to-earth. He hoped his friend was right about that. He missed rational male conversation.

And he missed Arabella. He had tried to contact her, had sent letters that were returned unopened, had gone to Leathorne House only to be turned away, every day until the knocker was down, signifying they had left London. He had tried. But she would be married by now. It had likely not been put in the paper because of the scandal associated with her name that still re-sounded throughout London, the scandal about that weasel, Lord Conroy. Within seconds of meeting the fellow, after Arabella had left town as the betrothed of Lord Pelimore, Marcus had written the fellow off as a hopeless mama's boy and weakling. He had heard the whole story repeated endlessly, and the more he thought on it, the less he believed Arabella had any part in it. It was all a mistake, or more likely Lady Swinley had managed the whole affair without her daughter's assistance. A woman like Arabella did not need to trick a man to have him marry her.

Arabella. He missed her so badly, and that puzzled him. Why could he not put Miss Arabella Swinley out of his mind? Even though he knew very well that she must be married by now, she was always there; it was not that she constantly came back to haunt him, she just never left his thoughts. He kept seeing her as she last looked, the very last time he had ever, or was ever likely, to set eyes on her. When she turned and walked away in that tiny park across from her London residence, sorrow had draped her like a dark veil. He had called after her, but she had fled like a swarm of demons pursued her. He couldn't have her and he couldn't forget her, and it was driving him wild.

And so on this fine August morning, with a mist rising from the hedgerow and birds flying up from the copse nearby, he rode—rode away from sorrow and responsibility and formality, and toward . . . well, toward something different. Anything! He had the letter in his pocket from his friend Captain Greyling, with an introduction to Major-General Prescott, and the admonition to treat Westhaven well, so he would not think so ill of his homeland as he had been wont to do in the colonies.

He arrived late in the evening and the hunting box, a smallish manse set in a clearing, was everything he had hoped; it was cared for by a slatternly couple named Brown, who ran a very casual household. They were obviously terrified when the new earl showed up on the doorstep unannounced and unexpected—after all, the old earl had not been there in almost twenty years, and it had only been loaned out to friends occasionally in all that time—but Marcus was cheerfully pleased to find himself forced to make do with eggs and ham for dinner, instead of a six-course meal with a footman standing behind his chair. Mrs. Brown soon understood him. She left him alone, tidying his chamber as best she could for the evening, and leaving him to stoke his own fire and pour his own washing-up water.

If privately the Browns were derogatory in their remarks about the new earl—they would have respected him more if he had been frosty and had threatened to sack them for their lack of industry—they were smart enough to be quietly respectful in his presence, without bowing and scraping overmuch.

The next morning dawned glorious and golden, and it was a happier Marcus who set off for Thorne House in response to the written invitation from Major-General Prescott to join him for some hunting. It was a little early in the year even for partridge, but he promised some hare hunting and perhaps a little grouse hunting, as the season was just getting started.

Major General Prescott, he discovered, was Viscount Drake, heir to the Earl of Leathorne, but for all that as unpretentious a fellow as he could ever hope to meet. Strange to think that he was the man at his side's social superior, he thought, glancing at him as they tramped through the meadows and fields toward a beech forest. Prescott, or rather Drake, as he must remember to call him, was a golden man, effortlessly regal, while he himself was rather lupine than leonine, he thought, more wolf than lion. Between them there seemed no barriers of rank though, and Marcus appreciated that so very much.

They didn't talk much throughout the day—Drake seemed to understand Marcus immediately, and other than conversation about the hunt, the area, and some generalizations about each man's part in the wars just over, they spoke little—but Marcus felt a kinship to the man he walked with. For almost the first time since landing on English soil, he felt at home.

Toward the end of the day, as they headed back to Marcus's temporary abode, he noticed his new friend limping slightly. "Blast, but I forgot! Greyling said you were injured at Waterloo, and here I've kept you out all day!"

"Think nothing of it," Drake said, cheerfully. "I welcome the exercise. M'wife will be the one you will have to face. She is a little termagant about my health. She is the reason I am even alive, so I suppose she has the right."

"Alive? What do you mean?" Marcus gazed over at him curiously as they entered the dark, ancient hall of Andover, as the hunting box was known.

"I had a bad spell with the fever—this was before I married her; she had come to visit with a cousin—and she nursed me through it." Drake sagged wearily onto a bench in the hall, handing his gun to his groom. "I was already half in love with her. I had wanted to ask her to marry me, but I thought her already betrothed. But even if I hadn't been in love, that experience would have made me so. She was so very tender, my little angel of mercy."

The depth of emotion in the viscount's voice choked Marcus. Lucky fellow, to love so deeply and have that love returned! "She must be a very special woman," he said, quietly.

"She is," Drake said, casting a side glance at Marcus. He rubbed his thigh, stretching his leg out in front of him, and said, "You can meet her if you will come for dinner."

Frowning, Marcus said, "Will that not put you out? You have a new baby, you said, and—"

"It is not as if m'wife has to cook the dinner herself while holding the baby on her hip," Drake said, laughing. He stood and flexed his wounded leg, then nodded as he put his weight on it, as if to say "That'll do." "Mind you, she could! She is a trooper, is my girl. Trust me, Marcus, we have adequate servants and our dinner will stretch to serve one more. Anyway, I told her I might bring you along if I liked the look of you."

Marcus chuckled. "So glad to have passed muster.

Well, if you are sure it will not put you out, I will gladly come."

"We dine at six. Country hours, you know."

It was only later after Drake had left that Marcus realized the fellow had never told him his wife's name. Oh, well, he thought, he would learn that soon enough.

"I hope we are doing the right thing, my love," Drake said, later, in his dressing room as he changed for dinner. He looked down at the old scar in his thigh from his near-death experience at Waterloo. The phantom pains shot through it when exercised for too long, as it had been that day, but he was lucky to be alive, and never mentioned when it hurt.

"It was too great a coincidence to ignore, Wy. Much too great! I could not believe when you got the note of introduction from the gentleman last night; it would seem that heaven smiles down on our endeavors." True, gazing at herself in the mirror on the dressing table, poked at a recalcitrant curl that would not behave and sighed, giving up on it. Her hair was as soft as spun glass, but for all that it would not be bullied into any particular style. Since she did not like to have a maid fussing around her, preferring the little rituals attending getting dressed with her husband's help, she let it go where it wanted. She stood and turned, and Wy did up the back of her dress, after laying a kiss on her neck.

"But what good will it do?" he said, continuing their conversation. "Arabella is engaged."

"But not yet wed," True said, with that stubborn cast to her bow lips. She had already sent away Drake's new valet—his former one had been his batman in the war, but was now managing the school Drake had set up to train retired soldiers for employment in peacetime England—because the poor fellow drove Drake to distraction. He was appalled at his new master's casual attitude toward clothing and harried him constantly in an effort to make him more elegant. Drake, tired from his long day, had been near the end of his patience and True, recognizing the signs after nearly a year of marriage, had sent the fellow down to assist the butler in the drawing room.

"But about to be wed in a week! Do not forget that, my dear." Wy pulled on his breeches and then struggled into a fine lawn shirt. "Will this not just cause more heartache if your surmises are correct?"

"I do not see how there can be any more heartache in Arabella's face, Wy. I know she cries herself to sleep, though she always stifles her tears when I come in. She needs to see him once more, the cad!"

"He seems like a thoroughly nice fellow, True," Drake objected, knotting his cravat around his neck and reaching for his coat.

"He cannot be such a nice fellow if he broke Arabella's heart."

"You do not know that," Drake said. "You do not know anything beyond her reaction when she heard the news that he had become the fifth Earl of Oakmont. It is just as likely that it is her frustrated money-grubbing that has upset her." He tugged on his coat while his wife worked her magic with his stiffly starched cravat. "Oakmont is a much bigger fish than Pelimore, and he is a very attractive sort of fellow in a wild way, the sort I imagine the ladies would like. Arabella is just piqued because she let a prime plum get away."

True sighed and poked his cravat into the final respectable fold. "You are ever ready to disparage Arabella, Wy, but you are not being fair! You did not see her that night she left Lea Park, when I was nursing you. She seemed almost desperate! Her mother has

been putting such pressure on her to marry well, and
the poor girl had gotten to think it was all she could
do, and that it was her duty to her mother. But she has
a heart, I know she does, and I very much fear she has
learned it too late."

It was the closest they came to arguing, and Drake
put his arms around his small wife and held her to his
heart. Lord, how he longed to be with her again, as
man and wife. But she was still so frail and delicate. He
would rather forgo that very private delight forever than
see her ill again, as she was after the baby was born.
"Very well, my love," he said, laying a kiss on the top
of her head. "Arabella is a princess in disguise and Oakmont is her secret prince. Miracles do happen, and they
will discover that the ugly troll, also known as Lord Pelimore, will be magically transformed into his true
guise, whereupon Oakmont will defeat him and release
the princess from her spell, after which they will marry
and live happily ever after." He dragged in a deep
breath after that long speech.

True pulled away. "Wy, do not mock me. I don't like
it."

Seeing that he had hurt her, Drake pulled her back
to him. "My love, I am sorry. I thought I was being a
tease; I never meant to be cruel."

She pushed him away again, but there was a tremu-
lous smile on her lips. "You could never be cruel. Finish
dressing, and come down to dinner. We shall see what
happens tonight."

"Have you told her there is to be a guest at dinner?"

"Yes, but not who it is," True said, grinning impishly
as she exited Drake's dressing room. "I want this to be
a surprise to both of them. I have a feeling about this!"

Drake groaned and shook his head in exasperation.

* * *

Arabella descended, realizing as she did so that she was a little late. She could hear voices coming into the hall from the drawing room, as though her cousin and cousin-in-law were just gathering to go in to dinner. True had said some hunting friend of Drake's was to be there for dinner and asked her to join them to keep the numbers even, or Arabella would have just had some toast in her room. As the wedding day drew closer and closer, she found herself descending into a pit of despair that threatened to close over her head like the quicksand she had once read about.

And yet she did not know what she could have done any differently. This was the life of her own making, and she would not whine or quibble about its downfalls now. If she had learned anything in the past months, it was to make the best of her life as it unfolded. She would concentrate on her good fortune, and let go of the rest. Her husband-to-be was a good man, if not appealing to her in any way. All she could do with her life now was try to be a good wife, and eventually, a good mother.

For True's sake, she wore her newest gown, the emerald green, and had her hair dressed up in a flattering Grecian style. She had taken to more casual country styles at Thorne House, especially since she seemed to spend all of her time out in the garden or up in the nursery, but tonight True had asked her to dress for company. She descended the stairs just as the company was coming out of the withdrawing room, just as she had expected. Smiling at True, she turned to meet Drake's new friend, and froze.

"M—Marcus . . . I . . . what—"

If she had suspected that this was all his doing, somehow, that thought was eradicated by the look of absolute shock and dismay on his face.

"Arabella," he said, moving forward but then stopping himself just before reaching out to touch her. "I thought you were m . . . I thought—"

"Do you two know each other?" Drake said, smoothly.

Too smoothly. Arabella cast him a venomous look. He knew she had met Marcus Westhaven, the new Earl of Oakmont. He had been at the breakfast table when True read that particular piece in the paper. In fact, True—Arabella turned to glare at her cousin, whose own face was a smooth oval radiating innocence. Had they contrived this meeting? Had they sought Marcus out and invited him here? Why?

"Yes, darling, these two met briefly in London. It *was* briefly, was it not, Arabella? You said you hardly knew the new earl."

Recovering from his shock, Oakmont, as Arabella must learn to think of him, she realized, said, "Yes, it was the merest acquaintance, was it not, Miss Swinley? It is still Miss Swinley, then?" As she nodded, his expression lightened a little, and he turned to his hosts and said, "Just enough that we need not be introduced again, but no more than that, I assure you."

"How about that," Drake said. "London, for all that it is the largest city on our island, is a very small place. And what a coincidence this is, that the friend of my old crony Captain Greyling, should be an acquaintance of yours, Arabella. One would almost think we had planned this, but one would be wrong." He shot Arabella an ironic glance. "Shall we go in to dinner?"

Arabella later had no memory of what they ate that night, whether the first dish was whiting or herring, whether they ate game or mutton, what the dessert was. She stared fixedly at her plate at first, only answering direct questions from True or Drake. At first she had thought Drake to blame; they did not get along well, but she did not think him cruel. How was he to know, though, what a shock seeing Marcus Westhaven would be? And his last words had been a deliberate challenge; sometimes it was as if he understood her thought processes too well. And so she must believe that their meeting this way was mere chance, coincidence.

After all, when the news report of Marcus's fortune was read to her, she had been careful to let no hint of her feelings for the man show on her face or in her voice—she thought anyway. But she began to see that True, usually the most open of ladies, had acquired a degree of cunning in the way she directed the conversation. Often shy around new acquaintances, True seemed immediately to take to Marcus.

"Lord Oakmont, how do you like your new home?" she asked, brightly, stabbing blithely at a piece of potato that was hiding under a leaf of her salad burnet.

"If you speak of the one at Reading, not well," he replied, shortly.

"Oh? Why is that?"

"It is too big, and people keep 'my lording' me."

"Mmm. I understand what you mean," Drake said. "Even though I grew up with it, it was rather a relief when I could order my troops to call me Major Prescott."

"Then imagine never having been called 'my lord' in your life, and suddenly being expected to answer to it." A bemused expression on his lean face, Marcus cut into a piece of meat, but paused with his fork raised halfway to his mouth. "I keep looking behind me to see who they are talking to."

Arabella found herself stifling a chuckle. She could see the scene so well in her mind's eye, the quick glance over the shoulder, then the dawning realization and belated response. But her merriment soon died. "You did have time to get used to the idea, though, *my lord,*" she said, coolly. " You were visiting your uncle for some time, the papers say, and had been accepted as the heir long before he passed on."

He understood her. It was in the hooded glance and downturn of his lips. "Getting used to the idea, then dealing with the reality, Miss Swinley, are two different things. And while my poor uncle lay dying in his bed, I did not while away the hours counting up my inheritance nor practicing being an earl in front of the mirror."

She flushed and bit her lip, while True sent a curious look her way. She could not meet her cousin's eyes. When first the piece in the paper had betrayed Arabella's inescapable interest in Marcus Westhaven, she had passed it off as the inevitable interest in someone's good fortune, and had downplayed it ever since, never voluntarily mentioning his name, though True had often raised the subject of the new earl. But it appeared that her cousin knew her too well and had suspected more. Arabella had not been able to hide her growing depression and anxiety as her wedding date drew near, but that was not solely to do with her newly discovered feelings for Marcus Westhaven, but also her despairing realization of what marriage would mean for her, and what marriage *could* mean, judging by her cousin's happiness. "I did not mean to imply that you did," she said, stiffly, in answer to Oakmont's acerbic comment.

Dinner finally over, the four moved to the drawing room, the gentlemen agreeing that there was no point in sitting away from the ladies when they had already spent the whole day together. Arabella played for them, losing herself for a while in a piece by Beethoven. His Sonata quasi una fantasia, op. 27, no. 2 was moody and quiet, working up to great lashings of emotion, a stormy finale that echoed her turbulent soul. She looked up once in the middle to find Oakmont's gloomy glance on her, and lost her way for a moment, but then found the thread again, and worked through to the finale.

There was silence when she finished, until Drake dryly commented, "I don't think I have ever heard you play like that, cousin. I must say, you have a riveting style."

Arabella searched for the sarcasm on his face, but was surprised by an expression that looked suspiciously like sympathy. She wanted to cry.

After, the nurse brought the new baby down to be fawned over. Arabella was genuinely fond of little Sarah, but soon she found the stifling atmosphere and cloying cooing too much, and she slipped away for a moment's fresh air out the French doors onto the newly created terrace. The soft breeze of late summer drifted, carrying the scent of night-blooming stocks and late roses up from the garden. True had not been up to much this summer, before or since the birth of her baby, but it had been clear that the sad state of the neglected gardens around her new home was bothering her a great deal, so Arabella took it upon herself to weed and plant and sort according to True's detailed plans. The resulting glory gave her a satisfaction Arabella had never experienced. It felt good to work toward something, toward a goal, and achieve it.

But this night she was not thinking of the lovely gardens, but of the man in the room behind her. It had been a shock to find out Marcus Westhaven was the fifth Earl of Oakmont, but more of a shock when she realized that this was the pitiful inheritance he had spoken of so disparagingly. Drake's stinging comment that morning True had read the piece in the paper, that the poor fellow had kept it a secret so as not to be overrun by fortune hunters, likely had some merit. But she thought they had become friends. Would he not have confessed the truth to a friend?

Ah, but she had early revealed her plan to marry a rich man to him. Was that what had kept him from

confessing the true state of things? Regardless, it hurt
that all the time he was kissing her and caressing her
and making her love him, he had the ability to marry
her and solve all her problems if he had so desired. Or
if that was not quite fair, then it hurt even more that
he did all that with no serious intention toward her.
While she thought him poor, she had believed that he
could possibly love her; he had not spoken, she believed, because he knew there was no future for them,
both poor as they were. But all the while if he had truly
loved her, truly wanted her, he could have just said the
word.

So he did not love her; she hugged that pain to herself. She had accepted that, had dealt with it. But he
had kissed her and tempted her to indiscretion, all the
while with his secret knowledge wielded like a shield.
He could hurt her, but she could not hurt him.

She heard the terrace door behind her and she knew
it would be him. She took a deep breath and turned to
face him in the spilled light from the drawing room.
Still so very handsome, she thought, gazing at him. He
had not trimmed his hair upon ascending to his new
lofty title, nor had he donned more fashionable clothing. His coat still fit too loose for a real gentleman, and
still revealed the power and almost arrogant healthiness
of the man more than a tight-fitting, fashionable jacket
would. There was ever a suggestion of wildness about
Marcus.

She spoke first. "So how do you like your new life,
Marcus?"

His brows pulled down and he stared at her, circling
her like a hunter would circle game. "I am not overfond
of it. It is like a snare, though, I find. The more I strug-
gle the tighter the bonds become."

Arabella turned, keeping him in her sight. "How so?
Does not wealth give freedom?"

"No, it does not. I have people depending on me now for their livelihood. Men with children, families, servants, dairymen, milkmaids, groundskeepers, farriers, schoolteachers—even a vicar or two! I was freer when I was poor."

She smiled at the despair in his voice. "You will become accustomed to it after a while."

"That is what I am most afraid of."

There was silence. A servant inside drew the curtains, shutting out the light from the drawing room, but the moon was rising and it cast a milky glow over the terrace, gilding the new-laid flagstones. The heavy floral perfume drifted around them, and Arabella stood staring up at the moon, finding that gazing at Marcus was too dangerous to her heart.

Marcus cleared his throat. "You know, I told no one about my inheritance for a reason. I have always despised toadeaters and fortune hunters. If I loved someone, I wanted to know they loved me back, not just craved my wealth. How can I ever trust any woman who says she loves me now? How will I know it is not just for my money?"

Arabella turned back toward him with an incredulous look. "What you really mean," she said, "is that you do not believe any woman could love you for *you.*"

"That is not true," he said. "I was engaged once, I will remind you, even though I was poor. And she was a better woman than you, Arabella Swinley!"

"Why a better woman than me?"

"Because she agreed to marry me even though I was poor," he said, his voice clearly indicating that he thought she *must* understand him.

She did. Chin up, she said, "You never gave me the chance, did you? You never asked me, never even let me know that you cared for me other than as a flirt.

You kissed me, but never asked me to marry you, poor or otherwise."

"Because you made it quite clear you would only marry a rich man. What would you have said if I had asked you to marry me?"

"Yes," she said immediately. And in that moment she knew it was the truth. If he had told her he loved her and asked her to marry him and go away, she would have. It would have cost her greatly to leave behind her obligation to her mother, but the temptation to be with Marcus Westhaven, to love him as his wife, would have been too great and the happiness offered too vast. But he would never believe that now. *Never.*

"Oh, really," he said, his voice dry. "Why do I have trouble believing that? Oh, yes, it may be because I have heard that you jilted that poor devil, Sweetan, who wanted to marry you, just because he did not have enough money."

"I did not love Daniel!" Her voice trembled and was so low she hoped that perhaps Marcus had not heard her. It was true. She had never loved Sweetan. She had only now discovered what love felt like, and it consisted mostly of pain, it seemed.

There was silence in the summer night air for a moment. Marcus approached, but did not touch her. "Do . . . did you love me? Tell me the truth and I will believe you."

"I d—d—" Arabella fell silent and turned away. No matter what, it was too late now. She owed Pelimore her allegiance as his future wife. Her heart breaking, she said, softly, "I am engaged. I will be married this day next week. Go away, Marcus. No matter what you think of me, I am not a jilt. I have made an agreement with Lord Pelimore, and I will uphold my end of the bargain. I will be a married woman the next time we meet."

Nineteen

Marcus stayed out in the soft evening air for a few minutes more, unable to master his expression enough to return to his host's company. Had any of what she said been true? Would she have married him? Had she fallen in love with him?

He did not trust her, and that was sad. And yet she had been honest with him always, had she not? Much more so than he had been with her. He had lied to her from the very first day of meeting, and perhaps that was what was behind his own mistrust of her. Could it be his own lies he was seeing? After all, did he really think that her marriage with Lord Pelimore had ever been touted as a love match by either of them? No, the baron was not being misled.

Maybe what she said was true; it was his own feelings about wealth that tainted his view and made him mistrustful. Never had she said she would pretend affection in order to entice a man to marriage. And the way she had kissed him at times surely showed a preference, even an affection—

But it was too late. He had vacillated, torn between the desire to tell her the truth about his inheritance, and his caution and mistrust. Because he had not trusted her, he had let her slip away.

He reentered to find that Arabella had made some excuse and fled upstairs. He sat for a while with Lord and Lady Drake, but soon left Thorne House to make his solitary way back to Andover.

Arabella was pale and quiet, but composed the next morning at the breakfast table. True longed to ask her questions—so *many* questions—but it was so clearly none of her business, she could not find a way to justify prying. When they were young Arabella had told her everything, but inevitably time had changed their relationship. And this last Season had seen the most change in Arabella ever. Once she had been a thoughtless flirt, but True had seen none of that in her this summer.

In fact, though she was clearly unhappy, she was indulging in none of the tantrums, none of the childish behavior she had been prone to in the past. Arabella Swinley had grown up, and though True knew she must be happy for that—after all, her new maturity could only be of aid to her in the coming years—she admitted to herself that a little more of Arabella's old openness would have been welcome, even if it came at the cost of a tantrum or two. There was a chilliness to her cousin's demeanor now, as if she were freezing her heart to avoid feeling the pain of a futile love.

Drake had ridden out early on some estate business, so it was just Arabella and True at the table. True signaled to the footman for coffee for them both. He was pouring True's when Lady Swinley, haggard and dirty from travel, burst into the breakfast room with a footman trailing behind her, bleating about announcing her.

"Never mind that, man, stay out of my way."

"Mother, what is it?" Arabella cried, leaping up from her chair and helping her mother to sit before she collapsed. She knelt beside the woman.

Lady Swinley waved a newspaper around in the air. "It's—it's—oh! It is horrible!"

War, famine, pestilence: all of those calamities stormed through Arabella's mind. She grabbed the newspaper and glanced over the first couple of pages. But the main stories were about the corn laws, the Luddites, and another demonstration by the poor, a rehashing of the political news that always took precedence in that particular paper.

Arabella smoothed back her mother's hair, normally so neat, but now escaping its tidy bun. "What is it? What is wrong, Mother?"

True busied herself with ordering a restorative for her elder cousin, and shooing away the curious staff. Annie, Lady Swinley's maid, followed in and was questioned by Arabella.

"What has upset my mother so, Annie? What has happened? Was it—was it the moneylenders again?"

"Oh, no, Miss Swinley," Annie said, collapsing in a chair, unbidden, an unusual thing for the girl to do. "The moneylenders are satisfied now, and all of Lady Swinley's gambling debts bin paid off, too. 'Tis something else entirely; it is—"

"Shut your mouth, girl," Lady Swinley ordered, sitting up straighter in the breakfast room chair, her face red with anger.

"Gambling debts? What—?"

But Arabella was not fated to have that query answered at that moment. Lady Swinley raised her hand and pointed at the newspaper. "Page eight," she said, wearily.

Together, True and Arabella spread the paper out on the breakfast table and read page eight over until they came to the gossip column. There was the usual tittle-tattle about who was seen where and with whom, but near the bottom they finally came to the piece Lady Swinley was in such a taking over.

"It is said," the column read. "That the elderly Lord P., who was so recently betrothed to the scandal-plagued Miss S., is being sued for breach of promise by Lady J., his 'particular friend' of some years' standing. She has a witness, it is rumored, who will positively state that the gentleman in question promised that if and when Lord P. ever married, it would be to her, Lady J. As a result of this suit, shall Lord P.'s name soon be amended to Lord Pay-her-more?"

Arabella shook her head in dismay. It was the work of seconds to identify herself, her betrothed, and his paramour in the story. "This is not pretty, Mama, and I certainly do not like my name being bandied about so. 'The scandal-plagued Miss S.,' indeed! But other than that, I do not see how this is to hurt us. Lord Pelimore certainly has enough money to pay Lady Jacobs to drop the suit."

Lady Swinley was on her feet, pacing and wringing her hands, though, and would not be cheered. "Oh, you do not understand! This is terrible. Terrible! What a scandal!"

Arabella shrugged. After what she had endured when the whole story of the episode at the Farmington estate came out, she was not acutely distressed over a little breach-of-promise suit. She had stayed in London long enough after her betrothal was announced to feel the full affect of the shunning she was subjected to. Suddenly doors that had always been open to the Honorable Miss Swinley were slammed shut. She was *persona non grata* in London society, and would be for some time to come.

This bit of news would just titillate the gossipmongers even more. But Pelimore would settle it out of court; men always did if they had the money.

Free of any worry about her status in the city and

among people who had turned their backs on her, her mind came back to something Annie had said. The girl had crept away, so Arabella turned to her mother. "Mama, what did Annie mean about your gambling debts?"

Lady Swinley looked guilty, but her chin went up in a gesture Arabella recognized in herself, and she stood stiffly. "The girl is an idiot! I play cards, but I really seldom gamble, and rarely—well, infrequently lose any amount at all."

"Has my dear, devoted husband-to-be settled any gambling debts? Was that a part of your . . . your agreement with him?" Arabella felt a dreaded calm overtake her, instead of the outrage she should be feeling. She saw True's worried glance, but had no time to reassure her that she would be fine.

Lady Swinley's gaze slid away and she stared at a candle sconce on the wall. "My dear, you know he agreed to settle *all* of our debts. I . . . I don't really remember them all! Life is so costly, and especially you, with three fruitless Seasons—"

"Mother, do not try to evade the question. Did you have gambling debts, and has Lord Pelimore paid them as a part of your agreement with him that I should marry him?"

Her beady eyes holding a sly light, the baroness said, "Well, no dear, Pelimore has paid no gambling debts for me at all."

Arabella knew there was more but could not think what it would be, until she saw where her wording had allowed her mother an out. "But he is going to, is that not so?"

Trapped, Lady Swinley nodded. "I . . . I feel faint. True, dear, may I have a room?"

* * *

Lady Swinley kept to her room for the remainder of the day, and all of the next. Arabella really did not want to see her mother anyway. She was terribly afraid that if she did see the woman, she would be unable to contain the ire that was building in her heart. She thought back to Eveleen's assertion that men treated women as chattel. How would that ever change when women were wont to do the same? Her mother had sold her for a shabby handful of gold; there was no other way to look at it.

True watched her younger cousin and worried. The revelations of the past couple of days had started her thinking, and she was deeply troubled.

"Wy," she said to her husband, "I think we have all misread Arabella, even I."

"How so, my love?" Drake curled one fine lock of her hair around his finger and kissed it. He whispered something in her ear, and she blushed a rosy color.

"Stop! I am trying to be serious."

They were sitting on a patch of lawn in the garden on a blanket, True curled up in her husband's arms. Arabella was working not far from them, ferociously weeding an until-now ignored corner of the garden. True had told her time and again that they had gardeners for the hard work. She was supposed to do the ladylike chores of planning and pruning, and no more. But she seemed to find an outlet in physical labor, so True let her go at it, knowing that this was how Arabella's restless nature found relief. And if she had callused hands at the end of it, a little peace was well worth it.

"I am always serious, my love," Drake said, kissing his wife's ear.

"I was saying I think we have all misread Arabella. I think she only agreed to marry Pelimore because her mother was having financial problems. I never knew

her before to be so avid about money, and from what
I heard in the breakfast room, I think Lady Swinley
forced Arabella into marrying because they were in financial trouble. I should have thought of it earlier from
something she said last autumn, but I was—well, I was
distracted at that time."

Both were silent. The previous autumn Drake had
been very sick and the doctors had despaired of his life,
but True had miraculously pulled him through with the
force of her love and a little herbal concoction.

"Say you are right. What has that to do with anything
now? She has agreed to marry the old codger, and
seems quite content to follow through."

True looked at her husband incredulously. "Content? She has been miserable! She is eating her heart
out over that cad, Oakmont! I do not know what happened between them; she will not speak of it. Not even
to me. But since he was here there has been even more
sadness in her eyes."

Arabella, too far away from them to hear their whispered conversation, sat back on her heels and passed
one hand over her brow, leaving a long smudge of dirt
there. Drake remembered how prim and proper she
had seemed to him the previous autumn during her
stay at his parents' home. She was more concerned
about her dress and gloves than about anything else.
Maybe there was something wrong, but whatever it was,
he had every confidence that she would survive. Arabella Swinley was much tougher than his wife thought.
Even if her marriage to Lord Pelimore turned out to
be the worst thing that ever happened to her, she would
live through it.

However, he hated seeing his wife as upset as she was
over her cousin's predicament. But he did not see what
he could do about it. She was betrothed to Lord Pelimore, and a betrothal, though not legally binding for

the lady, was a promise. If she broke it off there would be another enormous scandal attached to the Swinley name, and it might never recover. Right now, with her marrying respectably, it could be hoped that her reputation would recover.

As little as he cared about society and reputation, it seemed to him that Arabella had always cared very much about such things. Could she live ostracized from all that she held dear? And breaking away from Pelimore would not gain her Oakmont, or financial security of any kind. Drake would do anything for his wife, even allow Arabella to stay with them forever, but he could not support her and her mother's expensive habits, nor pay off Swinley Manor, if all that had been implied in Lady Swinley's unguarded moments were true.

He pulled True back down and nestled her against him. "Sleep, my dear. You are far from strong yet and I brought you out to this shady spot to get you to rest. There is nothing you can do to help Arabella right now. It is her own life, after all, and she must do what she thinks right."

The next morning, two mornings after Lady Swinley arrived, she finally deigned to descend for a meal. Arabella, after her initial alienation, had spent much of the last twenty-four hours in her mother's room and had apparently brought her some sense of peace, for she looked relatively cheerful, or as close as Lady Swinley ever got to that halcyon state.

All of them were gathered, Drake staying to breakfast when he normally did not, because he suspected his wife was not eating enough to regain her strength after almost dying in childbirth. He was fanatical about her health, filling her plate himself at most meals and assiduously making sure that she ate every morsel. He had consulted an old beldame in the village and was following her instructions, even down to buying a nanny goat and urging True to drink a cup of goat's milk every morning. He was starting to relax a little now that the roses bloomed once again in True's cheeks, but any little fluctuation in her eating, and he would become as guarded as before. The upsets of the last few days had brought him back to his role as her nursemaid.

True gazed at her plate in dismay, at the pile of eggs and cheese and kippers that she knew she would have to get through before her husband would rest his vigil. Manfully, she started, while Arabella picked at a piece of toast and Drake tucked into ham and kedgeree and a side dish of chutney. Lady Swinley took a cup of coffee and three buttered scones to her place and picked up one of the neatly folded London papers that lay on the sideboard.

There was silence for a while but for the rustle of the paper, and True's occasional sigh as a pleading glance at her husband was met with a shake of his head. She knew that he was only doing it for her own good, and if she really said no he would certainly never force her to eat; it was not his intention to make her uncomfortable. But it relieved his mind to see her eat, and she would do anything to spare him worry. She remembered too well a time when he was out of his mind with fever, and how *she* had felt. She knew he had suffered similar agony when she was ill before and after Sarah's birth. He would relax soon. And in the meantime she could not deny that she *was* feeling better for the diet he had prescribed.

A gasp from Lady Swinley, and a high shriek rent the peaceful morning, drowning out the birdsong from the open window.

Arabella leaped to her mother's side. "What is it? Mama, are you ill?"

The baroness could only gasp and point to a piece in the gossip column of the same paper that had caused her to come down to Thorne House in the first place.

Arabella snatched it from her mother's hand and read it out loud.

" *'Lord P.'*—why don't they just say his name, for heaven's sake— *Lord P. has gone to novel lengths to settle the breach of promise suit laid on him by the importunate Lady J. It can now be told that Lord P. and Lady J. have slipped off to the Continent to be married, as it appears that Lady J. is in an interesting condition, thus fulfilling Lord P.'s requirement of a bride!'* Do they mean she is going to have a baby? What bosh! *'Poor Miss S., to whom he was betrothed . . . will she now bring a suit for breach of promise against the gallivanting Lord P.?'* Not likely," Arabella finished, throwing down the paper.

She felt a curious lightness, as though a weight had been lifted from her. If this paper was to be believed, and she did not see any reason to doubt it, she did not have to marry Pelimore! She would not be tied for life to that snuffling, wheezing old man, a man she could not even respect, much less like. She was free, free!

But it only took a few seconds for her to realize that nothing at all was solved. If she was free of Pelimore, it was only to find her and her mother in the same tiresome predicament as before, and possibly even worse off. She looked over at her mother, who was weeping silently, tears streaming down her face. Nothing was solved.

Twenty

"I have a what?"

"You got a visitor, sir . . . I mean, my lord." Mrs. Brown fidgeted at the door of the decrepit library, twisting her work-roughened hands in her stained apron.

What on earth had made the woman start "my lording" him all of a sudden? Normally, in a twisted understanding of his new position, she called him Mr. Oakmont, or Lord Westhaven. He had begun to think it was deliberate on her part, an insolence he should abhor but instead found amusing. Marcus tossed the book he had been pretending to read down on the moth-eaten sofa and stood, stretching his long legs out.

"A visitor. No one knows me around here. Tell him—or her—to go away. I am in no mood for company."

"Beggin' yer parding, m'lord, I would ast that you do it yerself. He's a right proper swell, an' I wouldn't know how to—I wouldna know what to say."

Curious. Mrs. Brown always knew what to say. Once broken through, her outer taciturn shell proved to hide an inner magpie.

Feeling she had not expressed herself, she glanced once over her shoulder in a shifty manner and crept into the room, whispering, "He's like a god, sir, like one o' them Greek god fellers in one o' the books Lord Oakmont has in here. All golden and noble. He's the prettiest fella I ever seen, an' that is God's own truth."

Marcus thought for a moment, then put his head back and roared with laughter. It took a couple of minutes, but he got himself under control and said, "I do believe you have just met Lord Drake, known also as Major-General Prescott. Well, so that is the affect he has on the female half of creation. I am not surprised, and he is indeed the prettiest fellow I ever saw, too. Show him in, Mrs. B."

It had felt good to laugh for that minute. Since last seeing Arabella, he had had precious little reason to laugh or smile. Why was it that one often knew what one needed most in the world only when all possibility of attaining it was gone? It was like with Moira. If she had not become pregnant, he would not have asked her to marry him, but after she had died he missed her fiercely. His guilt over her condition, the reason for her death, was brutal and torturous and had haunted him for years, even though Moira's own father had not blamed him, but his grief was inconsolable beyond the guilt. Together he and Moira would have had a good life in the wilderness. She was a tough woman on the outside, but it concealed a streak of sweetness and goodness that many did not see.

Arabella, while on the outside being far removed from Moira's cheerful, bawdy good humor, was surprisingly like her inside. He thought that she was a far better person than even she realized. And he had lost her forever. She would be married in mere days, if it was not already done.

On that sobering thought, Drake entered the room.

Marcus managed a smile, and said, "Welcome to my humble home."

Drake's eyes widened at the ceiling-high shelves of books. "Lord Oakmont must have been quite a collector to have this array of books at his hunting box."

"More books than I have ever seen in a lifetime,"

Marcus said, glancing ruefully around at the thousands of tomes. "And this is merely the overflow from his other libraries; there are ten times this many at the Reading home. I'm not much of a reader, I'm afraid. More of a doer."

"I would give a lot to have an afternoon in this room," Drake said, his eyes scanning the titles and widening from time to time. "My God, is that a first edition of Hume's *The History of Great Britain?* I believe it is, and a complete collection of—oh, sorry Oakmont, I get carried away."

"Call me Marcus, remember? And you are welcome here any time to peruse the shelves, even if I am not here. I will tell Mrs. Brown to make you free of the place. I believe she stands in considerable awe of you, Drake. You transformed her into a proper servant in minutes. I can only hope she will go back to being the slattern I have become accustomed to after you are gone."

Drake tore his gaze away from the shelves of books and forced himself to remember the reason for his visit. He gazed steadily at the man before him. "You know," he said abruptly, strolling into the center of the room, "I was supposed to marry Arabella Swinley."

"What?" Marcus stared at him.

"Her mother and my mother are bosom bows from their days at school. They wanted to make a match of it between us. That is why Lady Swinley, Arabella, and True, who is her cousin, came to Lea Park to visit last summer, while I was still convalescing from a wound I received at Waterloo."

"I didn't know that. And you, you sly dog, never mentioned your wife's name before inviting me to dinner. I might have made the connection if you had, for Arabella—er, Miss Swinley, talked often of her cousin True, and it is not a common name." He paused and indicated a chair, but the viscount shook his head, and Marcus remained standing with his guest. "And so, to shorten your story, you didn't marry Arabella. You married Lady Drake and are now as merry as grigs."

Drake examined the man before him. Marcus Westhaven, now Lord Oakmont, was as tall as he was, but with a look of untamed wildness about him. His dark hair was straight and hung below his collar, and his eyes were a peculiar shade of gray, smoky, like the Atlantic after a nasty storm. And it appeared, if True was to be believed, that Arabella Swinley, who he had damned as heartless, had lost her heart to this fellow, the antithesis of every London beau Arabella had ever fancied in her previous Seasons. But how did he feel about her? True seemed to think there was something between them, but damn it, one did not interfere in a fellow's love affairs. He had never been the kind who could talk about that sort of thing, and still had trouble with anyone but True.

What could he say? How could he raise this subject?

"Get the newspapers here?" he queried abruptly.

"No. Who wants to look at the kind of rubbish the London papers carry? I cannot seem to care for the politics of this insufferably insular island, and the gossip pages are even worse. As if anyone cares who marries whom! London is a poisonous city, and I am venting my spleen for no better reason than that I am in a bilious and foul mood. My apologies, old man.

"The truth is, I came down here to Hampshire to get away from all of that. Now look here, Drake, what did you come for? You started to tell me that you were supposed to marry Arabella, and then you said nothing more." Marcus's eyes turned even darker. "Look, are you here to tell me—to tell me that she is married? Has it happened?"

Drake frowned as he watched the man before him

ball his fists, as though he were clenching his whole body against an expected blow. It seemed that True was right. Oakmont was in a fair taking as if—as if he *cared!* Damn if it didn't appear as if this fellow dreaded to hear that Arabella was wed, and if that was so, it could only mean one thing. He remembered when he heard—it was not true, but he did not know it at the time—that True was affianced; it was as if someone had driven a knife into his gut and twisted it. It was what had brought on the fever, indirectly, through his own lack of care of himself after he heard that terrible news.

And so he sympathized. And yet—

He glanced around him and sniffed the air. "This place is musty. Damp. Not good for books you know. Should have the place properly aired and a conservator look over the library."

There was silence, and Drake went back to the subject at hand, eyeing the other man curiously. "Why do you think I would come to tell you that news?"

"I thought—well, I thought that Arabella might have sent you, that she would want me to know—" He turned away.

"Actually, m'wife sent me."

Marcus's shoulders slumped and he sat abruptly, putting his face in his hands. "So it is true?" he said, his voice muffled. "I had lost track of the days. I did not want to know when she married that leprous old fiend, Pelimore. I should have ripped his heart out when I had the chance."

"So bitter!" Drake strolled around the room and stared up at the bookshelves. So many classics, shelved here where no one in the world could care for them, in this damp and dank hunting lodge. It was criminal. Perhaps in the future he and Marcus would be related and he would have free access—but he was getting ahead of himself. The way was not clear, not by a long shot. "Tell me, Marcus—you know, I am not one to pry normally, but, well, you seem to be in some pain. Do you . . . can you possibly—damn it, man," he said, swinging around and staring at his new friend. "Do you love Arabella Swinley?"

Marcus gazed down at his hands and twisted the ring he wore on his right hand, the ring left to him by his uncle as a symbol of his new position. He would give up everything, all his new wealth, his position, his houses, all of it, just to be with Arabella. He nodded slowly. "I do. I love her."

"Then go to her, man." He leaned over and grinned, staring at Marcus. "Lord Pelimore has called off the wedding and eloped with his mistress. Arabella Swinley is a free woman."

The first elation, the first delirious knowledge that she was free, was over. Arabella walked in the gardens she had helped to create, near the blooming roses that she had torn the weeds away from, past the thicket of sweet raspberries they had discovered when she pulled out a bramble bush that was choking it. In the same way when she tore all the debris away from her heart, all the conceit she had ever been victim to, all the care of position, and the love of money and clothes and jewels, she was left with the bittersweet knowledge that she could have had Marcus Westhaven.

If she had followed her heart and let him see how she felt, if she had not talked so constantly about how necessary it was to marry a wealthy man, he might have felt free to court her, marry her, *love* her. Eveleen O'Clannahan had seen it; she had even advised her to ask him herself. What would he have said to such an outré proposal?

But it was too late. Marcus Westhaven was now an

immensely wealthy man and the Earl of Oakmont. And he could never trust anything she might say to him now of love. Why should he? She had made it quite plain over the months that her prime requirement in a man was a fat purse. A hundred thousand pounds. She had even set her price. She had been for sale, just as surely as any Haymarket doxie.

She heard a rustle of fabric behind her and turned to find True approaching her. Poor True, she worried so about her. Once True had told her that she was a better person than she even knew; maybe there had been that potential there, but she had let things get in the way. Everything had seemed more important than who she was, and who the man she would marry was. And now when she finally understood herself, it was too late.

Hesitantly, True approached. "Bella, I need to talk to you."

Smiling, Arabella said, "Why don't we sit down? Drake will hang me up by my toes if I keep you standing in this hot sun too long."

They found a stone bench in a shaded alcove of the garden. True took Arabella's hand and they sat in silence for a few minutes, watching a small brown rabbit hop incautiously onto the pathway. It examined the greenery along the edge and then hopped away. "Bella, perhaps this is not the time to say it, but I want you to not worry about your future. You have a home here for as long as you need it, your whole life. I love having you here, you know that, and it is not as if we do not have the room."

Arabella squeezed her cousin's hand. "A poor relation; that is what I have become. I never wanted you to know about our financial problems, you know."

"You knew last fall, didn't you? You knew when you left Lea Park with Lord Conroy."

Arabella shuddered. "Yes. Mother told me; that is why I played that dirty trick on you about Drake, telling you I loved him and wanted to marry him. I knew your self-sacrificing nature would make you leave, even though you already loved him. It was a mean trick. A horrid deceit."

"But you told me the truth before you left," True said, squeezing her hand. "And it all turned out well in the end. Stay here, Bella. Be my friend, help me raise Sarah."

"Drake must still be head over ears in love with you to allow you to offer me a home. However did you talk him into it?"

True dimpled and shrugged. "He—we made a bargain."

Chuckling, Arabella said, "I hope the terms are not too onerous, cousin. Why do I have the feeling it was the kind of bargain you will both enjoy?" Unexpectedly tears came into her eyes, and she had to force down a wave of self-pity. What True had was because she was the sweetest, truest, most loving and giving person Arabella had ever met. One could not begrudge her her good fortune.

"I . . . True, I don't know. I have to think about Mother. I do not imagine Drake's offer extends to her."

Looking troubled, True said, "Well, Wy said that—"

At that moment a footman, resplendent in rust and gold livery, came along the path and bowed. "My lady, there is a visitor for Miss Swinley."

For some reason Arabella's first thought was of Eveleen O'Clannahan. She had not heard from her at all since her flight out of London to the Isle of Wight, and she was still worried about her, even though events in her own personal life had crowded everything out on occasion.

"Is it a lady? Is she—"

But in that second, around a bend in the garden path, came Marcus.

True's eyes widened and she curtsied to him. "Lord Oakmont, what a pleasure. I shall go up to the house and order tea." She glanced at Arabella, who still stood staring at the young man. "It will be served in the drawing room in half an hour." If privately she thought that champagne might be more in order, she did not say so.

Arabella was vaguely aware that True and the footman had left them alone. She could not think, her mind was so numbed.

"Walk with me?" Marcus asked, holding out his arm to her.

She nodded, mutely, and took his arm. They wandered for a while down the long pathway that led to a creek where willows dipped and swayed, drawing leafy fingers through the shallow brook. She remembered being there the previous summer with True and Drake and Lord Conroy. How things had changed since then. She glanced up at the man at her side. He frowned and stared off at the far, misty hills, his brow wrinkled into a series of horizontal lines. What on earth did he want? Had he heard of Lord Pelimore's defection, or did he still think her betrothed? Today would have been her wedding day.

There was now a bench down by the creek, placed exactly where Drake had slept by True while she smoothed his curls from his forehead, the second day after they had met. Marcus bade her sit. Avoiding his eyes, she did so, gathering her soft, moss green skirts around her. He dropped down on one knee in front of her and took both of her hands in his. She looked up, startled. "Arabella Swinley," he said, in determined tones, "will you do me the inestimable honor of consenting to become my countess? I realize that this is sudden, but—"

Arabella pulled her hands from his grasp. "Marcus, what are you doing?"

"Proposing, widgeon," he replied, brusquely. "You see, I know all. You have been jilted and are no longer betrothed. You are brokenhearted and vulnerable, and I am going to take advantage of your momentary weakness to gain my point. Now, where was I? Ah, yes." He cleared his throat and took her hands back in his. "I know this is sudden, but it must have been evident to you for some time that my heart—"

Yanking her hands from his grasp again, Arabella said, her voice sounding panicky and strange, "Marcus, stop this foolishness. What are you doing?"

"Proposing!" He sighed and looked up at the sky, now a lovely shade of deep blue. "One would think the girl would remember what this is like. She has heard this a time or two, after all." He settled his gaze back on her, took her hands up one more time, and said, "Arabella Swinley, will you do me the honor of becoming my coun—Arabella!"

She had jerked her hands away, clutched them behind her back, and was glaring at him. "Do not make fun of me, Marcus Westhaven—Oakmont, whatever! I will not be mocked, not even by you!"

"I am not mocking you," he said, gently. "Now, my knee is getting cramped, and I think you sprained my thumb that last time you jerked your hands away from me, so let me get this out. You know the drill. You have heard the question before. You have even said yes before, so none of this is new to you. Arabella, will you marry me?" He grinned up at her. "Now it is your turn to smile sweetly and say yes. Say it; say, 'Yes Marcus, I will marry you.' "

"I—I c—can't!"

He sat back on his heels. "What? Yes you can. Why can't you?"

She reached out one trembling hand and touched his face, trailing her fingers down his cheek, tracing the lines that led from his nose to his mouth. He was serious! He was really asking her to marry him, despite his joking demeanor. He really was asking her just as she had fantasized once. "I can't!" Blinking away the tears in her eyes, she continued. "Every time you looked at me, you would wonder if I married you for your money or for yourself."

He grinned. "I believe you once accused me of being too sure of myself. Marry me, and keep me on my toes. It will give me something to strive for, if I am not too sure of your love."

"Seriously, Marcus, I can't. I just can't. It would break my heart. I would spend every day trying to convince you that I loved you, and never being sure if you really believed it, if you knew it in your heart." She placed her hand over his heart.

"So convince me," he said, covering her slim, white hand with his larger brown one.

"Don't! Don't joke! I cannot have you doubt me like that. And you—oh, Marcus, you deserve to know how much you are loved, every single day. I have seen that here, with Drake and True. There is so much between them, so much love and trust. You deserve that."

"So convince me," he said, huskily. He took a seat beside her. "Convince me now." He put his arms around her and kissed her deeply, passionately, letting his love flow through her like honeyed wine. She succumbed, and he felt wave after wave of love and longing and pain and deeply felt need coming from her, shaking her, quivering in her lips and arms and fingers. He felt a deep exultation well up in him as he understood how *much* she loved him. In that moment, his heart needed no more convincing.

"I love you," she whispered in his ear. "I love you so

much it hurts to be near you! How can that be? Why does it hurt so much to love you?"

He claimed her mouth with his and kissed her deeply. "I love you, you tormenting little witch! I have loved you for so long, with no hope of return. That is when it hurts. The pain, my dear, is just fear, and I know you are brave enough to overcome it." He kissed her again. "I love you, Arabella, forever and always. Does it hurt a little less now?"

"Yes." She sighed. "A little less. Kiss me again."

Obliging as always, he did.

Twenty-one

It was September, but summer still. The fat, nodding roses still bloomed along the walk, the willows still draped leafy fronds into the brook, and the sun still gilded the verdant countryside. And in the garden of Thorne House, under a blue sky, Arabella Swinley became the Countess of Oakmont. But more important to her—far more important, she had learned at long last—she was marrying the only man she had ever loved.

"We are joining our lives together from this time forward, but more importantly, we are fusing together two halves of a whole. Life made us two, love makes us one," Marcus said, taking her ungloved hands in his.

Lady Swinley sniffed and whispered, "This is not at all the done thing, to say such nonsense during the ceremony. What is wrong with a few verses from the good old King James?"

But Marcus and Arabella had wanted to say something to each other during the ceremony, rather than just repeat the vicar's words. True, whom the baroness sat beside, just smiled and played with Sarah on her lap. She liked the informality of this rather hurried wedding, though Lady Swinley had spent the previous weeks condemning it. She had wanted a full court ceremony at St. George's in Hanover Square as befit such a brilliant match, though even she knew that was impossible.

The groom was still in mourning for his uncle, and the ceremony could only be small and restrained.

But still, Lady Swinley had said, they could have waited the required year and married in style. What was the hurry, after all, she asked, not understanding the nature of love, and the eagerness with which her daughter anticipated marriage. In her mind it was a social coup, a brilliant match, and she credited her daughter with more conniving than she had previously thought Arabella capable of. She had always known her daughter was going to marry well, and was on her way to convincing herself that *she* had arranged this marriage. Her only wish was that her new son-in-law was a little more generous to her, but she already had a few schemes in mind to enlarge her newly arranged allowance.

Arabella, with tears in her eyes, looked up at her groom, handsome and tall and incongruously wearing a colorful beaded sash given to him by his friend, George Two Feathers. "I didn't know what love was and that is the only reason I can give why I did not recognize it when it stole into my heart. But you taught me that life is not complete without it, and that all the wealth in the world, or all the *promise* of wealth, could not make me happy."

"Easy for her to say now," Drake, on the other side of True, whispered. "Oakmont is ten times wealthier than I am."

True put one hand over her husband's, determined not to let even his cynical observation destroy the day. He was just on edge because of all the hubbub surrounding the marriage and all of the guests at Thorne House. He preferred a quiet life, and life had been anything but quiet lately. He would be fine once Arabella and Marcus were gone, and Lady Swinley had departed for her now mortgage-free Swinley Manor.

The only thing that had mollified him somewhat was

Marcus's offer to sell him whatever he wanted out of the library of Andover, the hunting lodge. He was to go down there and catalog it all and decide what he wanted, while Marcus and Arabella were away on their extended honeymoon to Lakelands, Oakmont's proper seat up in Cumbria. Marcus had never yet seen it, and was curious now to see it with his new bride.

At last, as the morning sun reached its zenith, the wedding was over and Marcus and Arabella were now man and wife, earl and countess.

For Arabella the day went by in a swirl of dizzying tableaux, the wedding breakfast, gifts to be opened, trousseau to be packed—the same trousseau that had been prepared for her wedding to Lord Pelimore, who was now back in London with his new wife.

And then, at long last, as the afternoon sun slanted through the line of trees that marched down the long drive from Thorne House, farewells to be said. She was in the carriage and Drake, happy now that the end was near, held little Sarah, whom Arabella had come to love as if she were her own, up to the open window. Arabella took her, cuddled her on her lap for a minute, and then whispered in the baby's ear, "I shall try to give you a couple of cousins to play with very soon, my little love."

"I am in great anticipation of that event myself, my darling wife," Marcus said, his own lips close to Arabella's ear. "But maybe not too soon." They had finally spoken of children, and agreed that despite his fears for her health in childbearing, they would welcome the coming experiences together.

She blushed a fiery red, and said, "You were not supposed to hear that, sir."

"Nevertheless, I did." He took the baby, who promptly started crying, and gave her a kiss on her button nose. "Good-bye, little one, and now I think I should give you back to your papa." He leaned across his wife and handed Sarah off to Drake much as he would a valise or hatbox.

True came to the window and looked up at Arabella with tears in her periwinkle blue eyes. She handed Arabella a small package through the window and sniffed back her tears as best she could.

"Don't cry, True!" Arabella said, taking the package and holding on to her cousin's hand. "I am not a weeper, but if I see you sniffle I shall be off like a watering pot!" She gazed down at her cousin and thought how tired True looked. She felt a sudden streak of worry dart through her, and she set the package down on the seat and took both of True's hands in her own. "Say you will rest for days and days now that this is all over. Say it, or I shall worry myself sick!"

Her cousin cast a fond look over her shoulder at her husband, who still held their baby. "Do you think Wy will let me do anything? He has been beside himself for days, and only the promise that I would have a good, long, lazy period after the wedding would convince him to allow the wedding here at all."

"I hope this has not been too much for you. You must evict my mother immediately. She has Swinley back and her debts are all settled. She has no excuse to linger."

"Arabella, do not worry so much! Wy will do all that is necessary, and your mother will travel wherever she wants in our carriage. I do not think she will want to stay; she and Wy do not see eye to eye on anything. I think it is already arranged that she is going over to visit Wy's mother at Lea Park for a couple of days, and then she will travel on to Swinley." True's face took on a more serious expression. She squeezed her cousin's fingers, and said, "Bella, be happy. It is all I have ever wanted for you, and at last I think it is in sight."

"I am too—oh, too delirious to be happy yet, but I

think I will be. I think so, and soon." She glanced over
at Marcus, who was on the seat opposite her now, talking
out the window to Drake. "I am a little nervous
about . . . well, about *things,* but I will be fine."

True gave her a glowing smile. "There is nothing at
all to be nervous about, my dear. Please trust me."

"It is just that Mother made some things sound so—
so sordid, and unpleasant, and it is not that I believe
her, but what if—" She left the rest unsaid. Silent worries had plagued her that she would find the physical
side of marriage unpleasant, for she had never been
one of those women who felt a need for male affection.
She enjoyed Marcus's kisses and his caresses, but what
if she did not like the rest of what was to come?

"Don't worry. You will soon find that there are few
things as pleasant as the moments when you and Marcus
are alone together in your room."

Lady Swinley moved forward, her mouth working as
if she were having trouble keeping from crying, and
her beady eyes bright and fixed. True moved away, with
just a whispered "Be happy," as her farewell to her
cousin.

"Mother, are you—are you all right?" Arabella gazed
at her mother with worry.

"I am just fine. I do not know why Oakmont finds it
necessary to take you to the ends of the earth on a
wedding trip when the Little Season is just about to
begin. We could all go to London! You should be introduced to society with your new title! But I will be
fine, all alone."

Arabella was silent. She could think of nothing to say,
for she had her own cherished dream that would take
her much farther away before long, and she would not
give it up easily. She wanted Marcus to take her to Canada, and she wanted to sail before winter arrived. She

had not broached the subject yet, but planned to while they traveled to Cumbria.

"Mother Swinley, I am only taking her north for a month or so, and then we shall come back to London and see you." Marcus voice was stern, but he smiled at his new mother-in-law kindly. He had found the only way to deal with her was to tell her how things were going to be, and let her squawk about it. There had been many discussions in the past month where he had had to talk long and loud over her protests, and he had won every disagreement simply by dint of being persistent and insistent.

She gave him a look of dislike, but tempered it quickly. "You may call me Isabella, Marcus." She put her hand out and he shook it, then glanced at his wife, and kissed it. She sniffled and said, "I wish you well. Be . . . be kind to my darling daughter." Her voice broke on the last word and she turned away.

Arabella caught her hand before she moved off. "Mama?"

Lady Swinley turned back after hastily applying a handkerchief to her eyes.

"Mama, I . . . I love you." And she did. It was amazing, but after everything, even after finding that Lady Swinley had gambled away a good part of the money that had been left her to run Swinley Manor, even after the Conroy debacle and the Pelimore episode, she did love her mother.

Lady Swinley burst into tears and stumbled away to indulge in a private bout of weeping. It was all right. Arabella had left her a letter telling her things she had never been able to say. It had felt good to express some of it, but there was much less anger and much more love in the letter than she would have thought possible a month before. Happiness had made her forgive much that she had thought unforgivable.

Finally they pulled away from Thorne House as the sun sank below the treetops. They were alone, and Arabella felt a wave of shyness engulf her. She covered her nervousness by opening the package True had given her at the last moment. It contained a golden locket with the words LOVE IS ALL engraved on it. She held it for a long while, thinking how lucky she was to have found love when she had pushed it away with both hands.

They traveled for a time in silence, the interior of the carriage growing dim as night closed in. Marcus purposely let the silence go on, knowing his new bride needed some time to recover from the emotion of the day, and of the parting.

But finally he pulled her to his side. "I have reserved a room for us at the White Boar on the road into Basingstoke. It is a lovely little inn I discovered on my way down to Hampshire. They have clean sheets, good food, and a very private room." He felt her shiver. She was frightened. He was a little nervous, too, but it must be much more awkward for her, not knowing exactly what was to come. He needed to lighten the mood.

"I think I shall require some convincing, my elegant, lovely wife, that you married me for reasons other than my pretty purse and handsome new title."

"Marcus," she said, turning to him with a stricken expression in her glowing green eyes. "Please don't say that you don't believe me! Oh, this is what I was afraid of—"

He silenced her with a kiss and held her close. The repercussions of his ridiculous distrust still rippled. "My love," he whispered, "I am *teasing* you. Now, in that spirit, can you contrive to convince me that you love me for *me*?"

Swept up in a dizzying tide of passion and desire, fueled by his lips tickling her ear and his teeth nipping at her earlobe, she started to think that perhaps True was right. The physical side of the marriage was the last thing she needed to worry about. "I think tonight I just might be able to convince you, my husband."

He was grateful for the dark, for the surge of hunger that swept through him had its physical effects, and he wanted to go slowly, wanted to teach his beautiful wife that there was nothing to be afraid of in his love. Keeping his tone light with a great effort he nipped at her collarbone and said, "Perhaps I shall require nightly convincing, my heart's delight."

"I think—I think that I can promise you that," Arabella said, breathlessly, threading her fingers through his silky, straight hair. She gasped as his hand wandered over her curves, and began to wonder if they would ever get to the inn. It could not be too soon.

"Good. I look forward to that," he said, his voice muffled as his kisses trailed down her neck to her bosom.

And then no more words were said, as in the velvet-soft dark husband and wife made silent promises they would be delighted to keep.

ABOUT THE AUTHOR

Donna Simpson lives with her family in Canada. She is currently working on her next Zebra regency romance, A RAKE'S REDEMPTION, to be published in February 2002. Donna loves to hear from readers and you may write to her c/o Zebra Books. Please include a self-addressed stamped envelope if you wish a reply.